CW01661161

Taming You

ALEX TAYLOR

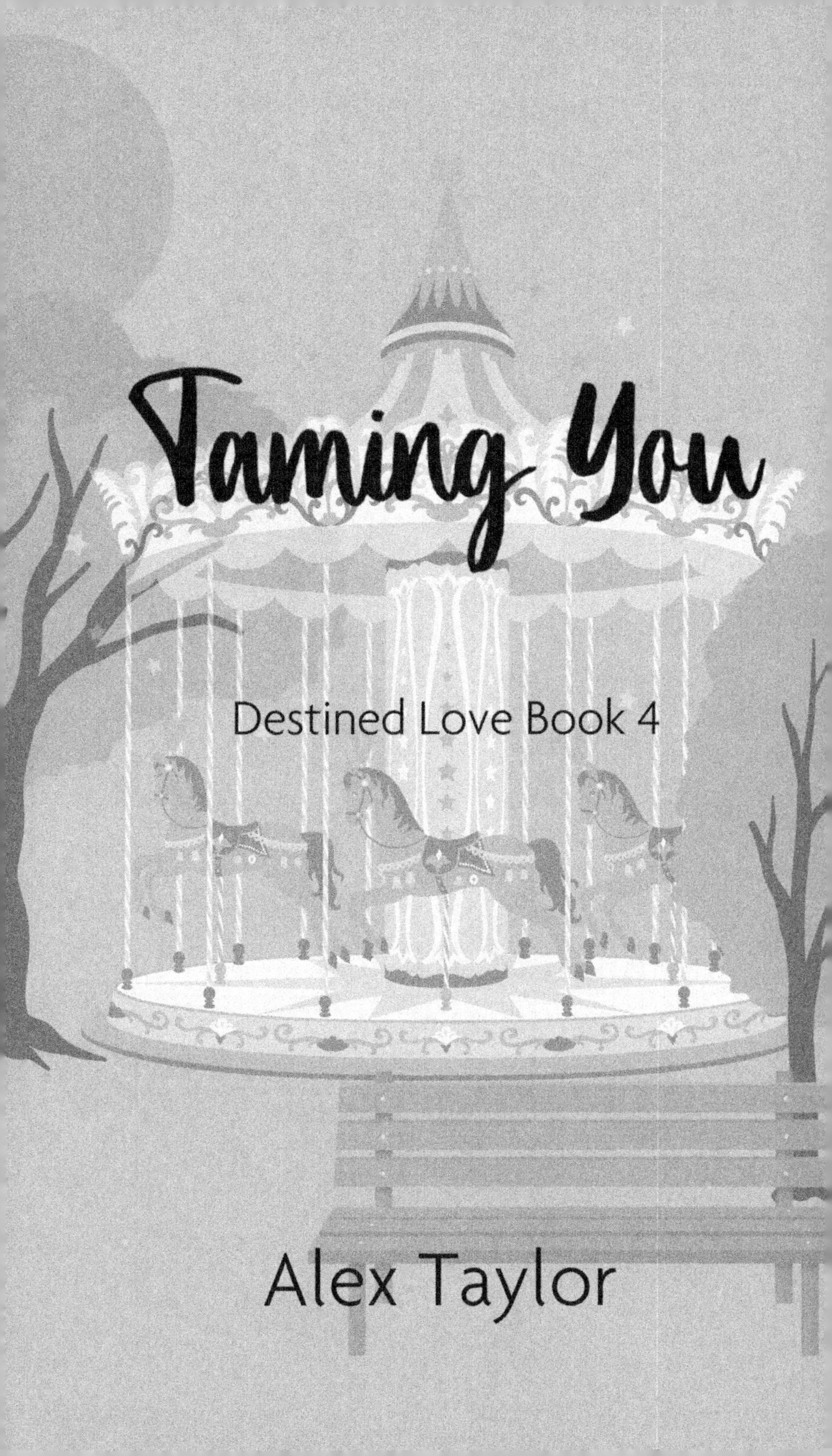
Taming You
Destined Love Book 4
Alex Taylor

Character art by Paige Moreland

Cover Design by Kimberly at KBG Designs

Editing by Editing by Andrea

Print ISBN: 978-1-7381786-6-7

Ebook ISBN: 978-1-7381786-7-4

To all those unsure about the future,
it's okay to pivot and change.
Chase happiness and joy.

Author's Note

Please note that some of the subject matter in this book may be triggering for some people.
If any of the following subjects cross a line for you, please do not continue.
Your mental health matters.

Discussions of parental neglect
Discussions of drug addiction and alcohol abuse
Child abandonment
Explicit sex scenes

Looking for a Dicktionary? Check out the back of the book.

Playlist

Changes
Hayd

Dear Son
Josh Brock, Rye Davis

Haunted by Potential
PIAO

Cursive
Billie Marten

that way
Tate McRae

I Turn to You
Christina Aguilera

When I Look At You
Miley Cyrus

People Don't Talk About
The Recklaws

Friends Don't
Maddie & Tae

More Than A Woman
Bee Gees

We're Not Just Friends
Parks, Squares and Alleys

Arms
The Paper Kites

River
Myles Smith

When You're Ready
Shawn Mendes

Dress
Taylor Swift

Adore You
Harry Styles

Like I Can
Sam Smith

Electric Love
BØRNS

Dangerous Woman
Ariana Grande

Best Part (feat. H.E.R.)
Daniel Caesar, H.E.R.

Nobody Does It Like You
Shawn Desman

Only Us
Laura Dreyfuss, Ben Platt

She Looks So Perfect
5 Seconds of Summer

ILYSB
LANY

Just You and I
Tom Walker

CHAPTER 1

Zoey

A baby!?

When I rolled off Matt's couch this morning to take my hungover ass home, I did not expect to see a baby sitting outside his front door. I close the door quickly before opening it again to see if my hungover brain is making things up. Nope, the baby is still there.

"Matt," I call.

The baby, who doesn't look any older than three or four months, sucks on a pacifier as they watch me through barely open eyes. I don't hear any noise coming from Matt's bedroom, so I yell, "Matthew James Carter!"

Shuffling comes from the other side of the apartment, and then Matt steps out wearing nothing but a pair of gym shorts that hang off his hips, showing off his stomach that's not quite abs but fit, as he rubs his eyes. His brown hair is unruly, only confirming he just rolled out of bed. I take in every inch of him and shake my head, reminding myself that now is not the time to be ogling my best friend's brother, no matter how good he looks first thing in the morning.

"What's with the yelling, Zo?" His voice is groggy as he makes his way towards me.

I turn and fully face him, needing to see his reaction. "Oh, maybe the fact there's a baby outside your front door."

He stops in his tracks as his deep-brown eyes that match his sister Liv's meet mine. "You mean Liv dropped off Cate?"

I shake my head. "No, I mean, a baby I've never seen before is sitting in a car seat with a diaper bag outside your door."

Even at six-foot-two, he slides around me with graceful ease. When he finally sees what I'm talking about, his jaw drops. "Whose baby is it?" he asks.

"How am I supposed to know? I opened the door to leave and almost tripped over the damn car seat."

He stares at me, dumbfounded.

I sigh. "Is there a note, Matthew?"

He side-eyes me at the use of his full name, but it always seems to come out when I'm frustrated with him. Years of spending time with him can do that.

"I don't know, Zoey, I haven't had time to really comprehend the fact that I'm staring at a baby that's been left outside my place."

I roll my eyes. Fine, I'll give him that. He checks the car seat first before he moves on to the diaper bag. The baby starts to fuss, and I place a hand on Matt's shoulder.

"Why don't we move inside?" I ask.

He looks at the baby and then back at me before nodding. I grab the bag from him while he grabs the car seat and takes it inside to the dining table. He attempts to soothe the fussy baby by rocking the car seat while I search for a note. I find one tucked in the outside pocket of the bag. We both stare at the folded paper, knowing whatever's written on it is going to change both Matt's and this baby's life.

I hand him the paper, and he takes it hesitantly while I take over soothing. He reads it silently before collapsing in a chair. I watch his eyes as he reads it again before he drops his hand with the paper between his legs.

"He's mine," he whispers. His voice is mixed with confusion and hurt. When his eyes meet mine, there are so many emotions swirling around them.

"He's yours?"

He nods and hands me the paper, and I also have to read it twice for it to really sink in.

Matt,

I tried to do this, but I couldn't. I never wanted to be a mother, but thought I'd change my mind after Jayden was born. I couldn't. Jayden is yours. I'm sorry for not telling you earlier, but I didn't know how you'd feel about having a kid. I now know he's better off with you than me. I've left his birth certificate and medical information in the diaper bag along with documents signing away my parental rights. I'm flying home to Winnipeg tonight. I can't stay in Vancouver any longer. Please take care of our boy.

Hazel

Holy shit. Matt has a baby. Matt, the playboy, knocked a woman up, and I'm not entirely sure how to process it. I've known for years he got around, but that he actually got someone pregnant is a different story. I have no idea who this woman is. I've never heard her name before, so she must be one of Matt's many casual flings or a one-night stand. If she had been a serious girlfriend, I would have heard about her from his sister.

The baby's eyes match Matt and Liv's. I don't know what his mother looks like, so he could have gotten those from her, even if it's unlikely. I'm too hungover and not fully awake to process or try to make sense of this all right now. I need sugar and a shower.

"At least she didn't give him a horrible name," I say, trying to bring some levity to the situation.

Matt looks at me unimpressed.

"I'm sorry. I'm just not sure what I'm supposed to say or do right now."

We both sit and stare at the beautiful baby boy sitting in front of us. He starts to fuss again, and I get up, grab some formula and a bottle out of his bag, and begin making it. Matt's still in shock. He hasn't moved one bit since handing me the letter, and I don't blame him. Having a baby randomly dropped on your doorstep and being told they're yours is huge.

I hold the finished bottle out for Matt. He stares at it, and I give it a little shake. "You should feed him. Use it to try and bond."

He takes it from me before grabbing Jayden and getting settled on the couch. It takes a minute, but Jayden eventually accepts the bottle. Matt watches him with rapt attention.

"I know nothing about him," Matt says, his voice soft as he stares at Jayden.

"Well, you'll get to know him. You're good with kids. You've got this."

"I'm fun Uncle Matt, Zo." He looks at me and shakes his head before looking back at Jayden. "I'm able to borrow my niece for a bit and then return her to her parents. I wasn't planning on kids for a while. I'm single, for God's sake. How am I supposed to do this on my own? I still have to work. How can I be sure he's even mine? If he is, I've got to figure out child care, make sure he's got all his vaccines. I need to learn if he has allergies, and I need to figure out where he's going to be sleeping. On top of all that, I have to tell my family."

When Jayden finishes, Matt burps him like a pro.

Stress and anxiety radiate off Matt. I know telling his family is probably the most difficult thing on his list. His family has always been the supportive type, but finding out Matt has a child no one knew about won't be easy news to hear.

"Why don't we tackle the first concern first. I'm sure there's somewhere in town we can get a paternity test run," I say.

He nods. I grab my phone and do a quick search, finding a place nearby, and text the information to Matt.

"I've just sent you a place in town that does them. I've got to head out, but I'll see you later," I say and move towards the front door.

Matt very deftly gets off the couch while still holding Jayden. "Whoa, Whoa, Whoa. Where are you going? You can't leave me here with a baby. I have nothing to take care of him."

I stop in my tracks and face him. "Matthew, you're not useless. You take care of Cate no problem and have since she was born. You can take care of your son."

The deer in headlights look he gives me and the soft spot I've slowly developed for Matt recently have my shoulders slumping. This better not bite me in the ass.

"Fine," I sigh. "Let me go home, shower and change, and then I'll come back so we can get you stuff to get him settled."

He relaxes. "Thanks, Zo."

I nod. "Of course."

As I pull open the front door, Matt stops me. "Hey, Zo? I'd appreciate it if you don't say anything to my sister or anyone before I get a chance to." He worries his bottom lip between his teeth, much in the same way Olivia does when she's worried. Liv's my best friend, and I tell her everything, or I guess almost everything, since I haven't told her how close Matt and I have grown over the last year and a half. Matt's no longer just my best friend's brother. He's my friend, too. So, what's one more secret?

"Not a word," I say before closing the door behind me.

CHAPTER 2

Matt

Any sense of calm I had leaves me the second Zoey closes the door. I stare down at the little boy bundled in my arms and feel myself sweating, wanting to throw up and pass out all at the same time. Waking up with a baby was not in my plans for the year, let alone this morning. I've always known I wanted kids, but only after I had found the person I planned to spend the rest of my life with and settled down. I'm not prepared in any way for a baby right now. Let alone one an ex casual fling dropped off at my door with no warning.

I know I can manage financially. I make good money as a financial advisor, but that's such a small part of being a parent. It's everything else that freaks me out.

That thought leads me into a spiral. How does one just abandon a helpless baby on a doorstep? Anything could have happened. She didn't even knock.

Jayden fusses some more, likely sensing my anxious energy. I bounce him as I pace my living room.

At least when I've had Cate, I've been able to plan for it, and I always know she's going home to Liv and Josh after. Having a kid on my own is way out of my wheelhouse. But I know I'd never abandon him like he just was.

When I finally get Jayden settled, I put him in his car seat and cover him with his blanket. Settling in a chair beside him at the dining table, I open my laptop and begin my research.

I'm not sure how much time has passed when there's a knock on the door. I nearly jump out of my seat. I was deep in research and every new thing I read put me more and more on edge. I quickly check on Jayden before moving to the front door and checking the peephole. I relax when I see Zoey on the other side.

She smiles her radiant, easygoing smile as her brown eyes shine and she tucks a piece of her short, brown hair behind her ear as she walks in, eyeing both me and Jayden before saying, "See, I told you you'd be fine."

I shake my head. "Fine. Really? I have nothing he needs. Did you know you need to make sure a baby sleeps with nothing surrounding them to ensure they don't suffocate while sleeping? Or that you need to cut their nails regularly, even at this young of an age, because they can scratch themselves? Or that he's fifteen weeks old, and by this age, they've usually formed an attachment to you and he's now been abandoned by the one person he knew?"

My chest tightens, and it feels like my lungs aren't taking in oxygen even as I take a deep breath. Zoey reaches out and grips my arm, and I release a breath and close my eyes, taking strength from her touch.

"Whoa. Started down the research rabbit hole, did we?"

I nod.

"Okay. Well, let's focus on the positives right now. Jayden is in a warm place with someone who will take care of him. We're going to go out and get him what he needs. Jayden will get to know you and form that attachment. Have you made the appointment for the paternity test yet?"

I release a deep breath, trying to let Zoey's words calm me. "Not yet."

She nods. "I'll watch Jayden while you make the call and then we'll head out."

The one positive thing I found in all my research was that Jayden's car seat is a baseless one, so I can take him in the car with us safely. I ended up watching a ton of videos on how I'm supposed to secure him in the car.

I look over at the cute sleeping baby before I head into my

bedroom to schedule the appointment that could very well change the rest of my life.

I didn't think they'd have an opening today, but they said if I could be there within the hour, they'd take us, and that is how I find myself sitting in the waiting room between Zoey and Jayden's car seat. My leg won't stop shaking, the only way I seem to be able to process my nervous energy right now.

After a minute, Zoey's hand comes to the top of my thigh and puts pressure on my leg, stopping the shaking. I look at her, and she offers me a soft smile. "I know you're nervous, but you're driving me batty with the leg shaking."

I try to hold my leg still, but I can't. Thoughts of what this test could mean run through my head. What am I supposed to do if he's not mine? I have to completely turn my life upside down if he is. Having a kid is so much responsibility, and I'm not sure I'll be able to change everything in my life quick enough.

Zoey's hand finds my leg again as a nurse walks out of the back and calls my name. A whispered, "Thank God," leaves Zoey, and I stand, grabbing the car seat and follow the nurse. She explains the whole process, but I'm barely paying attention. She swipes a cotton swap around the inside of my cheek and does the same to Jayden and tells me they'll put a rush on the results and call me as soon as they're in.

I take Jayden back to the waiting room, and Zoey stands immediately. "How did it go?" she asks.

I grip the back of my neck. "Good, I guess. She said they'll rush the results."

She nods and leads the way back to the car. I make sure Jayden is secured in the back, and then we head to the baby store.

Walking in and seeing everything is overwhelming. Every time I've been here, it's been to grab something for Cate or my friend Caleb's daughter Charlie. Being here to grab things for my own kid is entirely different. I stand near the entrance and stare into the store, taking it all in.

Zoey turns to me and takes charge. I'm so grateful she's with me right now. She was Liv's friend for the longest time, and is still her best friend, but around the time that Liv and her ex, Drew, broke up, Zoey and I became close, too. We both knew Josh and Liv should be together, and we worked together to push them towards each other. Our relationship grew from there, and I would now call Zoey one of my friends.

Liv and Josh started spending more time together, which meant they had less time for us. We started filling those spots for each other. When I got the flu last winter, Zoey came over with soup and sat and watched *Lord of the Rings* with me. When Zoey's needed a ride after a late night out, I've picked her up. That's how she ended up on my couch last night.

She leads me towards the cribs and turns to face me. "Okay, do you know what type of crib you want?"

"I didn't even know there were different types. I'm sure Liv did a ton of research. Why don't we just grab the same one she got," I say.

She nods. "Should we call Liv and ask her what else she got? Brands and such?"

"No," I practically shout, my hand shooting up. After taking a breath, I drop my hand and say, "I don't want to tell Liv until I know the test results. Until then, I'll have to make do with what the two of us know."

She holds my gaze before she sighs. "Okay, well, for what it's worth, I don't think Liv would say anything about all this." She waves her hand in front of Jayden and me. "I think she'd just be happy to be an aunt. Don't underestimate your sister."

Jayden starts to make noises of discomfort, and I look at the car seat sitting in the shopping cart and start pushing it back and forth, trying to calm him.

Looking back at Zoey, I say, "I know. This is just never how I imagined I would do this. I always thought one day I'd find the girl I wanted to spend the rest of my life with, we'd get married, *then* have kids. I never pictured it as me knocking up some woman who would then leave our child on my doorstep after never telling me she was pregnant. It's all been so much to process in the span of less than twelve hours. I'm still kinda freaking out."

She steps close and tips her head back, staring up at me, and I take in the softness of her gorgeous brown eyes and inhale deeply.

The delicate scent of her perfume has the stress slowly leaving me. Her hand comes to my bicep, and she gives it a quick squeeze before I take a step back, our proximity mixed with the smell of her perfume reminding me of a time I almost crossed the line with her.

"Matt, I know you didn't plan this, but you're in this situation now, and you're going to make the best of it. You're going to be an amazing dad. We'll grab the things you need and head back to your place, and I'll stick around to help you get everything set up. I've seen you with Cate, this is the same, just all the time," she says with a small laugh. Her words are comforting, and knowing she'll stick around tonight to help out makes me feel better.

We make our way through the store and start loading things into the cart. Zoey remembered the brand of Liv's crib from the registry she made months ago, and we grab a pack and play, a ton of baby clothes, a bottle warmer and few bottles, boxes and boxes of diapers, and wipes, and Zoey grabs a few of the comfort items she thinks Jayden will need.

When we leave the store, the receipt almost touches the ground and my bank account is significantly smaller.

Back at my place, Zoey makes Jayden a bottle while I carry everything upstairs. I take in my apartment, trying to figure out where in the world I'm going to put everything. It's insane just how much such a tiny person needs in order to survive. The crib is going to have to go in the corner of my room. Thankfully, the bedroom is pretty empty except for my bed, nightstand, dresser, and TV.

A few curse words and pinched fingers later and I have it ready for us to put Jayden to bed. He's been pretty chill today, but I have no idea what tomorrow is going to be like. We get him settled, and I order takeout for Zoey and me while we start going through the rest of the things we bought. We set up one corner of the living room with all of Jayden's things, and by the time we finish, our food has arrived.

We settle on the couch and pull up the last show we were watching together. After the day I had today, it's nice to be able to sit here with Zoey, relaxing and watching TV.

When she's done her food, she takes her plate into the kitchen and places it in the dishwasher before saying, "Well, I should be going."

I walk with her the few steps to the front door, and she grabs her coat and purse.

"Thanks for today, Zo. I'm not sure I could have done any of it without you. You're a better friend than I deserve."

"Of course. You're just as good a friend, Matt."

She squeezes my arm and opens the door. I watch her walk down the hallway to the elevator, not closing the door until she's inside and riding down.

The second I settle back on the couch, Jayden starts crying. I make a bottle before heading into my room and picking him up. Thankfully, he takes the bottle pretty easily, and I rock him, hoping he'll fall asleep again.

When he finally falls asleep, I decide to call it a night, too, climbing into bed. Jayden is up like clockwork every few hours, and I don't sleep for shit.

CHAPTER 3

Zoey

I don't know what I'm doing or why the hell when I got up this morning I decided to grab breakfast and go to Matt's.

I hold up my fist and stare at his front door, rethinking this whole thing. I really hope this isn't my heart playing stupid games with me and wanting to be close to Matt. I may have redeveloped a small crush on him over the last year as our friendship grew. I had one in eighth grade for a short period, but I thought it had gone away completely. Apparently, I was wrong. Our relationship started off as us trying to get Liv and Josh together, and it grew into us actually being friends ourselves, hanging out and watching movies, playing laser tag, and even doing some hikes during the summer. Matt's got this certain charm that's hard not to be sucked into. Not only is he six-foot-two and hot, but he's also caring and thoughtful and an amazing brother and friend. But I know I can't get sucked in too far, because the last thing I want to be is another notch in his bedpost. As much as I know Matt will eventually settle down with some lucky woman, I also know he's enjoying his freedom and doing that with a slew of different women, and I'm not built like that. I'm a relationship girl. I don't sleep with guys until after the third date, minimum, and more often than not, I don't sleep with them until after the sixth. If I were to sleep with Matt, it would fuck up the whole group dynamic and make things extremely awkward with Liv. I'm not going to do that. Liv has given me her blessing for something to happen, but I'd only do that if it was serious.

Matt is my friend, my best friend's brother. None of this makes him having a new baby my problem. But remembering just how flustered Matt was yesterday has me not backing down. I'm going to help him. Also, Jayden is just so freaking cute.

I finally knock, and a moment later Matt slowly opens the door, a smile spreading across his face when he realizes it's me, not his sister or someone else.

"Hey, Zo!" Enthusiasm fills his voice.

"Hey. I thought you could use some breakfast and maybe a check-in this morning," I say, holding up the Tim Hortons bag and coffee in my hand.

"You're a godsend," he says, pulling the door open and inviting me in.

I pass him the coffee and make my way to the dining table, where Jayden is buckled into his car seat. I start taking food out as I ask, "Heading out somewhere?"

Matt shakes his head. "No, it was just the easiest place to put him right now."

I nod. "You should probably get in some tummy time with him, maybe play some music."

Matt hums his acknowledgement as he joins me at the table. We eat in silence. His eyes locked on a sleeping Jayden.

"Do you have a plan to tell your sisters and parents?" I ask, and I feel the tension radiating off him.

"Not yet. I don't know how to drop the bomb on my family yet. I'm sure Mom will be upset she couldn't be around during the pregnancy and dote on Jayden's mom and do all those fun grandma things. I know she got to do all that with Liv and Cate, and Cate is the first grandkid, but I also know she's going to want to do it with all her grandkids. I don't know what Liv or Gi will say. I'm supposed to be their big brother, the role model, and here I am, only just now finding out I'm a father. What kind of example is that?"

Matt has always prided himself on being a good brother. He's always done everything he can to protect and support his sisters. I guess in all these years, I never realized the stress that put on him.

"You know both Liv and Gi look up to you, right? This isn't

going to change anything. They care about what's in your heart. How you treat them, your family, and your friends. When it comes to Jayden, all they're going to care about is how you respond to it all. How you take care of Jayden. Your parents are proud of you, no matter what. I don't think you should be as scared as you are when it comes to them." I feel Matt's eyes boring into me, but I continue. "Maybe when you get the results, you can make dinner and invite them over to meet Jayden. Then you're in your safe place and you know you have everything for Jayden and you can be more in control of the situation."

Matt doesn't say anything, and when I turn to look at him, he's staring at me with something in his expression I can't decipher.

He clears his throat. "You're right." He nods. "You know us all pretty well," he says, a forced lightness to his voice.

I laugh. "After nearly two decades, I probably know you as much as your siblings."

He laughs, too. "Again, you're right. You're an honorary Carter."

Those words make my stomach turn. Growing up, I always wanted to be a Carter. My parents were never around. It wasn't until I was older that I realized they spent most of their time either drunk in bars or looking for their next high. I was lucky as a kid, because my older brothers shielded me from so much of that.

I have five brothers, to be exact, and Henry, the oldest, took on the responsibility of taking care of the five of us younger siblings. He's twelve years older than me. He's now married to a wonderful woman named Maggie, and they've both agreed they never want kids; they want to travel and enjoy life. I can't blame them, especially after Henry raised five kids that weren't his and never got to enjoy his childhood.

After Henry moved out, the responsibility of taking care of the rest of us fell to Ezra, but that was only for a year or two until he moved out, too, and it fell to Kai for four years and then Riley. Even after they moved out, my brothers always made sure they'd come by and check on the rest of us. As I got older, I saw how the responsibility weighed on them. They don't talk about it much, but I know Henry, Ezra, and even Kai saw the worst of our parents.

"Zo?"

I shake my head as Matt pulls me from my thoughts. "Huh?"

"I asked if you'd be here for dinner when I tell my family."

"Matt—" I start, but he takes hold of my hand.

"Please, Zo. It would mean a lot to me if you were here. Plus, you and I are the only people Jayden knows so far, it might help him to have somewhat familiar people around."

His eyes are pleading, and for some reason, even though I know it's probably not the best decision for me, I find myself unable to say no. I nod. "Yeah, I'll be here."

He squeezes my hand. "Thanks, Zo, you're a life saver."

I slowly pull my hand free from his and leave the table. I need some distance from Matt. This pull I feel towards him is becoming too much. I'm agreeing to things that aren't my business, because I hate seeing how all of this is weighing on him. I'm not family. I shouldn't be at this family dinner when he tells his parents and siblings he now has a son. Being an honorary Carter doesn't actually make me a Carter.

I make my way to the corner where we set up Jayden's things last night. I pull out the box with the tummy time mat and the toys to put over it and begin setting it up. Matt joins me and tries to take over, but I tell him to feed Jayden while I finish.

When I'm done, I grab Jayden from Matt and lie on the floor with him. I put him on his back at first and show him all the toys above him, and he smiles and giggles as I shake the moon-shaped toy. His laugh is so light and full of joy it has me smiling back at him.

From the corner of my eye, I notice Matt lie on the floor on the other side of Jayden. Matt smiles at me as he grabs the sun toy and does the same thing. Jayden's attention moves to it, and I let go of the moon as Matt and I smile at the adorable little boy. After a few minutes, I help Jayden roll onto his tummy and run my hand over the edge of the blanket with a textured section that crinkles when you put pressure on it. Jayden focuses intently on it, a smile playing on his lips, as I continue to make it make noise. After a few minutes, I help Jayden roll onto his back and play with the hanging toys again.

We continue playing with Jayden for a bit before I can tell he's getting tired again and is ready for his nap. Picking him up, I settle him against me before heading in the direction of Matt's room, where the crib is. I quickly swaddle him before setting him in the crib and quietly backing out.

When I get back into the living room, Matt is sitting on the couch, running his fingers through his hair, leaving his curls a mess as a sigh leaves him. I grab my purse and stop in front of him.

"So, I'm just going to head out," I say, and Matt's head shoots up.

"What?"

I nod towards the door. "I'm going to head home," I say again and begin to leave.

His hand shoots out and wraps around my wrist. "Please stay." The look in his eyes is earnest, like he's not sure he can be by himself. "Watch a movie or something with me. Whatever you want, Zo. I just really need the company right now." He gives my wrist a quick squeeze, as if pleading more.

I nod and drop my purse on the table before settling beside him. I feel the anxiety slowly leave him as his shoulders deflate and he hands me the remote. I silently take it, pulling up Netflix and putting on the first comfort movie I know we'll both enjoy.

We're almost halfway into the movie when we both jump as his phone begins ringing loudly on the coffee table. He scrambles for it, flashing the screen to me where it says Granville Labs, and answers.

"Hello." His voice comes out hoarse, and he clears his throat.

The volume on his phone is loud enough I can tell it's a woman speaking, but I can't pick up what she's saying. I move to the edge of my seat, waiting and ready for him to hang up and tell me the results of the test.

He nods before saying, "Thank you," and hanging up.

He looks at me and swallows before his barely there words hit my ears. "He's mine."

I'm not shocked the way I thought I would be. If you look closely enough between Matt and Jayden, you can see Jayden has a lot of the same features. The shape of his nose, the colour of his eyes, even the little wisps of hair he has, which you can tell will grow out similar to Matt's curls.

I curl a leg up on the couch, allowing me to face him more fully. "How do you feel about that?" I ask.

He sits back on the couch, tipping his head back, and stares at the ceiling as a long breath escapes him. "Relieved, I guess, is the first feeling. There's no longer this is he–isn't he. I know he's mine. I'm also worried I'm going to fail him." He looks at me and puts a hand up, stopping me as I open my mouth. "And yes, I know, Zo, I'm great with Cate. And I love her, but she's my niece. This whole time I've known I get to watch and play with her when Liv needs help and I wouldn't be screwing her up. She'd be going home to loving parents who know what they're doing. Liv and Josh had months to plan for Cate. I just got a baby dropped on my doorstep. I'm going to do everything I can to be the best dad to Jayden and give him everything I can in life, but I'm scared shitless."

Matt's fear is palpable. I can see it in his face and feel it in his body language. I reach out and squeeze his leg.

"I'll let you in on a little secret, and you better not tell your sister I told you, because I'm not losing best friend status."

He nods.

"Liv was scared shitless, too, when she found out she was pregnant. Yes, she was so excited, but also, having a kid was a big change. She and Josh had only just gotten together. You had just found out about their relationship the night before. Everything in her life was changing. But she had a great family around her, your parents, you, and Gianna. Josh was so excited. Plus, she had all of us girls. You've got all the same people in your corner. You're going to be a great dad. Believe me, I know something about shitty parents, and you're not going to be one. I think being so worried you will be is the first sign you should take that you won't. Shitty parents don't worry about being shitty parents."

"Thanks, Zo. It means the world to me you'd say that. I'm not sure what I'd do if you weren't here."

He gives my hand a squeeze and runs his thumb over the top of it. That mixed with the look in his eyes has goosebumps scattering up my arm. Spending time with Matt over the last year and a half has been great, except I started to develop feelings for a man I know I can never have. Matt's always been attractive, but spending one-on-one time with him and seeing parts of him I never did growing up has not helped at all. I always knew he was a protective brother, but I never realized how funny he is, or how when he's home he likes to curl up on the couch in a pair of sweats with a blanket and popcorn and watch movies.

This last year and a half let me see his serious side, not just his goofball one. But I know he's not ready to settle down, especially now that he's had the major responsibility of a child dropped on him. When I said he'll be a great father, I meant it. I know he will do whatever is necessary to give Jayden the best life possible.

I pull my hand from his and pull them into the sleeves of my cardigan, crossing my legs in front of me. "Yeah, of course." Looking around him, I check the time on the stove and say, "I should probably head out, it's getting late."

He nods and pushes up from the couch, helping me up before wrapping his arms around me and pulling me into his chest. "Thanks for everything, Zo."

Nodding against him, I inhale his scent and close my eyes for a second, allowing myself to enjoy the feeling of him being close and the way his cologne envelopes me, before stepping back.

"Let me know when you want to do that family dinner," I say before making my way to the front door. My hand hovers over the handle for a few seconds as if my brain and heart are debating whether I should really go. My brain wins, and I leave Matt's apartment.

CHAPTER 4

Matt

Trying to find a date that works for my entire family, Zoey, and me is a pain in the ass. When I press the importance of dinner, we finally settle on Saturday.

Zoey is over every day for at least a couple of hours. I'm not sure how we both manage to go the whole week without seeing Liv, because that never happens. I've watched Zoey skirt Liv's calls when she's been over, and I've done the same, trying to keep all of our communication via text so I can hopefully not reveal anything until I can do it in person.

I'm a ball of nerves as I cook dinner. Finally, believing I have everything ready, I grab Jayden from Zoey. After I got the call from the lab on Sunday, I emailed my boss and took family leave, and I can take federal parental leave so Jayden and I can adjust to our new normal. I've picked up on some of his tells, like the way he squirms differently when he's gassy and I need to help work the bubbles out before he starts screaming, and the look of concentration he makes before he poops. There is still so much more I need to learn, but knowing those two things no one else does makes me feel better about this situation.

A knock at the door has me on edge. There is no more planning or running through hypotheticals about telling my family. I'm doing this. Zoey's eyes meet mine as she exhales slowly, and I follow her lead. I nod, and she moves to answer the door. Before pulling it open, she does one last check with me, and when I nod again she pulls it open.

"Zo?" Liv's questioning voice comes from outside.

"Hey, Liv."

They hug, and Zoey holds the door open for her and her husband Josh to come inside. Liv takes off her jacket and hangs it up, not even noticing me standing in the kitchen, but Josh does. I've never seen him as stunned as he looks right now with his jaw on the ground as he stares at me. Josh and I have been best friends since we were kids. We met in school and bonded and have never looked back. We played hockey together in school, attended Harvard together, play on the same rec hockey team, and now he's married to my younger sister and the father of my adorable niece. All that to say, I've seen Josh in a lot of states, but nothing compares to this.

Liv looks at him and asks, "What's wrong, babe?" She turns to look at me, and her jaw drops, too.

I smile at them, really out of my comfort zone right now. I guess I should at least be happy they're the first ones here, because it's going to be easier to tell them than my parents. I'm not sure how our younger sister Gianna is going to react, though.

"Hey," I say, and they close their mouths, Liv opening and closing hers a few times, trying to gather herself.

"How about we take a seat," Zoey says, helping usher them to the table and taking the car seat with Cate from Josh.

As soon as Liv's ass hits the chair, it's like she's magically gathered herself. She looks between Zoey and I before she asks, "Why is there a baby here, and who does he belong to?"

Zoey and I exchange a look that Liv picks up and has her diving into even more questions. "When? How? Why didn't you say anything? How long have you known?"

Zoey, knowing her best friend as well as I do, places a cup of water in front of her and a hand on her shoulder and says, "Breathe, Liv."

Liv turns on her. "And when did you find out? Why did you know before me? Why didn't you tell me? Is this the only secret you're keeping from me, or are there more?"

Something about seeing Liv interrogate Zoey has me breaking my silence. "Zo only knows because she was here when I found out."

She turns back to me so quickly I'm not sure how she doesn't fall out of her chair. "Why was she here? Oh my God, have you two been secretly hooking up behind my back? I told you guys you have my permission, why wouldn't you tell me?"

That's news to me. I had no idea she had given us her blessing. I shake my head, because it doesn't matter; we're not hooking up. Zoey is more of a relationship girl, and I'm currently in a "having fun" state—or I was, until Jayden.

"Zoey had a bit too much at the bar, I picked her up and offered my couch for her to crash. She went to leave in the morning and Jayden was in a car seat outside my door with a diaper bag."

Josh and Liv look stunned, more than they were first seeing me with Jayden. "You mean someone left a baby unattended outside your door in an apartment building where anyone could have taken him?" Josh asks.

I nod.

"Fucking hell," he mutters as he rubs a hand down his face.

"Look, I know you want all the answers right now, but I'd really love to tell this story only once. Can we wait until Mom, Dad, and Gi get here?" I ask.

Liv's eyes soften as she looks at me and nods. "Can you at least tell me this, is he yours?"

I look down at the small bundle in my arms and smile softly. Running my finger down his nose, I say, "Yeah, he's mine."

I pour Zoey a glass of wine and hand it to her before grabbing beers for myself and Josh and making a mocktail for Liv. She's choosing not to drink while she's breastfeeding. She wasn't a huge drinker before, so it doesn't seem to be the end of the world for her.

We settle at the table, and Josh, Liv, and I slip into talks of the NHL pre-season so far. Zoey's not as big a fan of hockey as the three of us, but I know she's enjoying the lull before the storm that will be this dinner.

When there's another knock at the door, I hold my breath.

Liv reaches for my hand and squeezes it in the same way we've done for each other our entire lives. "I'm right here. Know that no matter what happens or how this goes down, I'm always in your corner."

I squeeze her hand back and smile at Zoey, because she was right,

I had nothing to fear when it came to telling Liv. My sister has always been the understanding type, and above all, she's loyal and supportive.

Zoey reaches for Jayden, and I pass him to her and make my way to the front door, greeting my parents and sister. Mom immediately pulls me into a hug and kisses my cheek, giving it a couple of taps before she walks past me and into my place. I hug my dad before moving to Gianna. With my arms wrapped around her, I whisper in her ear, "I'm sorry it had to be this way." Pulling back, I give her a smile, and she gives me a quizzical look.

Stepping back inside, I move quickly to Zoey's side, running my finger over Jayden's nose again before taking him from her and standing in front of my parents.

"Mom. Dad. I'd like you to meet my son Jayden."

The look of hurt that crosses Mom's face as she clutches her chest and stares at me has me almost breaking. I'm not sure how I'm supposed to do this. I understand Mom's pain, I do, but I hope she understands mine, too. Having my son dropped on my doorstep was never my plan for building a family. I've always known that when I did decide to have kids, I wanted to be a part of the whole experience, the pregnancy, the planning, the birth. I'm hurt and angry I wasn't given the chance to be a part of everything. I lost out on so much because Hazel never told me she was pregnant. I'm still trying to process that I missed out on all of it.

Dad helps lead Mom to the table, where she takes a seat beside Liv while Dad shakes Josh's hand and kisses Liv's cheek. Gi takes a seat beside Zoey, and we let the silence wrap around us, all of us knowing Mom needs to process this. After a few minutes, she seems to do that and wipes at a tear that's started its way down her cheek. That tear is soul crushing.

She takes a deep breath and turns to me. "Okay, what happened, Matthew?"

My full name. *Great.*

I grip the back of my neck and settle into my chair. Mom watches Jayden as I tell them everything, every detail, so they have all the information. The more I tell them, the more tears build in Mom's eyes. When Jayden starts to fuss, Zoey gets up and makes him a bottle. I take it from her with a smile and thanks and feed him as I finish the story. They all hang on to my every word, not wanting to miss a thing, and I can't blame them.

When I'm finally done, Dad is the first to speak. "So, what's your plan?"

Dad's always been a pragmatist, making plans and trying to avoid anything that could go wrong.

Before I can say anything, Mom asks, "Can I hold him?"

I nod and pass her grandson to her. She stares down at him with so much love in her eyes.

"I'm going to start looking for a place to move. This works for now, but I know that very shortly, I'll need more space and that means a house, probably. I've been saving, knowing it's been in the plans, even if it wasn't in the near future. I've looked into the daycare program at the office, and it's good, so when I go back, I'll be able to leave him there during the day. I've taken some time off to adjust to everything. I've been looking for a pediatrician so I can make sure he's up to date on his vaccines. Beyond that, I'm not sure. It's only been a few days, and thank God Zo's been here, because she's kept me sane," I say.

Zoey gives my arm a squeeze. "Don't sell yourself short. You've been doing a great job."

Everyone looks at her, and her cheeks pinken.

"Thank you, Zo. For being there for Matt. I'm sure this was not on your plans for the week," Mom says.

She nods. "I'm happy to help."

We finally serve the food and settle in at the table, moving the conversation on to Liv and Josh's anniversary and our Thanksgiving dinner plans. My parents always host, and we now do a joint dinner with the Lincolns, Liv's in-laws, after she was so indecisive about how to spend the holiday. It's a good thing our families were close when we were all growing up. Zoey, like usual, will be heading to her oldest brother's house for their big dinner. I'm sad she won't be doing dinner with us. She's become my lifeline this week, and I'm not sure I can stay afloat without her for an entire day.

When we finish eating, Mom insists on getting to hold Jayden again, and no one has the heart to argue with her. I clear the table with Gi as everyone else joins Mom in the living room.

"So, you're a dad now," she says as she puts plates in the sink and starts rinsing them. She's been quiet tonight, not saying much when we were talking about Jayden. Gi has only been home from finishing her degree at Stanford for four months. She's changed a lot since she graduated from high school. She's become more observant and less carefree than she was then, and I'm not sure it's for the better.

"Yeah."

"I'm sorry," she says, and I stop what I'm doing and turn to face her.

"What do you mean?"

She looks at me over her shoulder and continues to rinse dishes and put them in the dishwasher. "I know this wasn't what you wanted. I know, I know, you've always wanted kids. But you've always wanted them after you settled down. It's the same as Liv and me. We had Mom and Dad to look up to, the Lincolns, too. I know you'll be a great dad, though."

She places the last plate in the dishwasher, and I wrap my arms around her. "Thanks, Gi. You know I love you, right? I never wanted to keep this from you guys. I just knew it would be easier for me to tell you all at once."

Her arms wrap around me, and she holds me tight. "I know. I love you, too, Matty."

I kiss the top of her head and step back to lean against the counter, crossing my arms over my chest and legs at the ankle.

"Okay, so tell me what's going on with you. We haven't had a ton of time to catch up since you've been back."

She shrugs. "Not much. Can't get up to too much while living at Mom and Dad's."

"What about Em?" I ask, referring to her best friend and Josh's sister. "Have you been hanging out with her? Any news on the job hunt?"

She shakes her head. "No, Em's been busy, and nothing for a job yet. I have a few applications out that seem to be making some progress, so hopefully soon."

We move into the living room and join the rest of the family.

"He looks like you," Mom says, staring at Jayden, who is now in Dad's arms. I smile, because he does. Zoey has pointed out a couple of features this week, and every time she points out something new, it has my body filling with warmth, and I can't stop smiling. Mom's holding Cate now, and seeing the two babies together has an entirely different feeling rushing through me. A *we're all grown up* feeling. It was one thing when just Liv had a kid, but now I do, too, and I'm sure Gi will eventually, as well.

The rest of the evening is a game of pass the babies, the two of them making it through all of us before Liv says they need to call it a night and settles Cate in the car seat and begins saying her goodbyes. Everyone else starts to pack up, too, and I meet them at the front door, exchanging hugs before watching them make their way to the elevator. When I turn around, I take in Zoey, who's stuck around a little longer.

She fiddles with her hands in front of her. "I'm going to head, too. I'm so glad tonight went well."

"Thanks for being here. I'm not sure I could have done it without you. And seriously, thank you for everything you've done this week. You were literally my saving grace in this disaster."

We hug, and then she makes her way out to her car while I get my boy changed and settled in his crib for the night.

CHAPTER 5

Zoey

I roll over as my phone rings for the second time. Grabbing it, I see Matt's name flash across my screen. Two calls in a row have me shooting up in bed and my heart racing.

"Is everything okay?" I answer.

"Ummm... Yes, but I could I really use your help, Zo."

I exhale deeply, and my shoulders relax. "What is it?" I ask.

"Could you meet me at the rink in twenty minutes?" His voice comes out hopeful.

I pull my phone away from my face to check the time. "I guess. Why will you be at the rink at six in the morning on a Monday?"

"You're a life saviour. I'll explain everything there."

We say goodbye, and I quickly change into a pair of jeans, a T-shirt, a hoodie, and knee-high boots, not sure how long I'll be in the cold. I grab a peppermint mocha on my way, needing something to help wake me up. Caffeine has never really done the trick for me, but sugar does.

When I pull into the parking lot of the hockey rink Matt and Josh's rec team plays at, it's full. I manage to find a spot on the far side of the lot and make my way inside. I check my phone quickly and see he's told me which of the rinks inside he's at. I make my way through the building, taking in all the kids in their hockey gear and their very tired-looking parents bundled up and sitting either on the bleachers or standing at the boards. Every time I've been here, it's been with Liv to watch one of the guys' games. This is a whole different environment.

Rounding the corner, I see Matt dressed in his skates, pants, and a hoodie with Jayden strapped to his chest.

He smiles when he spots me. "Aren't you a sight for sore eyes," he says.

"You going to tell me why you dragged my ass out of bed at the ass crack of dawn?" I ask, a little grumpy about the situation.

He grips the back of his neck like he does when he's nervous, one of those ticks you tend to pick up from people when you spend enough time with them. "So... I... Ummm... I coach this kids' hockey team, and I need someone to watch Jayden. No one knows I coach, and you're the only one that's spent a ton of time with Jayden, and I really didn't want to bother Liv when she has Cate, and I really, really didn't want to drive all the way out to my parents'." The look he gives me is pleading, and as much as I try and hold my resolve and say no because I'm not some on-call babysitter, I deflate and give in.

I reach my hands out, and he passes me Jayden before taking the baby carrier off and leaving it for me.

"Thank you, thank you, thank you. You really are a life saver," he says, kissing my cheek before moving towards the ice.

"We'll be talking about this afterwards, Matthew," I call.

He gives me a solemn look and nods.

I watch as Matt calls the team to meet at centre ice. The kids look to be seven or eight, and I'm surprised by how well many of them move in skates. He runs them through some drills, and I take in how good he is with these kids. He takes the time to work one-on-one with some of the ones that are struggling.

I get the baby carrier secured on me and Jayden settled, pulling up a book on my phone. As I'm halfway through the first page, a man sits next to me.

"So, which one's yours?" he asks, and I look over at him. He's handsome, probably in his late thirties with dark-brown hair with a little salt and pepper around his temples. The smile he gives me is soft and inviting. The start of a dimple appears in his left cheek, obscured by a light dusting of stubble.

I smile. "None of them. I'm friends with the coach, I'm just babysitting for now."

He nods. "I didn't know Coach Carter had any kids," he says.

I'm not sure what to say; it's really not my place to go around spilling his secrets. Avoiding the whole story of what's happened, I settle for, "Yup, this is his son."

He runs his hands up his thighs, rubbing them on his jeans. My eyes can't help but snag on the veins in his hands and arms as they move. Something about them has me wanting to feel them under my hands.

"So, you and Coach Carter..." he starts.

"Are friends," I finish for him. "His sister is my best friend. I'm just helping him out this morning."

He nods a few times, like he's formulating a plan of some kind. We sit in silence until Matt dismisses the kids and one of the boys comes up to this mystery man. He taps him on the head, and the kid makes his way to the dressing room with the rest of the kids. Matt eyes me and the new guy before joining the kids.

We enjoy some small talk until his son is done.

As he gets up to leave, he turns to me. "I'd love to take you to dinner sometime," he says, and I smile. It's been a while since I've met a nice guy organically like this. All of my recent dates have been horrible online dating experiences.

"I'd love that."

His grin widens. "Great." He reaches into his pocket and pulls out a business card. "Here's my card, my cell's on there. Just shoot me a text, and we can make plans."

I take the card from him, and our fingers graze. I immediately notice there's no instant spark that has me wanting him to pull me into him, but maybe that's something we can build over time. "Sounds like a date," I say, and he leads his son out of the rink.

Watching them leave, I see Matt leaning against the wall outside the dressing room. His jaw looks tight as he stares at me. He pushes off the wall and walks towards me. "Going on a date with Dean Baxter?" His tone is on the edge of accusation and something else I can't quite decipher.

"Yes. Do you have a problem with that?" I ask, really not liking the way he's acting. He has no right to say who I can and can't date, so what is the point in asking?

"Nope, just curious," he grinds out.

"Good. Now can we circle back to you calling me to come babysit for you?"

He sits beside me and looks down at his son, who's peacefully asleep in the carrier. I can't help but to look down and take in the adorable little boy snuggled against my chest right now.

"I'm sorry for calling you," Matt eventually says, breaking the silence. "I didn't know what to do. You're the only person I could think of that was close that I knew I could trust unconditionally with him and didn't have children of their own they'd have to wrangle. I know it wasn't cool to just expect you to drop everything and show up. I appreciate you. I know I've asked a lot of you recently, so whatever you need from me, you've got a no-questions-asked favour."

"I think you owe me a few," I say with just enough levity in my voice to not sound like a bitch, but seriously enough that he knows I mean it.

He looks at me, making eye contact, and nods. "You're right. You've got a few no-questions-asked favours from me."

"Okay, well, now that we've cleared that up, why don't you take me to breakfast? I'm starving."

Matt laughs. "Why am I not surprised?"

I grin. "Because you know I require my daily dose of morning sugar and food to function."

"Let's go."

When we walk into the restaurant, it's extremely empty. I shouldn't be surprised, it's a Monday morning and everyone else is either at work or school. We find a booth in the corner and settle in. While I browse the menu, Matt makes a bottle for Jayden and feeds him. Jayden seems to be beginning to form an attachment to Matt, which is amazing. I know it was one of the things he was most worried about. He takes his bottle from him easily, and Matt tells me he's been sleeping in longer stints, which has been great for Matt's sleep, too.

"It must be weird being home all the time with a baby all of a sudden," I say.

Matt nods while watching Jayden guzzle down his bottle. "It is, but it's also been kind of amazing. I never planned Jayden, but even just having him for a week, I can say I'm glad he came into my life. I still have so much to figure out and life is crazy now, trying to make a new schedule around his feedings and naps, but it's so worth it. He smiled at me for the first time the other day, and I swore my heart stopped in my chest."

Our waitress comes over and takes our order. She can't seem to look away from Matt feeding Jayden, and I can't blame her. Matt's a good-looking guy, always has been. His brown hair is thick and has a slight curl to it that when it grows out a bit, like it has recently, it flops onto his forehead. He's let his beard grow out more than I've ever seen him do before, and something about it sends tingles through me.

I mentally slap myself. Matt's always been forbidden fruit. I can window shop with Matt. I can stare at him from afar and acknowledge it would probably be amazing to go for a roll in the sheets with him. He's probably picked up some techniques over the years. But I also know I do relationships. I don't do one-night stands, and I don't do casual. Matt is very much the opposite. So, to prevent any issues, I'll watch and never touch.

"He looks just like you," the waitress says to Matt as she puts a cup of coffee in front of him.

Matt looks up at that. "Thanks," he says.

When she leaves, I ask, "So, how long have you been coaching this kids' team?"

His eyes flicker to me then back to the bottle. Seeing Jayden's finished, he puts the bottle on the table and moves to burp Jayden. He does it all in silence, as if he's taking his time to answer the question.

"I started my first year back from Harvard. I felt like I was missing something. Especially with Gi being in San Fran for school and Liv was living her own life, and I had moved out of my parents' house. I found a posting looking for a coach for a kids' team, and I sent them an email. The dad had heard of me from my time in high school and even looked up some of my university games. They said they'd love to have me, and I've stuck it out since. It's been amazing watching the growth of the kids. I'm not coaching the same team I started with. I started with these kids about two years ago."

I run my finger over the lip of my cup of orange juice. "You looked like a natural out there with the kids. You really took the time to have little one-on-ones with some of them and listen to them. It only goes to show how great of a dad you'll be. And just wait, one day you'll be out there coaching Jayden's team, and maybe he'll follow in daddy's footsteps and play hockey for many years to come."

Matt clears his throat and readjusts himself, looking anywhere but my face.

"What's wrong?" I ask.

"Nothing," he says as he pulls at the collar of his shirt. He settles Jayden in his car seat and takes a long sip of his coffee. "Enough about me, Zo. How are you? How is it adjusting to being done with school?"

It's my turn to take my time answering the question, because I'm not entirely sure how I feel except lost. I'm still not sure what I'm going to do. I've passed my bar exam, and I'm an officially licensed lawyer and could apply to a ton of firms, but the thought of doing that day in and day out doesn't bring me the joy I hoped it would. The most content I've felt in the last few months was being at Matt's with Jayden. Something about helping someone who desperately needed help brought me joy.

"I'm not exactly looking forward to moving in with Henry again, but it is what it is," I say, and Matt raises a brow. Over the last year, he's begun to do that when he can tell I'm holding something back from him.

"Zo, you know you can tell me, right? I won't tell anyone, not even Liv."

I know he's telling the truth. Matt has always been a vault for his sisters' secrets, and he's kept a few of mine, too. I really need to talk about this because I'm just out here floating in the open ocean with no land on the horizon.

"I'm not sure I want to be a lawyer," I finally say.

He settles back in the booth. "Okay. Wow. I was not expecting that. You know you don't have to be one if you don't want to, right? It's your life to do with as you please."

I run a finger through the condensation on my glass. "I feel like by not being one, I'm letting my family down. My brothers did so much to make sure I could get into a good university and succeed in life. By not using the degree they worked so hard to make sure I could get feels like a slap in the face to them, like I'm not grateful. I watched them work all those jobs to make sure we had food at home and the bills were paid. They helped me with my homework and were always there when I needed them." I wipe at an errant tear that slips through my barriers. "I couldn't stomach letting them all down, Matt."

Matt reaches across the table and takes my hand, and I take a deep breath. "Oh, Zo, you need to know you'd never be letting your brothers down. As an older brother, I can tell you that all I want for both my sisters is for them to be happy and live the life they want. I don't want them changing or doing anything to fit what they think I expect of them. I know it's not entirely the same, your childhood was very different from mine, but I do know your brothers love you dearly." He squeezes my hand, and I offer him a weak smile.

"Thanks, Matt."

"Zo, you should talk to Henry, maybe having a one-on-one with him will be easier than all five of them. I'm sure they'll understand."

I nod, because I know there's some truth to his words, but I don't think I'm ready yet.

CHAPTER 6

Matt

Adjusting to having a baby in my life is no easy feat. I've told the guys I wouldn't be able to make any of our hockey games for the next little bit, being vague and just telling them I had a lot going on. Josh knows about Jayden, but the others didn't pry. Zoey has been a literal godsend. She's been over to check in on Jayden and me, and I'm not sure how I got her to, but she agreed to meet me at the rink on Wednesday morning as long as I brought her coffee and took her to breakfast after, and I couldn't turn that down.

I had originally agreed to watch Cate last night while Liv and Josh celebrated their wedding anniversary, but we both agreed that it might be too much for me with Jayden right now. Luckily, Gianna and her best friend, who also happens to be Josh's sister, headed over instead.

We're heading to my parent's today for Thanksgiving and it's going to be weird not seeing Zo or talking to her all day. Even before Jayden, we talked often. It varied between telling the other about seeing things that reminded us of them or sending memes to just wanting someone to talk to. Now, we talk practically every day. She asks for updates on Jayden, and we talk about how she's processing everything around finding a new job and what she wants to do.

Pulling up in front of my parents', I take a deep breath. I haven't brought Jayden here yet. We've only been at my place, the rink, and out to run errands. I've thought about what it would be like to bring my kids here to spend time with my parents, about them being able to do cousin sleepovers with Liv's and Gi's kids. But I also imagined that with us all being settled down, being married to people we love and excited to grow our families. I can't help but feel as though I'm failing Jayden by not having his mom in our lives or being settled down with someone.

The front door opens, and Liv leans against the doorway, watching me. I guess I can't keep sitting out here lost in my thoughts.

I get out and grab Jayden and his bag before making my way up the front steps of my parents' place and kissing Liv on the cheek.

"Happy Thanksgiving, Liv."

"Happy Thanksgiving, Matty."

We walk into the house, and Gianna is the first one to me, immediately taking Jayden out of his car seat.

"Well hello to you, too, Gi," I say.

She smiles up at me. "Hi, Matty, you know I love you, but I also need some time with my nephew. Grab a beer relax, Aunty Gi's got this adorable little boy." She makes her way to the couch and settles down beside Emily, who is all over Jayden, too.

"Looks like I've lost my kid," I muse.

Liv laughs. "Get used to it. I walked in and Eleanor had Cate before I could even blink. Enjoy the kid-free time. Trust me, take advantage while you can. I'm just grateful Emily doesn't have kids yet, because we can monopolize Josh's parents' grandparent time right now. Eleanor and Logan love spending time with Cate, and I know Mom and Dad do, too, but with Jayden now, I'm not sure they'll love taking two babies at a time. Just wait, Mom will be asking you when she can take him off your hands shortly."

I laugh, because I can see it. I know how much Mom has looked forward to being a grandparent. I follow Liv into the kitchen and kiss Mom on the cheek and shake Dad's hand before grabbing something to drink and following Liv into the den. Mom doesn't like when people interfere while she's cooking a large meal like Thanksgiving or Christmas, so we've all learned to say our hellos and make ourselves scarce unless she calls us.

"So..." Liv starts, running her teeth over her bottom lip.

"Just ask, Liv," I say.

She nods and turns on the couch to face me. "Have you heard from Jayden's mom at all?"

I shake my head. "No, and I don't think I will. Her letter made it seem like she was pretty content to just sign her rights away and never see Jayden again. As much as I hate that for Jayden, if she was willing to abandon him in the first place, I'm not sure I want her back in his life to up and do it again. She could have always told me she was pregnant and we could have done this together. I could have helped her when she was overwhelmed. Instead, she left me in the dark and abandoned our son. I'm not sure that's something I can ever forgive. How do you just leave a baby? She didn't even knock to see if I was home or to make sure that was my place. She left him defenseless where anyone could take him. I'm not sure how much longer I would have slept if it wasn't for Zoey yelling for me when she went to leave that morning. I had no plans to leave that day. How long would he have sat outside my door before I found him?"

I run a hand through my hair, and my chest heaves as I finish word vomiting on my sister. I haven't said those words out loud before now. I've thought them and tried to process all of my feelings about my son being abandoned, but to put those feelings into words is freeing.

Liv squeezes my leg. "Matt, you're entitled to your feelings. And please know I will always be in your corner no matter what. But I don't want you to write her off just yet. You don't know everything that she was dealing with when she was pregnant or when she left Jayden with you. Some women experience heavy depression during and after pregnancy. She may have thought she had no other choice. Do I think what she did was right? Of course not, but I'm also not going to pretend to know what she was feeling or thinking. So don't waste your time and energy being mad at her. Spend it getting to know your little boy and building a life for him."

Why does my little sister have to be so wise? I offer her a soft smile. "I know you're right, but I don't think I'm ready to move past the anger yet."

"Fair. If I was in your shoes I'd feel the same way. I don't blame you for your feelings, and I'm here anytime you need to talk. About anything."

I pull Liv into a hug and kiss the top of her head. Liv and I have always been close. Even when we were young and fought or wanted to strangle each other, we were close. I'm glad we didn't lose that as we grew up.

"I'm thankful for you," I whisper into her hair.

She squeezes. "I'm thankful for you," she whispers back.

"What did I miss?" Josh asks, leaning against the entryway of the den.

Liv pulls back and smiles at her husband. "Just a little sibling bonding."

He kisses her forehead and hands her a drink. "I think our sisters are experiencing some baby fever. They've managed to get both babies and are in the spare room with all the toys right now. My mom's joined yours in the kitchen, and our dads are in the living room watching a football game."

"Sounds like them," Liv says.

Josh picks her up as she squeals and holds onto him before he takes her seat and she settles in his lap.

I shake my head. "You couldn't have taken the chair that's literally right beside you?" I ask.

He chuckles and shakes his head as he tucks a stray piece of Liv's hair behind her ear. "No, I want to be as close to my wife as possible."

Liv's cheeks turn pink, but I watch as her smile grows. Watching them together has me feeling nothing but happiness for them. I watched for years as they both danced around the fact they liked each other but neither of them said anything. I know Josh worships her and is an amazing husband and father. I've never seen either of them as happy as they've been since they started dating. It was a change in Josh I noticed first that tipped me off that they had indeed started dating. He didn't want to go out as often, and when I did see him, he was always in such a good mood. The fact that Liv was so worried about how their relationship would impact his and mine only reminded me of how selfless my sister is, but them being married has only brought us closer. Josh is now my brother in every way that matters.

"So, who do we think ends up with a baby first, Gianna or Emily?" Liv asks.

Josh stills under her. "I'm not ready for my baby sister to have kids," he says, and I throw my head back with a laugh.

"You're telling me. I love Cate and wouldn't change anything about you two or her, but it was a lot to hear that my baby sister was expecting."

His hand finds Liv's stomach, and he smiles at her softly.

"Are you guys expecting again?" I ask immediately, and Liv's head turns to me so quickly I'm surprised I don't hear a pop.

"No, why would you ask?"

I tip my chin at Josh's hand.

She shakes her head and smiles. "No, but one day. We want more."

"Soon," Josh says, and I shake my head.

"You two are going to have your own little hockey team."

"Not that many," Liv says. "But a full house, yeah."

She leans into Josh more, and he tightens his arm around her waist. "What about you? Do you want more after Jayden?"

I sit with the question for a minute. I think I do want more kids. I want Jayden to have built-in friends like I had with Liv and eventually Gi. I want to hear a house full of laughter. But in order to have that, I need to find someone.

Mom saves me by calling us all for dinner.

The rest of the night moves smoothly. We all laugh and enjoy dinner. As I finish getting Jayden settled at home, my phone rings in my pocket. I quickly fish it out and smile as Zoey's name flashes across the screen. Lying on the couch, I answer. "Hey, Zo."

"Hey," she says, her voice soft and almost hesitant.

"How was your Thanksgiving?" I ask.

"It was good. Henry and Maggie made an amazing dinner. It's been a while since all of us could get together. How about yours?"

"Amazing. It was the first time taking Jayden to Mom and Dad's, and I basically lost him to Gianna the second I walked in the door, so I spent a lot of time with Liv and Josh. As always, Mom made enough food to feed an army, so I brought leftovers home."

I hear shuffling on the other end of the line. "Where are you?" I ask.

"I'm just getting settled into bed," she says, and I stiffen as thoughts of Zoey in slinky pyjamas as she climbs under the sheets fill my head. The way the fabric would strain against her chest and her nipples would press against the fabric, leaving nothing to the imagination. I shake my head quickly. These kinds of thoughts about Zoey have come more and more over the last year and a half, but specifically over the last two weeks. I woke up so hard the other morning after a dream about her, that if she had been here in pyjamas just like I was imagining, I probably would have come in my boxer briefs.

"Matt?" Zoey's voice breaks through my fog, and I clear my throat.

"Hmmm?"

"How did Jayden do today?" she asks.

"Oh, he did great. He didn't fuss when Gi took him, and he slept well in the guest room when we put him down."

"I'm glad," she says as a yawn tears through her.

"I should let you get some sleep."

"Nah, I'm fine. I wanted to check in on you guys."

I can't help the grin that spreads across my face. Knowing Zoey was thinking about us today makes me happier than it should.

"Get some sleep, Zo. We can talk tomorrow."

She yawns again. "Promise?" More shuffling comes through.

"Yeah. Promise."

"Okay."

"I'm glad you called. Sleep well, Zo."

"You, too," she says before the line goes dead.

CHAPTER 7

Zoey

Spending the last week at Matt's has led me to forget about my own reality, which is that I have one week to pack my apartment up and get ready to move into my brother Henry's spare room. Now that I'm done with law school and articling, my scholarship is up, which means my funding for housing is up and I need somewhere to live. I don't have a job lined up yet, so of course my extremely protective eldest brother said I was moving in with him. I know his heart is in the right place, and I love my brother dearly, I'm just not sure I love that at twenty-six my life is moving backwards.

When I first started university, I thought when I finished I'd find a job in a nice downtown firm and begin working my way up. Find an apartment downtown, walking distance from the office and meet some nice guy and settle down. Well, none of that is happening. I've now spent eight years of my life working towards a degree I'm not even sure I want anymore. I really don't know if I want to be a lawyer. It's not calling to me the same way it did when I was eighteen.

I know one thing that pushed me to the profession was money. Growing up the way we did, barely making ends meet and having to watch my older brothers pick up jobs to help cover the bills because our parents would either spend their money on other things, or be too out of it to even make it to work and end up getting fired, really shaped the way I picked my profession. But now, watching my friends do the things they love and my brothers finding some joy in their jobs, I'm not sure I can push myself to get a job I'm not sure I want.

I haven't exactly expressed any of this to anyone. When people ask about my job hunt, I keep it vague. *It's going well. I've got a few promising options.* Whatever it takes to get them off my back. I saved up enough money from working while in school that I'm okay for basic expenses for a bit, but I don't want to live at Henry's forever, which means I need to figure out my shit.

Matt and I text during the week, but I'm too busy to pop by, knowing if I do, it won't be a quick visit, but I'll end up there for hours. On Thursday, I'm staring at my apartment, overwhelmed by all the stuff that still needs to be put in boxes. Remembering Matt saying his parents wanted to take Jayden on Friday, I text him.

ZOEY

Can I call in that favour?

MATT

Shoot

ZOEY

I need help packing. I need to be out of my place by noon on Saturday.

MATT

You're moving??? Yeah, of course. Just let me know what time to be at your place, I'm dropping Jayden off with Mom at 10 a.m.

ZOEY

Can you come right after?

MATT

I'll be there.

I release a breath, relieved I'll have some help to finish this.

I'm racing around my apartment, throwing things from the kitchen drawers into a box when there's a knock on the door.

"Come in," I call, and Matt walks in holding a Timmies bag and tray of coffee.

"Oh, my saviour." I rush towards him, and he holds out a cup towards me. I take a sip of the sugary goodness. He holds up the bag of food next and follows me into the kitchen. We stand around the island as we both dig into the food.

"Okay, what's left to do?" he asks.

"My bedroom, bathroom, and a few things in the kitchen. I've got most of the kitchen done, so I'll finish that up."

He nods. "Sounds good. I'll start on the other rooms, then."

Throwing our wrappers in the garbage, we move to our separate rooms and get to work. When I finish in the kitchen, I move into my room and stop dead in my tracks as I see Matt standing in front of my nightstand, holding a boxed toy.

I quickly gather myself before saying, "Oh my God," and rushing towards him, grabbing the box, and shoving it into the open drawer and shutting it.

He stares at me and then back at the now closed drawer and then back at me.

"I'll take care of this room," I say, and he nods, staring at me for a few long drawn out seconds before moving into the bathroom.

Fucking great. My best friend's brother just got a peek at my very extensive toy collection. I quickly find a box and empty the contents of the nightstand into it before closing it, making sure I clearly label it DO NOT TOUCH, and putting it in the living room with all the other boxes. Matt can't seem to look at me for the rest of the morning as we work together to finish packing. When I ask him if pizza is good for lunch, he gives me a grunt of acknowledgement and continues packing.

When we sit to eat, he tries to scroll on his phone, and I hate this awkward energy that's between us now. We've never been this way with each other. We've been teasing and comfortable, but never awkward. I grab his phone out of his hands, putting it on the counter behind me and out of his reach.

"Hey," he calls indignantly.

"No phones," I say.

"Why?"

"Because you're making this awkward and we've never been awkward."

He grips the back of his neck, a tinge of pink hitting his cheeks. I've never been one to shy away from topics, so I decide to lean right into it.

"Ask me," I say.

His head shoots up, and his mouth opens slightly before he closes it. "What?"

"Do you have questions?"

"Zo—" he starts.

"Matt, please, just ask me."

"Okay. Fine. Why so many?"

"Variety. Plus, they're great teammates," I say with a smirk.

"Teammates," he draws out the word.

I study him, not sure if he doesn't get my meaning or if he's sitting there picturing them being teammates. "Yup."

"And the new one in the box, was that for a specific someone?" he asks, and I can see the wheels turning in his head. He wants to know if I bought that toy with the purposes of using it with the dad from the rink. His eyes search out an answer, and I let him sit in the silence, watching him squirm as though not getting an answer was more painful than asking the question.

When I feel he's squirmed enough, I finally answer. "No, I didn't buy it with anyone in particular in mind. When I end a relationship, I like to get a new one. That's been sitting, packaged, in my drawer for a while."

That answer seems to please him as he nods.

Taking mercy on him, I move the conversation away from my collection of sex toys and onto more mundane things. He seems to relax into the conversation, and the weirdness between us fades.

When we finish lunch, Matt helps me load boxes into both of our cars. Henry is out of town for work right now and can't help me move, Maggie is working on a major fundraiser for her job and couldn't get the time to help, and I didn't want to bug the rest of my brothers, so I'm doing this move solo, except the newly recruited help from Matt. I text him Henry's address, and we make our way to his place.

Henry lives in a very family-friendly part of the city. Him and

Maggie bought a house with enough space for the two of them, plus room to host. Even though they've decided against kids, I know they plan on being the fun aunt and uncle who have sleepovers and host family dinners.

Pulling into the driveway, I take in the two storey house and the groomed front lawn. This house is very different from the run-down one I grew up in. The grass is green, the front porch is clean, the paint on the front door isn't peeling, and an inviting fall-themed welcome sign leans beside the front door. The curtains on the front windows are open, and you can see that Maggie has already gone all out in her fall decorations inside.

I take a deep breath, settling myself. At least it's not my parents' place, I tell myself. I may be moving in with my brother, but I'm not moving back to that run-down home that didn't always have heat and very often felt cold the second my parents walked in the front door.

A knock on my window startles me, and I clutch my chest as I look over to see Matt standing beside my door.

"You okay?" he asks.

I nod and reach for the door handle, pushing it open. "You nearly gave me a heart attack," I say, leaning against the car.

He chuckles. It's light and airy, the perfect sound to remind me I'm not moving one hundred percent backwards. "Sorry, Zo. You got the keys so we can start getting you moved in?"

I reach into my purse and hold up the spare key Henry gave all of us the minute he bought this house. He wanted us to all know that no matter what happened in life we have a safe place we can go.

"Right here. Let's start with your car," I say.

He nods and makes his way back to his car while I unlock the front door. The second the door opens, the smell of fresh-baked cookies hits me. I move immediately into the kitchen and see a covered plate on the counter with a note.

Zoey,

I'm sorry I couldn't help you move today, but I wanted to welcome you home. I'll be home in time for dinner. Can't wait to see you.

Maggie

It's very like Maggie to make sure I feel welcome here. Henry was always so cautious about dating, because he had a lot of damage from dealing with our parents and having to raise his five younger siblings. He wanted someone who would be able to accept the responsibility he put on himself to make sure the six of us stayed close so he could be there for us even as we became adults. I was only twelve the first time Henry brought Maggie around. They were just friends at the time, but it was nice to have another woman around. Maggie was the one to talk me through my first period. She gave Henry a list of items to get at the store and told me how to use all the products and then sat with me on my bed and watched Disney movies, shunning Henry to go hang out with the guys while she chilled with me.

Maggie's been a constant in our lives since then. I was so ecstatic when they started dating three years later. I'm not sure who was happier when he finally proposed, Maggie or me. I finally got the sister I always wanted, and Maggie was getting to spend the rest of her life with my brother. Maggie is more than a big sister, though. She took on a motherly role I never got from my own mother. She became a trusted friend who I could tell those secrets to that I couldn't tell Liv, like the brief stint in eighth grade when I had a crush on Matt.

Liv is and always will be my best friend, and I love her dearly and she is my sister in every way but blood. Watching her get to grow up with Gianna and have a sister she could connect with always left me wanting that for myself. I'm grateful for my friends and how they've always had my back and become the sisters I didn't have as a kid. They've made all these years fun and exciting and less lonely than they were before our group.

"Zo," Matt's voice pulls me out of my head as I stare at a cookie in my hand. He leans over as he takes a bite of it, and I glare at him.

"What the hell, Matt?" I huff.

"You weren't answering me, and I know the best way to get a response is to take your food," he says with a grin.

"Maggie made those for me," I say indignantly.

"And I'm a growing boy moving boxes. I needed the fuel." He smirks, and I punch him in the arm.

"Growing my ass. You're twenty-nine. The only thing you'll be growing is a dad bod."

He raises a brow before taking another bite of my cookie, causing me to huff again. "I thought you guys were into the whole dad bod thing? Weren't you girls just talking about the hot single dad you were reading about?"

I roll my eyes. "Of course, you were eavesdropping. And for your information, it's not the body we love about the single dad's in our books, there's so much more to it. And some of them are well toned athletes or cowboys, and some of them are office guys, they don't all fall under one type. We were just swooning over the single dad who knows how to take care of his kids and his girl." I plop the final bite in my mouth. "We look at more than a man's body, Matthew."

I turn, leaving him, and head into the entryway and grab a box before making my way up the stairs and to my new room. Thank God it's on the opposite side of the house as Henry and Maggie, because I don't want to hear any of their extracurriculars.

I drop the box on the floor at the end of the bed and notice the new desk Henry set up for me. I rented my place furnished for the most part, so all of that stuff stayed behind. I run my hand over the top as I walk past it, noticing a comfy chair in the corner next to an empty bookshelf. I squeal as I run towards it. A note sits on the top shelf, and I snag it as I settle in the chair.

HEY KIDDO,

I KNOW MOVING IN HERE WAS NOT YOUR IDEAL SITUATION, BUT I WANT YOU TO KNOW YOU'RE ALWAYS WELCOME HERE. I'VE SET UP A NEW DESK AND A READING CORNER FOR YOU. WE'LL HAVE A MOVIE NIGHT WHEN I GET HOME.

I love you.

Henry

I smile at the note. Henry has always known how independent I've wanted to be, but always remained that safe place to fall.

"Nice," Matt says, and I look up to see him now leaning against the doorframe.

I take stock of the room in its entirety and agree. This room is nice. It's my perfect little oasis in this house while I get back on my feet. "It is."

I look back at him and he's got an unreadable expression. His eyes trail over me, and goosebumps erupt in their wake. No. This cannot be happening. I've grown up. I'm not a kid anymore. I know Matthew Carter is not a good idea. I cannot let myself react this way to having his eyes on me. His sole focus.

I clear my throat and put the note back before pushing up from the chair. "We should probably get the rest of the boxes," I say.

He runs his hand through his hair and nods. "Yeah."

He follows me out to the cars, and the entire time, I feel his eyes on me. After a few more trips, we get my boxes moved into the bedroom, and he follows me to the kitchen.

I hand him a cookie with a smile. "For your help today."

He takes it. "No need to reward me, Zo. You're the one who's been doing me endless favours recently. I'm not sure what I would have done without you at family dinner or if you hadn't come to meet me at the rink."

I run my teeth over my bottom lip. Matt's eyes are glued to the movement. "Happy to help," I say, swallowing as heat rises through my body. I really need to start dating again and get laid if a single look from Matt has my throat going dry.

"So, I'll see you at the game tomorrow," I say, and his eyes snap to mine as he reaches up and squeezes the back of his neck.

"Yeah, I'll be there. I was going to see if Liv could watch Jayden, too, otherwise I'll watch."

I sigh, because I know what I'm about to do is not the smartest decision, but I'm going to do it anyway. "I'll watch him," I offer.

He breaks into a grin. "Really?" he asks hopefully.

"Yeah."

He pulls me into a hug. "Thanks, Zo."

I pat him on the back and step out of his arms. "Of course." I look at the clock on the stove and say, "You should probably head to your parents' if you're hoping to beat rush hour."

He follows my gaze. "Shoot, yeah." He kisses my cheek before heading for the front door. "Have a good night, Zo."

"You, too," I call just before he closes the door behind him.

I lean against the counter and take another cookie as I try to figure out why I've put myself in the position to be babysitting for Matt once again.

Walking up to the rink, I'm excited to see the girls. Between avoiding them so I didn't spill the beans about Matt's secret baby and us all being actually busy, I've missed them. If you had told me two years ago I was excited to go to a rec hockey game, I would have told you you're out of your mind, but ever since Liv moved in with Josh and started coming, it's become a new regular activity for us. Now that our other friend Hannah is married to Matt and Josh's friend Grayson, who plays on the same team, it's just another reason for us to all meet here.

As I step onto the sidewalk outside the building, I spot Matt making his way to me. He's got Jayden strapped to his chest, his hockey bag over one shoulder and his sticks in his hand. The first word that comes to mind as I watch him get closer is *hot*. This man looks hot with a baby strapped to his chest as he makes his way to play a very physical and often violent sport. I quickly look around to see if anyone caught me gapping at him, and I'm lucky this time. Thankfully, Matt was too busy talking to Jayden who's making noises at him to pay attention to me.

When Matt gets close enough that Jayden spots me, a smile spreads across his face and I instinctively reach forward and pinch his chubby cheeks.

"Well hello there, my little man," I say.

He smiles even more, some drool escaping the corner of his

mouth, and I can't help but smile even bigger. He babbles, and I release his cheek.

"Aren't we just the talker tonight?"

"So, no love for me, just the baby?" Matt pokes, and I look up at him.

"You're not as cute as the baby."

He holds a hand to his chest and feigns pain. "Oh, Zo, you wound me."

I throw my head back with a laugh. "Matt, you and I both know you've got enough ego that you're not wounded."

That makes him laugh.

"It's not ego, it's confidence," he says.

I roll my eyes. "You keep telling yourself that. Now let's get this adorable little munchkin in where it's warm," I say, bopping Jayden on the nose.

Matt and I walk into the lobby, and I spot our group chatting when all of a sudden the entire lobby gets quiet and they're staring at us, except Liv and Josh, who look like they've been hiding secrets.

"What the hell?" Hannah practically yells, and I jump in place.

"Oh, man, what did you do?" Grayson asks, humour filling his voice.

We make our way closer to the group, and their eyes only seem to get wider as they get a better look at the baby strapped to Matt's chest.

Liz, one of my best friends and someone who's great at reading people, narrows her eyes at me. "Zo, why are you not the least bit surprised about the baby strapped to Matt's chest?"

Okay, I did not think I'd be the first one under fire. I'm not the one with a baby strapped to them. I'm not the one dropping some surprise bomb on all our friends right now.

I shuffle from foot to foot and look at Matt. He shrugs, knowing no matter what, it's all going to come out one way or another. They'll just continue to hound us for details until we give them. I've also noticed he has no shame when it comes to claiming Jayden as his. He's definitely expressed how upset he is that he didn't know about him before, but that was entirely out of his control. It's not like he just abandoned his son.

"I'm kinda the one who found Jayden when he was dropped off at Matt's," I say.

"What do you mean you found him?" Bailey asks. Bailey joined our group after she started dating Caleb, Matt and Josh's friend. She was a single mom when she first met Caleb. Her daughter Charlie is running around with some other kids who are here with parents for games.

"I crashed on Matt's couch and when I woke up the next morning to head home, I opened the door and found Jayden in his car seat," I say.

Matt and I do a quick retelling of the story, and when Jayden manages to grab a fistful of my hair, I take him from Matt, securing the carrier on me now.

The guys eventually leave us and head to the dressing room while the girls and I head to the bleachers to watch the game.

CHAPTER 8

Matt

I guess I should have been prepared for all the questions I was going to get today when I showed up with Jayden. Josh already knows all of this, and Caleb is more observing and taking in information as Grayson peppers me with questions.

"So, who's the mom? Where is she?"

"Some woman I was seeing casually a while ago. We called it off, and she never told me. She's in Winnipeg with her family," I say.

"Is she coming back?" Grayson asks.

I shrug. "I have no idea. I have no idea what it will mean if she does. I've been taking this all day by day. Not looking too far into the future past looking for a place to move. My place isn't big enough for him to grow up in. I've been saving, and I think it's time I look for a house."

Caleb nods and says, "There are a few nice houses up for sale in our neighbourhood. I'm sure you could find one you like. We're in a great school district. I can send you the listings tonight."

"Thanks. That would be great."

"Can you send them to me, too?" Josh adds, and I turn to look at him.

"You guys moving?"

He shrugs. "I know Olivia wants a backyard for when Cate is grown up and more space for kids. Our place works for now, but I get it, she's always wanted to be more out of the city. We can't fully escape the city right now because of me and the company, but we can get out of the heart of downtown. And what Olivia wants, she'll get."

Liv liked the way we grew up in a nice family-oriented neighbourhood, and I'm not surprised she wants the same for her kids. With them potentially trying for more soon, it does make sense for them to try to find a place now, and we all know that Josh, the CEO of his own company, can definitely afford it, even without selling his current place. He dotes on Liv and Cate, and I know he means it when he says whatever Liv wants, he'll give her. It would be nice if we could find places in the same neighbourhood so our kids can grow up together.

We finish getting ready and head out to the ice to warm up before the game. Before I step on the ice, I make my way to Zoey and check on Jayden, who is perfectly content curled up against her chest. I smile as I lovingly run my finger over his nose. Zoey smiles and wishes me luck before I join the guys.

As we get ready at centre ice, I feel Zoey's eyes on me. I turn my head slightly and see her soft smile from earlier still there. I'm not sure what comes over me, but I wink at her as I lower my upper body, ready to accept the puck from Josh if he wins the face off. The slight blush that filled her cheeks gives me a little more drive, and as the other team wins the face off, I'm driving towards their forward, vying for the puck. I check the one with possession into the boards, and Luke, one of our players, takes the free puck and makes his way through centre and towards the other team's goal. He passes to Josh, who makes his way to the left and fakes the shot before quickly moving right and getting the puck just between the goalie's left side and the post.

We gather around him and cheer before heading to the bench. Josh leads the line in fist bumps before we do a line change. The game is intense and physical, just the way I like it. I love using these games to process things I'm dealing with in a physical way. We barely scrape through with the win, 3-2.

When we skate off the ice, I immediately head to Zoey and Jayden. I feel drawn to both of them, this need to be close to them. Jayden is barely awake, offering me a weak smile when I brush my finger over his cheek and smile at him.

"He was good?" I ask Zoey.

She smiles down at him. "Yeah, he was gem. I've got him while you change."

"Thanks, Zo."

"Of course."

I meet the guys back in the locker room, and Grayson grins at me as I sit.

"Someone played with a little extra pep in their step," he says.

"Just working through some things," I say, brushing it off.

"Felt more like you were trying to impress someone," he pushes.

"No one to impress. My kid's a little too young."

"Mhhh, sure. Maybe a certain brunette who was holding that new kid of yours?"

"Zo? Why would I be trying to impress her?"

I avoid looking at any of the guys and focus on removing my gear, because I think he might have a bit of a point. Something lately has had me wanting to be closer to Zoey and maybe have her look at me differently. As more than just a friend. I know that's crazy, though. I've got a kid now, and she's my sister's best friend. I'd never forgive myself if I ruined their relationship because a relationship with Zoey didn't work out. I'm also not going to put Zoey into the position of taking on a parental role when that's not something she's signed up for.

"You tell me. Why don't we start with why she was at your place the night before you found Jayden," Grayson says.

I sigh. "Zo was out the night before on a date that didn't end well and she got super drunk. I picked her up and she crashed on my couch. That's all."

"Why'd she call you?"

I look up and see all the guys in the room trying to look like they're not paying attention to the grilling Grayson is doing right now, but they aren't very subtle about it and Josh and Caleb do nothing to hide their interest.

"Because Liv has a baby at home and she didn't want to bother her, same with Bailey having Charlie, Liz was out of town, and she figured since you and Hannah had the night off together, there was no point in trying to get ahold of your wife because you two would be occupied in other ways. She doesn't like to call her brothers because she's the youngest and has always felt bad that they took care of her so much when she was younger. I'm her friend and I always told Liv and her friends when we were growing up if they needed a safe ride home, they could always call me. They've each called me at least once in the last ten years."

"Sure know a lot about Zoey," Josh points out.

I shrug. "She's Liv's best friend. I've known her pretty much as long as I've known you."

"Yeah, but I don't remember you two being close back then."

"We weren't, but when Liv and Drew broke up and we needed you two idiots to see what was right in front of you, we spent more time together and we've grown close."

He quirks a brow. "What exactly did the two of you do? I know you put the bug in my ear about Liv needing a place to live, but what else?"

I raise a brow back at him. "Wouldn't you like to know."

I push up from the bench and head to the showers, making quick work before getting dressed to go get my boy. As I'm about to leave, Caleb calls my name. I turn back to him, and he addresses Josh, Grayson, and I.

"So, Bailey and I were hoping you guys could come for lunch at our place tomorrow."

We exchange looks; Caleb doesn't often ask us over for things. Before he met Bailey, we were only ever really at his place when it was his turn to host poker night. Bailey's hosted a few group dinners, but they aren't frequent. She knows Caleb enjoys having his space, and he lets her host us all from time to time because he knows how much she loves it, but they're usually planned well in advance. A last-minute invite is not the norm for him.

We agree, and Caleb says he'll text us the details.

I head upstairs to the restaurant in the rink we usually eat dinner at after Saturday games. Bailey and Hannah are deep in conversation at one end of the table while Charlie draws beside them, and Liv is making faces at Cate while talking to Zo. The second I see Jayden and Zoey, I break out into a smile. I take her in, the way she's laughing with the girls while she sways and rubs her hand over Jayden's back. Longing takes over me as images flash through my mind of what she'd look like in a couple of years with Jayden more grown while she's pregnant and holding another baby. I stop in place, quickly shaking my head of the image. I don't need shit like that filling my head, especially right now.

When I join them, Cate sees me and does grabby hands at me, and I take my niece from my sister. I pinch her chubby cheeks before burying my face in her tummy, and she giggles. I spend a few minutes with her before passing her back to Liv so I can take Jayden from Zo. When I turn to her, I see he's completely passed out.

"I'll take him," I say and she shakes her head.

"I've got this little cutie-patootie. I'll carry him to your car so you jostle him as little as possible." She smiles lovingly at him, and it makes me instantly think about raising him without his mother. Not that I'd want to be in a relationship with Hazel, but to think my son won't have that relationship hurts. I love the relationship I had with my mom growing up.

My parents were always a safe space for me, Liv, and Gi. We always knew no matter what, we could count on them. If we ever needed them, they'd be there, no questions asked. While some kids hated the father-daughter or the mother-son dance our schools would host, we always loved them. Our parents never went out of their ways to embarrass us or scold us in front of our friends. I remember the awkward feeling of being at a friend's house in eighth grade when his mom reamed him out in the other room and we all had to sit there and hear it.

I felt comfortable going to Mom when I was interested in a girl and wanted her advice. I want Jayden to have that kind of relationship, too. A woman in his life he can always turn to.

Liv snaps her fingers in front of my face, and I give it a shake and focus on her. "Huh?"

"Earth to Matt," she says.

"What's up?"

"I was asking how it was leaving Jayden with Mom on Friday. She mentioned she took him for the day."

I run my teeth over my bottom lip, memories of what I found in Zoey's nightstand flashing through my mind. She had an impressive collection of toys and lube in there, but the one that really caught my attention was the unopened one just sitting beside the rest of them. Zo seemed flustered when she caught me staring at them, but while we were eating, she asked me straight up if I had questions, and if I'm being honest, the fact she was willing to have that conversation was hot. Her mentioning using them as teammates had images of her naked on her bed, legs wide open for me while I teased her with one of them flooding my mind. But the unopened one was the one that piqued my interest the most, bold white text at the bottom had me wondering just how she planned to use it.

I force a cough to stop my mind from wandering any further down this path.

"Um, it was fine. I dropped him off, ran some errands, and picked him up. Mom said he was good for her and she wants to schedule another day to take him."

Liv nods but raises a brow. She's paying way to close attention to me, and I need to move her focus so she doesn't start asking questions I don't want to answer.

"So, you and Josh heading to Caleb and Bailey's tomorrow?" I ask.

She stares at me for a few seconds, well aware I'm moving the conversation along on purpose. "Yeah, we'll be there." She lowers her voice and leans in closer. "Do you know why they asked us to all come over? Bailey never asks last minute."

I shrug. "No idea."

Our food is delivered as the rest of the guys join us. Conversation fills the table as we eat, and it hits me how content I am sitting with my friends and enjoying a meal after playing a hockey game. I've got my son, my sister, and my best friends, the only thing missing is my person.

CHAPTER 9

Zoey

I've got a bottle of Bailey's favourite red wine in hand as I make my way up the walkway to their front door. The sound of a car has me looking over my shoulder, and I watch as Matt pulls up to the curb and quickly gets out, collecting Jayden out of the back. I stumble as I watch how much of a natural he's become handling Jayden and all of his things. His comment about how the girls and I were raving about the single dad in our book comes back to me, and I bite my lip to prevent me from smirking, because seeing Matt as a dad is hot.

In just two weeks, he's completely dove headfirst into it all. He texted me the other day asking if it was too early to get Jayden on a waitlist for a Montessori preschool. I had to text him back that I had no freaking clue. I have no idea when you're supposed to register kids for that kind of shit and that he should be texting Liv those kinds of questions.

When he turns around and spots me, his smile grows, and I can't help but smile back.

"Hey, Zo."

"Hey. Need any help?"

He shakes his head. "Nope, I'm all good. I'm slowly getting the hang of managing him and everything else."

"That's good."

Matt joins me on the walkway, and I peek in on Jayden in his car seat. He smiles, and spit bubbles form as he makes baby noises, and I smile as I reach in and use the spit up cloth to wipe his mouth.

"He's been a happy boy today," Matt says.

I dance my fingers over Jayden's tummy, pulling a giggle out of him. "I can see that," I say in the tone my voice tends to hit when I'm talking directly to babies. "I can see we're a happy boy today, aren't we?"

Jayden giggles more as he waves his arms in jerky movements in front of him, and my smile widens.

Grayson and Hannah pull up, and as they're getting out of the car, Hannah calls, "Loitering on the lawn now, are we?"

I look at Jayden as I respond to Hannah, using the same tone. "I just was saying hi to the cutest little boy, wasn't I, Jayden? Aren't you just the cutest boy."

He gurgles in what I'm going to say is agreement, and I smile at Hannah. She joins me and looks in on him, too.

Grayson and Matt exchange nods as Grayson says hello to me.

She brushes her fingertips over Jayden's tummy much in the same way I did earlier and smiles as she says, "Okay, I'll give it to you. He's pretty darn adorable."

"Right!" I exclaim.

"You Carter kids make adorable babies," Hannah says to Matt.

He grins at her. "That we do."

"We should probably head inside," Grayson says.

We make our way up the front steps, and Grayson knocks. Caleb quickly answers and ushers us inside. Lily, Bailey's best friend, and Liv and Josh are already here, but I don't see Bailey or Charlie.

"Where are the girls?" I ask.

Caleb grips the back of his neck in a way I haven't seen him do much in all the years I've known him. "Um, they're upstairs. They should be down soon."

I nod and follow him into the kitchen and join Liv.

After a few minutes, I hear the running footsteps of Charlie, and she calls, "Aunty Liv, Aunty Lily."

We all turn to watch her charge into the kitchen as she runs up to them.

"Hey, Charlie girl," Liv says while Lily stares at her slack jawed as her hands come to cover her mouth and she turns to look at Caleb. Tears are starting to run down her face.

"Really?" Is all she manages to squeak out.

Caleb is grinning like a fool as he nods. Bailey finally walks into the kitchen and Lily is throwing herself at her. The rest of us are looking around confused until Josh finally offers his hand to Caleb and says, "Congrats, Man."

"Thanks."

Caleb can't stop grinning, and Bailey and Lily are both wiping their tears.

"Charlie, what's up?" I ask, and she turns to me, allowing me to read the front of her shirt.

Best Big Sister

Everyone must have gotten a chance to read it now as congratulations fill the air and hugs are exchanged. Something in me twists as longing pulls at me. I push it to the side, needing to stay in the moment and celebrate this amazing milestone with my friends.

Once I've hugged Bailey and Caleb and they tell us she's three months along and due in April, I excuse myself to the back porch and take a seat on the top step and look out on their backyard. Charlie has toys all over the place. A covered sandbox sits in the back corner next to the little jungle gym Caleb built for her this summer.

Hannah comes out and sits beside me. "You good?" she asks.

I nod, not sure what to say.

"You know you can be happy for them and have other feelings as well, right?"

I bite my lip and nod again. She extends her legs, crossing them at the ankles as she leans back on her hands. We sit in the moment, silent for a while before Hannah speaks again.

"Before Grayson, I was beginning to lose hope." She chuckles. "Actually, even in the beginning of our marriage, I was losing hope I'd find someone who I could feel soul consuming love with. Give it time, Zo. You've still got so much time."

Of course, my friend can tell how I'm feeling right now. Hannah's the hopeless romantic of the group, too, so I'm not surprised it's her sitting with me right now.

I wipe at a stray tear. "I feel so lost, Han." I take a deep breath. "You, Bailey, and Liv are all getting settled. You're all in careers you love, even starting families. I have no idea what I want. Even Liz is happy with where she is with her job and life. I have a law degree I thought was going to make life so much better. All I had to do was get it. I'm now living with my brother again, and I've just had shitty date after shitty date. I can't remember the last time I made it past a third date with a guy." I wipe away another tear.

Hannah pushes herself up and wraps an arm around me as she leans her head on my shoulder. I lean into her, too, resting my cheek on her head.

"Zoey, you are an extraordinary person. You'll figure it all out, maybe it's just taking some time so that what you find is as amazing as you are."

I smile as I sniffle and feel nothing but gratitude for my friend.

Hannah sits with me for a few more minutes before she pats my arm and says, "Okay, so Bailey might not be able to drink, but we can. Why don't we open that bottle of wine you brought? And didn't you mention the other day that someone asked you out? Maybe tomorrow you text him and set up a date? Who knows, maybe he's the one and you've just been putting off learning it."

She's right, I do have the card from the dad of the kid Matt coaches. I sit straight and pull my phone out, determined to stop feeling sorry for myself, and text him.

ZOEY

Hey, this is Zoey. We met when my friend was coaching your son's team last week. I was wondering if you'd like to get dinner?

I shove my phone into the pocket of my jeans and follow Hannah into the house. She pours us each a glass of wine, and we join the girls while Caleb handles the food in the kitchen.

Matt and I are helping with the dishes when my phone dings on the counter.

"Can you check that?" I ask Matt, and he taps the screen. A look

I don't recognize flashes across his face. He doesn't say anything, just keeps rubbing the dish towel over the already dry plate in his hand.

"Who was it?" I ask.

"Dean." His voice is laced with something that sounds like a mix of anger and jealousy. But that can't be right. There's no reason Matt would feel either of those things when it comes to me dating.

"What did he say?"

Matt grabs the next plate and starts aggressively drying it. "He said he'd love to grab dinner. He wants to know if you're available Tuesday night."

I can't help but grin to myself. Maybe Hannah's right and this could be my luck turning around.

We finish the dishes, and as I turn to make my way into the living room with everyone else, Matt stops me with a hand on my wrist.

"Are you really going to go out with him?"

"Yeah, Matt, I am. I texted him first. Is there a reason I shouldn't?"

His eyes bounce around my face, and he obviously finds what he's looking for because he lets go of my wrist and shakes his head. "No, no reason at all." The words almost sound pained. I stare at him for a few more seconds, hoping that whatever he's holding back, he'll finally spit out. When he doesn't, I head into the living room.

After a minute, Matt comes back in and says he needs to leave and get Jayden into bed. I can tell that's not the real reason he's suddenly decided he needs to leave, but I don't press. I say my goodbye to him and Jayden.

Before he walks out the front door, he drops his voice to a whisper. "You still good to meet me in the morning?"

I sigh. I forgot I agreed to watch Jayden again tomorrow morning while Matt coaches. "Yeah, I'll be there."

"Thanks."

Before he can close the door, I say, "I think I'm feeling a peppermint mocha for tomorrow morning."

He grins and shakes his head. "Sounds good, Zo."

I close the door behind him and lean against it. I shoot a text to Dean, agreeing to meet at an Italian restaurant Tuesday night. As much as I'm excited about this date, I almost wish Matt had told me not to go on it.

The minute I see Matt, I grab the hot coffee he extends to me and take a large sip, relishing the taste of it. I finish almost half of it before putting it on the bleachers to take Jayden from him.

"Didn't sleep well?" he asks.

"Nope, and I'm not sure just one sugary drink is going to do it this morning."

"I'm sorry," he says and runs his fingers through his hair. "If I had anyone else I could ask, I would."

"What about Gi?" I ask, because quite frankly, I don't want to keep meeting him here at the ass crack of dawn.

"Nope. She's living with my parents right now."

I nod. As much as I don't want to be here right now, I have to admit what he's doing is nice for these kids and I'm not going to leave them all in the lurch.

"I'd offer you an energy drink, but I know you can't stand the stuff," he says, and I make a face. That crap is disgusting. I don't know how he drinks the stuff.

"Well, you might as well get out there," I say, settling on the bleachers and pulling my Kindle out of my purse.

"Thanks, Zo."

"Yeah," I say waving my hand, dismissing him.

When he comes out with the kids, my mind can't seem to stay focused on my book. It keeps turning to Matt and watching him with the kids. I'm startled when Dean sits next to me. I offer him a small smile, unsure what I should do. Should I start a conversation? Try to read my book?

Thankfully, he answers that question by asking, "So, you're helping Coach Carter out again?"

I rub my hand over a sleeping Jayden's back and smile. "Yeah. This boy's pretty easygoing, so it's not too bad. The early morning kind of sucks, but at least I can try to get some reading in," I say, shaking my Kindle.

He nods, and his eyes dart towards Matt. "So, how did he manage to convince you to come out here this early to watch his kid?"

I sense jealousy in his question, like he's not sure why I'd help Matt out.

"He's a friend. Plus, he's promised to make sure I get my sugar in the morning."

He pinches his brows. "Sugar? In the morning?"

I nod. "Yup. Caffeine doesn't seem to do it for me, only sugar."

I feel the judgement radiating off him, but push it to the side. Maybe he's right and sugar in the morning isn't the most normal thing.

"Your son looks pretty good out there," I say, wanting to move the conversation along.

That perks him up a bit. "Yeah, he's one of the best on the team. He gets it from his dad."

I side-eye him, but he doesn't seem to see it. *What an odd way to brag about yourself.* "Oh, you played?"

"Yeah, best centre on my university team until I tore my ACL."

"That sucks, I'm sorry."

"It is what it is, just wasn't meant to be. I was able to focus on my studies, and now I have my own business management firm. I guess it's for the best." His words come out in a humble brag that just isn't doing it for me.

"So, where did you go to school?" I ask.

"Harbour View."

From what I remember when I was doing my research years ago for university, Harbour View was a decent school, nothing great, but they also didn't suck. I do remember Matt and Josh both said they'd never attend the school for hockey when they had teams trying to recruit them in high school. That has me wondering just how good of a player Dean could have been.

Matt's whistle pulls my attention back to the ice. He gathers the kids and talks to them before dismissing them and sending them off the ice. Matt's eyes are locked on me as he makes his way off the ice.

"Hey, Bug," he says, and I swear my heart stops in my chest as my mouth opens slightly. Did he really call me Bug? He hasn't called me that in over a decade. Why the hell is he bringing it out now?

"Bug?" Dean asks.

Matt grins bigger and comes to my side, tucking a piece of hair behind my ear, and I must be fucking dreaming. *What the hell is going on?*

"Yeah, just a name I've had for Zo here since we were kids."

Dean's eyes bounce between the two of us, and he nods. "Ahhh. Well, it was nice talking to you, Zoey. I'll see you tomorrow night."

I smile. "See you tomorrow."

When Dean rounds the corner, I turn to Matt and slap his arm. "What the fuck was that? Bug? You haven't called me that since I was like fifteen. Why are you bringing it back now?"

He looks at me with a blank stare and then shrugs. "I don't know, but I'm thinking I should bring it back full time." He's grinning now. "What do you say, Bug? Ready for breakfast?"

"Can we not with the nickname?"

He shakes his head. "I forgot how much it bothered you hearing that name in public."

"Yeah, because it's a weird name," I huff.

He throws his head back and laughs. "But it was so you."

"No it wasn't."

He sits and pulls at the laces of his skates. "Whatever you say, Bug. How about some pancakes?"

My stomach growls at the mere mention of food, and he grins at me. He knows my weaknesses and it fucking sucks.

I follow him to his car, helping him get Jayden settled before we head to the restaurant.

CHAPTER 10

Matt

I have no idea why I'm pacing my living room, but I do know I'm anxious as hell. I can't stop thinking about Zoey being on a date with *Dean*. What could she possibly see in a guy like him? He's got a few years on me, which means he's got several on her. Zoey is smart and beautiful. Why would she feel the need to date someone so much older, and so… I nearly drop my phone when it starts ringing. Liv's picture fills the screen and I answer.

"Hey, Liv."

"Hey! What's going on?"

I look around my apartment like a weirdo, as if my sister is watching me and knows I was just thinking about her best friend in ways I probably shouldn't be.

"Nothing, just hanging out at home. You?"

"Same. I actually just got off the phone with Gi. We were thinking about doing brunch on Saturday and wanted to know if you wanted to join us?"

"Yeah, that should work," I say.

"Oh, good. Josh said he can either take Jayden for you or I'm sure Mom would love to take him."

"Josh is willing to take on two kids under one?" I ask, surprised.

"Josh will be fine with both of them." I hear the smile in her voice. "Plus, if we're going to have more, we've got to get used to it."

"I guess…"

"Oh, stop it, Matty. Josh will be just fine for a few hours. We haven't gotten together just the three of us in a long time. Indulge me, please?"

Damn it, her pouty voice is coming out, and I've never been able to say no to it.

"Please, Matty."

I sigh. "Yeah, I'll drop Jayden off at your place and pick you up."

"Oh, yay. I'll let Gi know. I'll see you Saturday! Love you!"

"Yeah, love you, too."

The line goes dead, and my mind immediately goes back to wondering what Zoey is doing on her date. Is she having fun? Is she leaning in as he talks? Is she making him her sole focus?

Jayden wakes up and starts to cry, and I feel horrible for thinking it, but I think *thank God.* Jayden being awake means I'm forced to focus on things other than my friend across town on a date.

I may have bought Zoey two coffees this morning on my way to the rink. I'm not sure how I convinced her to come watch Jayden again, but I did. I've got Jayden in the car seat today, and I'm hoping the two coffees can help to butter her up so she'll spill details about her date last night, because I couldn't sleep not knowing what was happening.

Zoey offers me a soft smile when she rounds the corner. Her eyes light up whens she sees both coffee cups I'm holding out for her. She grabs them both and takes a tasting sip of each, her eyes remaining on me as she evaluates them.

"Pumpkin spice *and* peppermint mocha. You did good, Matthew."

I hold back the face I want to make when something akin to butterflies start in my stomach. I, Matthew Carter, do not get butterflies, especially when it comes to girls. Never have. I've always been able to get whoever I wanted, and I don't mean that as a brag, it's the truth. Every girl I've ever asked out has said yes. So why the fuck does Zoey fucking Williams have me getting butterflies when she uses my full name and praises me for my coffee choices?

I clear my throat, trying to push this feeling aside.

"Uh, so how was your date?" I ask, and I sound so pathetic. I grip the back of my neck, the tension in my muscles growing.

She looks up and to the left as she rolls her bottom lip between her teeth. I can see the wheels turning as she tries to figure out what to say. "It was…" she trails off as she moves her coffee cups up and down. "Fine. I don't think I'll be seeing him again."

Fuck me if that doesn't take a weight off my shoulders. I physically feel myself perk up at this news.

"Really?"

She rolls her eyes so hard I'm sure she gets the start of a headache. "You don't need to seem so excited I've had another failed date," she says.

"Not excited," I say. "I just thought you could do better than him."

The vulnerability in her eyes is like a stab to the gut. "Really?"

"Of course, Zo. There's no way someone as smart and beautiful as you has to resort to someone so much older than her and who's kind of a pig."

She snorts, a full on, sounds like a pig snorts. "You noticed that, did ya?"

I can't help the laugh that leaves me. "Yeah, I noticed that."

She guffaws. "The way he kept calling our waitress hun was disgusting."

I think she actually gags as she says it, and I laugh again.

"Why didn't you say anything?" she asks.

I look her straight in the eyes and say, "Because no one should tell you who you can and cannot date, and I believe you're an excellent judge of character. You would have picked up on it eventually, and I was right, you did."

She nods. "Yeah, I did. Thank God he's not here this morning. Not sure I could put up with being that close to him for your entire practice."

The sound of the kids exiting the dressing room fills the rink, and I watch them get on the ice. Zoey follows my line of sight and tips her chin their way.

"Go. Jayden and I will be fine here."

I reach out and squeeze her shoulder before walking past her and joining the kids.

Practice goes by relatively quickly today. The kids pick up on the new things I teach them, and I manage to steal several long glances at Zoey. Zoey may hate mornings, but I can't help but notice how beautiful she looks right now. She's fresh faced, not a stitch of makeup on, and is relaxing with a book while she occasionally looks lovingly at my sleeping son. When he begins to wake up, she takes him into her arms and starts rocking him.

I have to force myself to look away and focus on the group of kids I'm coaching. I blow my whistle and bring the kids in for a huddle before sending them off to change. As I step off the ice, one of the overeager mothers stops me, and I have to bite my tongue from rudely asking her to get out of my way so I can get to Zoey.

I offer her a practiced smile, and the one she gives me is flirtatious as she runs her hand from my shoulder and down my arm. I'm no stranger to a woman making her interest known. In fact, over the years, I've grown to love it because it's less work for me, but I've also never shit where I eat. That means no sisters of friends, no friends of sisters, and definitely no mothers of kids I coach.

"I wanted to thank you, Coach Carter," Ms. Johnson practically purrs. "Benjamin has improved so much since you took over coaching the team."

Her fingers dance back up my arm, and it takes everything in me not to step back in revulsion.

"I was hoping to thank you for everything you've done. I make a really good pot roast, maybe you'd like to come over Saturday night and I can make it. Maybe open up a bottle of wine?"

I gently grab her wrist and remove her hand from me, keeping in place my practiced smile. "While I'm flattered, Ms. Johnson, I have plans on Saturday. I do this because I enjoy coaching, not for any rewards."

That only has her doubling down her efforts. She steps closer and practically shoves her breasts against my arm as she leans in and whispers, "That just makes the reward so much better."

I take a step back again, and immediately, I'm looking for Zoey. When I spot her, I plead with my eyes for her to come save me, but she just shakes her head slightly with an amused smirk. Of course, Zoey is getting a kick out of my being uncomfortable and needing to find a way to tell this overeager mom I'm not interested.

Taking another step back, I say, "Well, Ms. Johnson, I should really get back to my son, and the boys should be finished soon."

Her eyes flick to Zoey then back to me, and her mouth drops into a little O shape. "That's your kid?"

I nod.

"And your girl?"

I go to open my mouth to say no, she's not my girl, but the thought of her being mine fills my mind and I can't help but think about what it would be like if she was.

That seems to be enough, though, because Ms. Johnson takes a step back and nods before quickly turning and leaving.

When I join Zoey, she's rocking Jayden's car seat while holding back a laugh. I do an over exaggerated mock laugh and that breaks the dam. Her laugh is contagious, and it has me smiling and shaking my head.

"Laugh it up, chuckle bunny. I know, very funny watching me squirm as she had her hands all over me."

"I swore," she says through her laughter, "that I saw you gag." She bends over clutching her legs as she rides out her laughter. "Oh, man." She wipes are her brow. "Thanks for that. I needed a good laugh."

I roll my eyes. "Harty har har har. Laugh at my misery."

"I think that was just karma for some of the shit you've done to me over the years. The universe wanted me to see you suffer in a way."

"Oh, pray tell, Zoey, what do you think that was karma for?"

She levels a look at me, telling me with her eyes she thinks I'm an idiot for not knowing. "How far back we going? Childhood or keeping it to adult years?"

I roll my shoulders. "Zo, there's no way you have that much."

"The time in sixth grade when you showed up to walk Liv home and called me Bug so loudly everyone could hear." She starts ticking them off with her fingers. "The time I brought my first boyfriend to your family's Canada Day celebration and you proceeded to tell him all about the time I got food poisoning during a sleepover with Liv. New Year's Eve last year when you caught me and the guy I was seeing outside Josh and Liv's place and interrupted us, making it so awkward he left."

I put my hands up in submission. "Okay, you may have a point."

"May?" Her voice rises an octave.

"Okay," I sigh. "You have a point."

She nods, and I move to check in on Jayden. He's been pretty decent about sleeping. It sucks I have to wake him up so early on Mondays and Wednesdays, but coaching happens so early so the kids can go to school after, and by the time we get to the rink, he's usually ready for his first nap and sleeps the whole time for Zoey. I get to feed him after practice.

Zoey and I have developed a routine now for these early mornings. I bring her coffee, she reads and watches Jayden, and then we go to breakfast before we head in separate directions.

When she leaves after breakfast today, I'm immediately looking forward to seeing her at my game on Friday.

CHAPTER 11

Zoey

I chastise myself for missing Matt after we go our separate ways. With Maggie and Henry working during the day, I have the house to myself, and I'm not a huge fan of the quiet. It makes me want to crawl out of my skin. I watch TV and read books, but sitting at home by myself has it really hitting that I have no idea what I'm doing with my life. I'm not attending classes, and I'm not working. I don't know what I want to do now. Do I go find a job serving just to keep myself busy and to find a source of income?

I'm so glad I told Liv I'd go to the guys' game tonight. Getting out of the house and spending time with my friends will hopefully help pull me from this funk. When I get to the rink and see Hannah holding Jayden and Matt nowhere in sight, something in me twists. I don't know why. I should be happy Matt's not relying on me once again to watch Jayden, but I also enjoy the feeling of being needed. I smile as I join the girls, and my heart skips when Jayden spots me and is immediately reaching for me.

I enthusiastically take him from Hannah, and the four girls grin at me.

"Someone is growing attached," Hannah says.

I respond to Hannah but speak to Jayden. "Oh, who wouldn't grow attached this adorable little guy? Aren't you the most adorable little dude?

Jayden giggles, and my smile grows.

"Does that mean you're growing attached in... other ways?" Eliza asks.

I stop bouncing Jayden for a second before resuming. I won't admit it to them, but I am, and it sucks. No matter how much I tell myself I'm a relationship girl and Matt likes the fun flings, when I see him with Jayden, or he brings me my favourite type of coffee when we meet early when he coaches, or I see how good he is with his team, I can't help but want to be around him more.

"No," I say, avoiding eye contact. "I just can't help falling for this adorable little guy."

Liz doesn't say anything, but Hannah hums in a way that says she doesn't believe me.

Wanting to change the subject, I turn to Bailey and ask, "So, where's Charlie tonight?"

"She's with Grandma. Caleb's mom asked to take her for the weekend." She's grinning from ear to ear. I know how alone she felt before she met Caleb and she all of a sudden got the four of us girls and his family. Bailey fit in immediately with us. She was hesitant at first, but Liv wore her down and we all fell in love with her and Charlie.

"So, in other words, you and Caleb won't be leaving your bed all weekend," Liv says with a laugh, and Bailey's cheeks pinken.

"Caleb and I will be enjoying time together," she says, and we all know what she means.

"Well, you can't get any more pregnant," Hannah says.

I laugh. "What do you think got her into this position? Caleb's mom was probably offering to babysit all the time, hoping she'd get another grandkid."

Bailey's jaw drops, and I see the wheels turning in her head. The rest of us can't help laughing.

"Oh God, she really did, didn't she?" I ask. I was only half joking, but this is hilarious.

"I think she might have," Bailey whispers.

When the guys come out of the dressing room, Bailey calls Caleb over. "Do you know why your mom was always offering to babysit?" she asks.

"We think she was doing it to help facilitate another grandkid," Hannah adds.

Caleb grips the back of his neck. "She may not have offered all those times, I may have asked," he admits.

Hannah bends over, laughing. "Man, you really wanted to get Bailey pregnant," she says through her laughter.

"We had already agreed to try. I was just putting in some extra work," he says, beaming with pride. "And look at us, it didn't take us long after agreeing to try. I'd say that just means I'm an over-achiever."

"That you are," Liz says.

He flashes us a grin before joining the guys on the ice.

"So, you had decided to try?" Hannah says as she turns to face Bailey.

Bailey nods. "The night we got engaged, Caleb said he wanted more kids with me. He wanted Charlie to be able to be a big sister and he was ready to grow our family. We threw out my birth control that night."

Liv reaches over and squeezes her arm. "I'm so happy for you guys. And now your new little one can grow up with Cate and Jayden, built in friends. And Charlie is going to make an amazing big sister."

A tear escapes, and Bailey wipes at it quickly. "Thanks. Ughhh, I've been so emotional with this pregnancy. I'm glad this little one" —she rubs her hand over her stomach—"will have all of you and have so many kids to run around with."

"Aunty Hannah is looking forward to spoiling all these little ones."

"What about you and Grayson?" Bailey asks.

She smiles softly. "Kids are not in the cards for us right now, and that's okay. We're content being the fun aunt and uncle and spending time with your little ones. Maybe one day, but we're not in any rush."

"Kids aren't for everyone and that's okay, as long as you're happy, that's all that matters," Liz says.

Hannah beams. "I'm so happy. Grayson and I are planning a trip to Willow Valley for Christmas, and I think Dad's going to join us. I'm excited to see his parents' place in the snow and build a proper snowman. The snow here is so damn wet it never really works, but Grayson has assured me we can make them there."

"You're not going to be here for Christmas?" Liv asks with pouty eyes.

Hannah wrings her hands in her lap. "Yeah, I've been meaning to tell you. I know we usually do friends Christmas on Boxing Day, and you guys should still totally do that, and we'll be back for New Year's, but we both really want to spend the holiday with his parents. He hasn't gone home for Christmas in years."

"I get it," Liv says. "But we call dibs on you for New Year's. Josh and I will host again. We'll do dinner and snacks and then watch the ball drop. We'll make sure we have the guest rooms set up for the kids so they can sleep."

We all nod, and Hannah says, "Promise."

The game moves pretty quickly tonight, with very few whistles or penalties. Jayden is strapped in the baby carrier, and I have him facing out so he can see what's going on. When Matt is on the ice right in front of us, he reaches for him as he babbles.

I point to Matt and say, "Is that dada? Yeah, that's dada."

Jayden continues to babble as we watch the game, and when it ends, Matt makes his way towards us. His smile widens as he looks at Jayden and me. As soon as he stops in front of us, he bends to Jayden's eye level. "What's up, little man? Did you have fun with Zo?"

Jayden babbles at him.

"Oh, that's good," he says as if he can actually understand what Jayden is saying, and my smile grows. He leans and kisses Jayden's cheeks. "Be a good boy for Zo." He stands straight and looks at me. "Thanks for hanging with him."

"Well, who could say no when this cutie is reaching for them?"

"Seriously, Zo. I appreciate it. He's obviously recognizing you, which just tells me I have you around a lot. Don't get me wrong, I love having you around, more than I can say, but I don't want to be taking advantage."

I rest my hand on his arm. "Matt, I promise you I'll tell you when it's too much. I'm actually quite enjoying spending this time with Jayden. Helps me not focus on my personal crap."

His eyes are soft as he stares at me for a few seconds before nodding. He leans back down and kisses Jayden's cheek. When he stares into my eyes as he stands straighter, I swear he's going to kiss me, and my heart beats faster. His eyes flick over my shoulder, and he pulls back. Disappointment radiates through me, and I mentally slap myself.

Matthew Carter doesn't do relationships, and why would he want me when he can have any woman he wants?

I plaster on a smile as I grab Jayden's hand and wave at Matt as he makes his way to the dressing room.

I spin around and face the girls and quickly say, "So, food? I'm starving."

They agree, and we grab our stuff and head upstairs to the restaurant. The first thing I do is order myself a stiff drink. The second it's delivered, I down half of it.

"Whoa, slow down girl," Liz says, and I wipe my mouth with the back of my hand.

"I'm good, just thirsty," I lie through my teeth.

Thankfully, our waitress comes by to deliver our orders, and the guys join us.

As I pick a fry off my plate, Hannah asks, "How did your date go?"

My eyes flick to Matt, who is sitting beside me. "It was fine, but I won't be seeing him again."

I've had this conversation with Liv already and was planning on telling the rest of the girls, but at a girls' night, not in public.

"Why?" Liz asks.

I stick a fry in my mouth, hoping to buy myself some time because I'm not sure how to say it with other people around. Unfortunately, Liv beats me to the punch. "He wasn't into her... tastes."

I kick her under the table, thankful Josh is holding Cate now.

"Owww."

I glare at her, eyes flicking to Josh and the rest of the guys.

"Tastes?" Grayson asks. I see the mischievous look in his eye and know he's stirring shit. Hannah covers her mouth as she holds back a laugh, because she knows exactly what Liv means. The girls know I enjoy certain things when it comes to the bedroom, and one of those things is I like to take control and maybe dish out some praise. I learned real quick that's not something Dean would be into.

"It's nothing," I say.

"Oh, Zoey, are you into some kinky shit?" he asks, and the girls burst into laughter.

I'm not going to back down, because he should know his wife talks. We're her best friends, so of course we know some of the shit they've done. I lean forward on the table and stare him directly in the eye. "Grayson, Grayson, Grayson."

He leans in as he stares me down, too, not backing down.

"I wouldn't say kinky, unless you think your wife calling you a good boy is kinky."

He immediately leans back in his chair, mouth open a tad.

"I'd be careful about poking fun at me, because I won't back down. I'm not ashamed, but I also know little things about you guys from your wives. See, girls talk. We have all shared things with each other."

"There's no way she's shared that much," he says, skeptical.

"How should I prove it? How about the spot by the pond at your parents, or Caleb and Bailey's wedding?"

"Those were good, I stand by those," Hannah says.

"What the fuck don't you share with them?" he asks.

She shrugs. "Not much. Honestly, we have a great sex life. Would you rather me be complaining"—she leans into him—"or sharing that my husband keeps me satisfied?"

He leans in and whispers something in her ear, and she blushes. "Okay, so if you're not ashamed, what tastes was he not into?"

I ponder how to word it delicately. "He's very… I don't know, old school in his thinking. Very much someone who would not be willing to relinquish control."

Matt starts coughing as he puts his drink on the table.

"You okay there?" I ask, humour filling my voice.

"Yeah. Yup. Just went down the wrong pipe."

I shake my head before taking a bite of my burger. "He just ended up not being my type."

"Well, why don't you let me set you up with this guy I met at this teacher development seminar I just went to. He teaches high school math here in the city and seemed nice. I can send him an email and see if he'd be interested in something," Liv offers.

"Is he anything like the last guy you set me up with?"

About a month ago, Liv tried to set me up with one of the new teachers at her school and that did not end well either. The guy ended up trying to mansplain everything to me. I ended up excusing myself to the washroom during one of our dates, sneaking out of the restaurant, and texting him that I had an emergency to attend to.

"I had no idea he was like that, and no, from the conversation we had at the seminar, he did not seem like a mansplainer."

"There's a new doctor at the hospital I can set you up with, too. He's cute," Hannah says.

"Dr. Bardot is cute?" Grayson asks, sounding offended.

"Oh, don't sound so butt hurt. You know I love you and find you much better looking. As I've said, you're stuck with me."

Grayson looks at her with hearts in his eyes. "I would never say I'm stuck with you."

"Someone has gone soft," Caleb says, holding back a laugh.

"Well, you guys were right. When you find the right person, you'll do anything for them."

"Is there a reason you two are trying to throw men at me?"

"We just want you to be happy. We know you're looking for something long term, so we're just helping you find someone," Liv says.

"Okay, I'll meet the math teacher." I relent, knowing her heart's in the right place. And I would love to find a fulfilling relationship.

"Amazing! I'll email him tonight and let you know what he says."

The conversation moves on, and we finish our dinner. The entire time, Matt is acting weird. I can't put my finger on it, but he seems to be more reserved and distant, which isn't him. He kisses his sister on the cheek and gives a brief goodbye before waving to the guys and telling Liv he'll see her tomorrow before taking Jayden and leaving.

CHAPTER 12

Matt

I slept like complete and utter shit last night. I kept having recurring dreams of Zoey out with different guys, and I was forced to sit and watch them. Watch her laugh with them. Flirt with them. In a couple, I had to watch her kiss them, and it had my blood on fire. I'm not sure what's caused it, but I've developed this possessive attachment to her. I don't want to share her. I don't want her to be going on dates with the guy my sister wants to set her up with or some hotshot doctor Hannah wants her to go out with. I wanted to slam my drink on the table and say no, she's not going out with either of them. But I can't do that. I have no claim over her. The most I can say is she's a friend.

Her saying Dean wasn't in to giving up control only made me more interested. I want to know exactly how she takes control.

I'm grumpier than Jayden as we get ready to leave the house for sibling brunch and for him to hang out with Josh. I'm still not sure how I feel about Josh juggling both kids, but I also know Josh is a great dad and won't let anything happen to either of the kids.

With the diaper bag over my shoulder and Jayden in his car seat, I make my way up to Josh and Liv's apartment. I knock, and Liv almost immediately pulls it open, a huge grin on her face when she sees me.

"I'm so glad you're here!"

The look on my face must show I've had a rough night, because she asks, "Did Jayden not sleep last night?"

I shake my head. "He slept fine, it was me who had the issue."

Worry etches her face. "You okay?"

"Yeah, I'm fine. Just some weird dreams."

Josh comes out of the kitchen and joins us, Cate on his hip. "Hey, man," he says, tipping his chin at me.

"Hey. Thanks for watching Jayden for me."

"Of course. It will be great for Cate and Jayden to get some cousin time, and Liv's been going on about how she wants a sibling breakfast."

She smiles at me. "I just miss you and Gi. It's been too long."

"It has. Well, I've packed everything you should need: bottles, diapers, wipes, some of his toys. If you have any problems, I'll have my cell."

He chuckles. "Matt, I'm sure I'll be fine. I've done this before."

"I know, but you've never managed two kids at once."

"Go. Have fun."

Liv ushers me out of her apartment, and we make our way down to my car to pick up Gi. Liv catches me up on some of Cate's milestones she's hit recently. Cate has recently started blowing raspberries and is very entertained by them, but with that has also come the fascination of putting things in her mouth, and that's a stage I'm not looking forward to. Cate is only two months older than Jayden. I never thought Liv and I would have kids so close in age, but I'm glad they have each other. If Josh and I both end up finding places near Caleb's, our kids will all end up going to the same school, which will be nice.

Gi is waiting for us outside when we pull up to the house, and she hops in the back. "Hey!"

"You're chipper this morning," I say.

"I am! It's been so long since the three of us have gone out and done anything together. I'm excited," Gi says.

"See, even Gi agrees it's been too long," Liv says.

"I know. Life's just been kind of crazy."

They nod, and I drive us to the restaurant they picked earlier this week. The place is bustling with people. We manage to snag the last booth in the corner and settle in. I order coffee, needing a pick me up.

The three of us seamlessly slip into conversation, catching each other up with what's going on in our lives. When our food is delivered, Liv manages to maneuver the conversation to a bet she still has to cash in with me. Last December, I bet her Josh could slip in Taylor Swift song titles into conversation and no one would notice, but I lost when Caleb figured it out. I now have to let Liv set me up and I have to go on three dates with her.

"Why are you cashing in on this now?" I ask.

"Because I think you're now in place to settle down, and that you might actually stick it out with her."

Something about going on a date doesn't really sit well with me. I can't seem to stop thinking about Zoey, but maybe dating is exactly what I need to get her off my mind.

"And what am I supposed to do about Jayden?" I ask.

"Oh, I'll watch him," Gi says.

"Gi, I'm not going to make you come all the way out to the city to watch Jayden, and as much as I want you to spend time with him, I don't really want to do the drive to and from Mom and Dad's to drop him off."

"No, it's no problem. I can spend the day with Emily and then sleep on your couch, or I can bring an air mattress." She looks determined to do this.

"Are you sure?"

"Yeah, one hundred percent. As much as I love being home and seeing Mom and Dad all the time, I would also just love to get out of the house. I miss being in the city. Back at school, I was always out and about. Now I feel like I never leave the house and all I do is binge watch TV while I crochet or read books. This will be a great excuse to force me out of the house, and I want to bond with my nephew."

I nod and turn to Liv. "As long as the date also works for Gi, you can set it up."

"Oh, yay! You're going to love her," Liv exclaims. "I'll text you both the details when I get it set up."

"You're not going to let me pick the restaurant?" I ask.

"Nope, I'm going to plan the whole thing. All you have to do is show up."

I furrow my brows but accept it. I'm far too exhausted to fight her on any of this, and if it makes my sister happy, I'll let her do it.

Brunch with the girls today reminds me of how much I miss when we all lived close to each other. We got to have that while I was home for the summers when I was in college, but by the time I was back from the east coast, Gianna was heading off to Stanford. It hasn't worked out in eight years for us to all be in the same city for long. I may be their older brother, but I also like the people they've become and enjoy spending time with them.

When the waitress drops off the bill, I quickly snag it before either of them can. I know Liv is going to fight me for it, but I'm not going to give in. Liv insists on getting the next one, but we'll see about that.

I spend the drive back to Liv's excited to see Jayden. I haven't spent much time apart from him since he was left with me, and being so far away is giving me anxiety, no matter how much I know Josh has everything under control. The second I step into their apartment, I'm looking for him. I barely make it into the living room before I see Josh has the two babies asleep on his chest while highlights from last night's games play on the TV.

I know Jayden needs to sleep, but a hint of jealousy that he'll sleep so easily for Josh courses through me. It makes the annoying, doubtful voice in my head pop up.

You're replaceable.

He's not that attached to you.

You're going to fail at this.

No matter how hard my rational brain tries to fight the thoughts, they linger. It's the same voice that told me I couldn't raise Jayden on my own when I first saw him.

Liv makes her way towards Josh, kissing him on the cheek before she tries to take Cate from him, but he levels her with a look that has her smile growing and her taking a seat beside him.

"Daddy's not ready to give up his princess?" she teases. There's a warmth to her voice that tells me she loves that he wants to be close to her and spend all this time with Cate.

"No, I'm not. These two have been inseparable all morning. I could not take one of them into a room without the other. The only way they'd sleep was together, but Cate also wanted to be held, which is how I ended up here."

Liv and I share a look. Our babies wanted to be close to each other. It's like they can feel the familial connection without even knowing about it. There are big enough age gaps between Liv and me and Gianna and me that I was conscious of the fact I was getting baby sisters before they were even born. But these two seem to just know.

"I'm sorry if he was a hassle," I say, and Josh shakes his head.

"No hassle. I'm glad Cate gets to grow up with the ability to be so close to her cousins, and to have the two of them so close in age, it will be wonderful to watch them grow up together." There's a softness to his voice, similar to what was in Liv's. These two have always been family oriented. I'm not surprised one bit by how happy they are to be growing theirs or having their families so involved with Cate.

Needing to lighten the mood, I say, "Who knew Joshua Lincoln was such a softie."

He stares lovingly at Liv. "Your sister brought it out of me."

I hold back a groan. As much as I love that they found each other, seeing my best friend and my sister being sappy isn't my favourite pastime. I leave them to gather all of Jayden's toys and make sure his diaper bag is packed before returning to collect him off Josh's chest.

"Thanks, guys. I should probably get this guy home," I say and make my way towards the front door. Liv follows me, and I pull her in for a side hug and kiss the top of her head.

"Thanks for today, Matty. I'll text you with the details of your date."

"Thanks, Liv."

Liv closes the door behind me as I make my way down to my car.

Luckily, Jayden sleeps the entire car ride home. Upstairs we get in some tummy time and a feeding before he's out again. Just as he passes out, there's a knock at the front door, and I quietly close my bedroom door and head to answer it. Checking the peephole, I can't help my smile when I see Zoey standing on the other side.

I enthusiastically pull the door open as I say, "Hey, Zoey."

She smiles up at me, and I take a step back, allowing her to come in.

"What brings you by?"

She holds up a bag, and I furrow my brows.

"What is it?"

She reaches inside and pulls out a plush hockey puck attached to string. "I saw these and thought they were the most adorable things ever and needed to grab them for Jayden," she says excitedly.

I follow her to the couch, where she digs out a few more before making her way to the toy that hangs over the tummy time mat and secures them to the bottom of each line. She grins as she sits next to me.

"Now he can see something to remind him of his dad every time he lies there and looks up."

I'm stunned into silence as I stare at her. The fact that Zoey was out and bought something so my son could have it to always remind him of me is everything.

She reaches forward and digs in the bag again. "Is he asleep? I have something else for him, but I'd love to be the one that gives it to him."

"Yeah," I barely squeak out, and she turns to look at me.

"Oh God, please tell me this is all okay. I didn't overstep or anything, did I?"

I scoot closer to her and place a hand on her leg. "Zo, of course, this is all alright. I'd never say you can't buy him thoughtful gifts. I appreciate it more than you'll ever know."

I stare at her, fully taking in the smattering of freckles that dust ever so slightly over her nose and cheeks. Her brown eyes are locked on me as her lashes flutter and lips part slightly. The next thought that passes through my mind is *I wonder what her lips taste like.* Her tongue slowly glides over her bottom lip, and I can't help but wish it was my tongue instead.

As I feel myself beginning to lean in to give in to temptation, she clears her throat and her head snaps to the bag her hand is still inside of. She pulls out a blue stuffed elephant and turns so that her legs are now between us, creating more distance.

"I grabbed this for him, too. I had something similar when I was a kid and absolutely loved him, I thought Jayden might, too."

I hold out a hand and ask, "May I?"

She nods and places the stuffed animal in my hand. He's soft with flappy ears and nose. It looks like something Jayden will happily play with and probably stick in his slobbery mouth.

"He's adorable," I say, handing the stuffie back to her.

She smiles as she looks down at it, flopping his ears a few times.

"You're welcome to stick around and wait for Jayden to wake up, if you want," I say. "I've got to do some dishes, but you can chill and watch something."

"Are you sure?"

"Yeah. Of course. One hundred percent." I'm starting to ramble. I never get this way. I don't get flustered around women, but I want her to stay. I want to be close to her, and something about her has me losing all my footing.

"That'd be great."

I nod and hand her the remote before making my way to the kitchen. She puts on some home renovation show and provides commentary as I load the dishwasher and clean the counters. When I'm done, I quickly whip us up some food as the next episode comes on.

When I approach the couch with two bowls, she looks at me with a raised brow.

"KD with sausages," I say, and excitement practically radiates off her. Her and Liv loved mac and cheese growing up, and it's a food they still love to eat. I only really keep boxes of the stuff in the house for them.

I pass her the bowl, and she immediately adjusts herself, crossing her legs and getting comfy as she digs in.

As the TV shows the kitchen pre-renovation, Zo makes a face.

"What was that?" I ask.

"Hmmm, pardon?" she says as she takes a bite.

"You made a face."

She looks at me and then back to the TV. "Oh, that kitchen, it's hideous."

I chuckle. "Okay, what did you hate about it?"

"Those cabinets were such an ugly colour, and don't get me started on their lack of storage and all the appliances on the counter and their full outlets. Their countertops don't match the rest of the kitchen, and the whole space just looks super cramped."

I nod. "So, you like open kitchens with brighter colours and clear countertops?"

"Oh, one hundred percent. I like an open kitchen that encourages conversation. I don't want to feel cramped in the space. Realistically, you spend so much time in that space, I don't want to feel anxious about it."

Her reasoning makes total sense, and I get what she means about the colour of that kitchen—definitely not appealing.

She points out a few more things she dislikes about the place pre-renovation and then oohs and awws about the finished product. The episodes roll into one another, and when Jayden starts to cry in the other room, Zoey is up and off the couch faster than me and making a beeline straight to my bedroom.

"Oh, is my Jaydie boo awake?" she coo's as she approaches his crib.

His arms flail upwards as she leans over and reaches down for him.

She bounces him as she talks to him. "Did you have a good sleep?"

His sobs die down, and he settles for her.

She leans forward to put her mouth on his tummy, and her face pinches. "Oh, someone needs a diaper change," she says.

I reach for him. "I've got it."

She lets me take him and helps gather the necessary things while I get him settled on the change table.

"Did someone go poop?" I ask as I dance my fingers up his front and bop him on the nose, causing him to giggle before I undo his onesie.

Zoey and I work in perfect sync as I change him and she hands me things. We don't have to say anything, anticipating the other person's move and it feels so natural. I never thought I'd be standing over a dirty diaper thinking I love how effortlessly I move with someone, let alone Zoey.

When Jayden's all cleaned up, Zoey takes him into the living room and I make him a bottle. His giggles fill the room as Zoey entertains him, and my heart feels as if it might explode in my chest. I can't be feeling this way. I can't be standing in my kitchen watching Zoey play with my son, wishing every day was like this, because that's not realistic. She's my sister's best friend, but I also don't want to bring her into some instant family. Jayden and I are just gaining our footing, and pulling Zoey into that full time is too much. She deserves better.

I finish the bottle and join them. Zoey feeds him while we settle back in and play the show. When he finishes his bottle, she shows him the stuffed elephant, and he's immediately obsessed with it. I eventually order us pizza for dinner, and she helps me bathe Jayden before he settles in for the night.

I walk her to the front door, and all I want is to ask her to stay. "Thanks for the gifts for Jayden."

She smiles at me. "Of course. Thanks for letting me hang out with the two of you today. I can only handle so much of being at Henry and Maggie's." She gives her head a little shake, and a stray piece of hair falls from her ponytail.

I step closer and tuck it behind her ear as I say, "You're always welcome here, Zo."

It feels like our breaths sync as our eyes lock. It's like she's pulling me in with just the soft look in them. I could get lost in them, watching as little flecks of gold appear depending on how the light hits them.

"Thanks," she breathes out softly.

The urge to lean forward and dust my lips over hers is strong. It's as if we're magnets, and I'm struggling to fight her pull, but I do. I drop my hand and shove it into the pocket of my jeans, hoping that will stop me from touching her more.

Her chest deflates, and she looks down at the ground. I've seen that look of rejection before, and I hate more than anything that she looks like that because of me.

"Well, I should get going," she says.

"Have a good night. Text me when you get home safe."

She stares at me for a few extra seconds before she leaves my apartment, and I watch her until she's out of sight.

CHAPTER 13

Zoey

When I get in my car, I sit and stare out the windshield. I thought Matt was going to kiss me twice today. The first time, I pulled away because there's no way Matthew Carter wanted to kiss me, right? But the second time, I knew it. From the look in his eyes and the way he delicately tucked that piece of hair behind my ear, I knew it. Then when he didn't, my stomach bottomed out. It was like I built it all up in my head and was being delusional. I hate that I was disappointed he didn't kiss me. I hate that I stood there waiting for him to close the last few inches between us.

I bang my head back on the headrest a couple of times as I shout, "Ahhhhh."

I know better. I know I shouldn't get my hopes up when it comes to Matt, because not only am I not someone he'd go for, I'm a relationship girl, and as much as I know a roll in the sheets with Matt would probably be mind-blowing, I'm not going to change all my ways just for him.

Needing to get out of my head, I blast music on my drive back to Henry's. I haven't been staying there long, but I've already noticed their house is not necessarily where I want to be when they're both off. I've heard things I wish I could go my whole life never hearing. The night after Henry got back from his work trip was truly horrific. I couldn't look either of them in the eye for a couple of days.

I breathe a sigh of relief when I pull into the driveway and see Kai's car. Kai is nine years older than me and three younger than Henry, so the two of them were always closer. When I open the front door, the smell of baked goods hits me and my mouth waters. One bonus to living here has been Maggie's food. She's not only a great cook, but also an amazing baker. She always has something made and ready in the house for people to graze on.

Maggie comes out of the kitchen in her apron and smiles at me. "Hey! You're home," she says cheerfully.

I nod and follow her into the kitchen. The living room is right off the kitchen, and that's where I see Henry and Kai sitting, each with a beer in hand as they watch some hockey game. Growing up, whether I was at the Carters or at home, the sport was always on, but I never bothered to learn it. I've learned some things since Josh and Liv got together and we've started going to more of their games, but I couldn't understand a game on my own.

I grab a bottle of water from the fridge and take a seat at the kitchen island as Maggie opens the oven and pulls out a cake pan.

"There's dinner leftovers in the fridge if you're hungry," she says over her shoulder.

"Oh, I'm good, thanks. I ate already."

"What did you have?" she asks.

"We ordered some pizza."

She turns and faces me, raising an eyebrow. "We?"

I take a sip of my water, prolonging the need to answer her. "Um, yeah. Matt and I."

That catches my brothers' attention.

"Matt, as in Matt Carter?" Henry asks.

I nod. "Yeah."

Kai sits forward and turns to get a better look at me. "What were you doing with Matt Carter?"

I play with the lid to my water bottle, watching as I spin it on the kitchen counter. "He's my friend, I thought I'd stop by when I finished shopping." I avoid telling them about Jayden, because quite frankly he's none of their business, and I also don't want to deal with the Spanish Inquisition right now.

"Your friend," Kai drags out.

"Yes, my friend. Nothing more."

Henry opens his mouth, but before he can say anything, I say, "I'm going to head upstairs and read." I slide off my chair and climb the stairs two at a time, wanting to be as far away from my questioning brothers as possible. After changing into comfy pyjamas, I slide into bed with my Kindle and open my latest book.

I have pre-date jitters the entire week. Liv texted me on Sunday morning with a restaurant, date, and time, saying the reservation was under my name. She didn't tell me anything about the guy I'm supposed to be meeting, so I have no idea what to expect.

I spend hours getting ready on Saturday, cycling through different outfits, showering, doing my hair and makeup. I finally settle on a navy sweater dress and some knee-high boots with a heel. I adjust myself in the mirror, taking in every inch, and I look hot, if I do say so myself.

Grabbing my purse and jacket, I make my way downstairs and into the foyer.

"Well, don't you look nice," Maggie says as she stands with Henry in the kitchen, pouring a glass of wine.

"Thank you. I have a date."

Of course, that piques Henry's interest, forever the protective brother.

"Date?" he asks.

"Yes. Liv set us up."

Knowing he at least knows one of my friends and she has my best interest at heart seems to relax Henry a little.

"Where are you going?" he asks.

"Alchemy."

His eyes widen slightly. "That's a nice place."

I nod. "It is."

"Call me if you need anything," he says.

I roll my eyes. "Henry, I'm sure I can handle myself on a date. I'm not a kid anymore if you hadn't realized."

"Still my baby sister." He rounds the island and stops in front of me. Leaning down, he kisses my cheek before saying, "Seriously, Zoey, please call me if you need anything."

"I will."

He steps back and nods. "Have fun."

I leave and make my way to the bus and Skytrain and head for Alchemy. I don't know much about the restaurant. I know they're newer in town and have a reputation for being upscale and hard to get a table at.

Inside, I give my name to the hostess and she guides me to my table. I take my seat and settle in, and she returns with a man in toe, but he's one I recognize. I could spot those waves and brown eyes anywhere. Why is Matt here?

I hold my breath as I watch the hostess lead him to the table beside mine. As she leaves the menu on the table, he spots me and stops removing his jacket as he stares at me.

"Zo," he breathes out, and I swear goosebumps erupt over my entire body.

He stares at me, and I take him in. He's very clearly dressed for a date in black dress slacks that fit him perfectly and a deep-red, almost burgundy, button-down. Despite the cool temperatures outside, he has the sleeves rolled up to his elbows. His hair is styled perfectly so the stray curl that usually flops onto his forehead is held back. He's started growing out his facial hair since Jayden came into his life, and I'd be lying if I said it didn't make him a tad more attractive.

"Zo." His voice is so low I barely hear it.

"Matt."

So much is running through my head right now. Why is Matt here right now? How am I supposed to sit through a date knowing he's at the next table? He settles into his chair, and I flag the waiter and order a glass of wine. At this point I'm saying fuck it to waiting for my date. If I'm going to make it through the evening, I need some booze. Matt must be thinking the same thing, because he orders a scotch. Usually my go-to would be to text the group chat or Liv, but I can't. What am I supposed to say? *Liv, your brother, who I've started to develop feelings for, is here.* Nope. Nope. Double nope. Texting anyone about this situation takes these thoughts and puts them out in the open, and I'm not ready to accept that reality. I'd rather live in the land of delusion than admit to someone I might have more than platonic feelings for Matthew Carter.

When my wine is dropped off, I fight the urge to take a gulp of it, instead sipping it politely. I can't help myself and watch as Matt takes a sip of his scotch, his tongue catching a stray drop on his bottom lip. I hold back a groan. Why am I all of a sudden having this reaction to Matt? How have I gone years—literal years—knowing him and spending holidays with his family and him just being my best friend's brother to me sitting here in a restaurant fantasizing about licking a stray drop of scotch off his lip, maybe pulling it between my teeth and watching as his eyes dilate?

I force my eyes away and check my phone, confirming the time Liv texted for the date. Seven p.m. It's now 7:10 p.m. and no word. I tell myself I'll give him five more minutes and then I'm writing him off and calling this date a dud. I mindlessly scroll, only stopping when Matt makes a noise of frustration. I look up at him, and his eyes are now locked on me.

"So, it looks like my date stood me up," he says, flipping his phone face down, his eyes never leaving me.

A small laugh escapes me. "Same."

His smile is soft and grows. "What do you say, Zo? Join me for dinner?"

I gnaw on my lip as I contemplate the implications of this. Because years of knowing me means he can pick up on subtle things, he notices my hesitancy.

"Come on. It doesn't mean anything, Zo. Just two people who have been stood up and are looking to make the most of their evening. After all, this is one of the hardest restaurants to get a reservation in, especially during busy season."

I stare at him, pursing my lips, as I wonder if Liv used Josh's connections to get a table. After a few seconds, I relent. I grab my wine and purse and slide out of my chair before slipping into the chair across from Matt. A look of triumph shines in his eyes. We each take a sip of our drinks, awkwardness filling the air between us. Matt focuses on his drink as he runs his finger up and down the side of the glass.

"Who were you here to meet?" he asks.

"The guy Olivia set me up with," I say, taking a sip of my wine.

He nods slightly before leaning forward. "Well, he's missing out, because now I get to enjoy your company."

I roll my lips together, holding back my smile. "And who were you meeting?"

"Someone Liv was setting me up with. Liv just texted and said the girl had an emergency come up."

"So, you and I get to enjoy one of the top restaurants in the city together," I say, matching his position.

We stare at each other for a few moments before we finally pull back and settle in our seats. I quickly open the menu, needing to stop looking at him and just how good he looks tonight.

We both pick something to eat and opt to share an appetizer. Conversation is stilted and awkward for a few minutes, but we eventually slip back into our comfortability. We laugh, and I'm genuinely enjoying my night. The food is good. I share some of my mushroom risotto with Matt, and he shares some of his steak with me.

As the waiter walks away with our new drink order, I hear Matt's name called from across the restaurant. Over his shoulder, I see a stunning tall blonde approach our table. As soon as she's at his side, she's leaning down and kissing his cheek and saying how nice it is to see him.

"Melinda," he says, smiling politely at her.

"Oh, Matt, that's all you've got to say? I've missed you. We should totally catch up."

Her tone is extremely flirtatious, and it's obvious she's one of the many women Matt's had fun with over the years. She's stunning, so I don't blame him. I watch as she drags her fingers up his arm and bats her lashes at him. She's not being very subtle in letting him know she wants another round with him. Thinking of him leaving with her has my stomach turning. I don't want to be here anymore. I have no right to feel this way, but I thought we were having a good time, even if it was just as friends.

"I'm here with someone, Melinda," Matt says.

Her eyes flick to me, and her smile turns fake as she turns and leans into Matt more.

"Hi," she says.

"Hi." My voice comes out soft.

"Melinda, this is Zoey, Zoey, this is Melinda."

I nod and start to gather my jacket and purse. "I should get going. Matt, dinner was nice, I'll get you back this week." I move to quickly get out of my chair when Matt grabs my wrist.

"Zo, don't go. We just ordered new drinks."

My eyes move to Melinda quickly before back to him. "I'm sure Melinda will enjoy it." I pull my wrist free and push past her, making my way out of the restaurant, the cool air hitting my skin. I start to make my way towards the Skytrain station. I'm glad I didn't drive. I need the walk to clear my head. I need to go on an actual date that's good so I can get these stupid thoughts of Matt out of my head.

I'm almost two blocks from the restaurant when Matt's car pulls up beside me and he rolls down the passenger window.

"Zo," he calls, but I keep walking.

The sound of his car door closing echoes through the air before I hear him working to catch up with me. He grabs my wrist and stops me in my spot.

"Zo, look at me." His voice is pleading.

I reluctantly turn around, and his eyes slowly take in my face.

"Why did you leave?"

I roll my eyes, using it as my defence to prevent me from saying it hurt to watch that woman fawn over him knowing I mean nothing to him besides being his sister's best friend.

"Just thought I'd leave and give you and Melinda the chance to catch up," I say.

His eyes widen, and he shakes his head. "I didn't want to catch up with Melinda. I was enjoying my time with you."

"Matt, you don't need to lie. I know neither of us planned to be having dinner together, and I'm sure you went into that date thinking you'd be getting more at the end of the night. I was giving you the chance to get that."

He sighs. "Yes, neither of us planned for the night to go the way it did, but I don't regret it. I enjoyed having a nice meal with you. Talking, seeing you laugh."

His words warm my blood, but I can't fall into that feeling.

"Just go find Melinda, Matt."

"No." The word comes out strong, sure. "Zoey, I'm not ending our night like this. I'm definitely not letting you take the train home when I can drive you. If you want to call it a night, fine, but I'll be driving you home."

I open my mouth to argue, but he takes a step closer, and it's like the air in my lungs freezes. He tucks a piece of windblown hair behind my ear. "Let me take you home, Zo."

I melt, wishing there was more meaning to those words. A gust of wind comes through, and I shiver slightly. His hand moves from my face to rub up and down my arm.

I know that, like his sister, Matt is stubborn and won't let me just walk away. I nod, relenting, and he leads me to his car, opening the passenger door for me.

I don't want to talk right now, because I'm sure the second I open my mouth, I'm going to say something stupid. Relief hits me when Matt puts on music, and we make the drive to Henry's in silence. When he pulls into the driveway, he quickly rounds the front of the car and opens my door, helping me out. I thank him, and he walks with me to the front door. I stop and face him, unsure of what to say.

"I had fun with you tonight, Zo."

I can't help my soft smile, and even though the night didn't end in the best of ways, I did enjoy myself. "Me too."

He leans down and places a soft kiss on my cheek, and I fight the urge to lean into it.

"Sleep well, Bug."

My heart skips a beat. Matt is fucking with my head. I slip inside the house and wait until I see his headlights pull out of the driveway before I make my way to the kitchen for a glass of water.

"So, you're dating Matthew Carter." Henry's voice scares the shit out of me, and I jump.

I fully enter the kitchen and see him standing at the sink with his ankles crossed and his arms folded over his chest.

"No, I'm not."

"You said before you left you were going on a date, and he just dropped you off. How does that not equal you guys dating?"

I fill a glass with ice and water from the fridge and turn to face my brother. "I got stood up, he was at the same restaurant for a date and also got stood up, we decided to make the most of it and had dinner. Nothing more."

No matter how much I wish that were the case.

His brows furrow. "That seems like quite the coincidence."

I shrug. "I guess. I don't know. It's not like I chose to be stood up."

"I'm not saying that, Zo. I'm just saying be careful with him. I don't want him hurting you."

Anger boils in me. What is that supposed to mean? Does Henry really think I'm not capable of taking care of myself?

"And how exactly do you think he'll hurt me, Henry?"

He runs a hand over his face, probably sensing my frustration. "Zoey, I'm just looking out for you. I remember what he was like in high school, and if he's anything like that still, I just don't think that he's the guy for you."

I scoff. "You're nine years older than Matt. What do you mean you remember what he was like then? Do you really think that people don't change or that I can't take care of myself?"

I can tell I'm overstimulated and emotional, because I'm picking a fight with Henry, and I haven't done that since I was a teenager.

"Do you really think I wasn't checking out who you were hanging out with when you were growing up? Of course, I think people can change, but it's never a guarantee. I'm your big brother. I've spent years taking care of you, making sure you're safe and taken care of. I can't just turn that off."

I slam my cup on the counter. While my anger grows, tears gather behind my eyes. I hate that when I feel any emotion strongly, I cry.

"I'm not some kid anymore, Henry. I can take care of myself. I appreciate everything you did while I was a kid—" A sob leaves me as the tears begin to fall. I'm feeling too many things at once right now. Disappointment over what really happened with Matt, anger at my brother for treating me as if I'm still a kid, and sadness about being stood up and still living this single life.

"Zo?" Maggie rounds the corner into the kitchen wearing her bathrobe, and her eyes bounce between Henry and me. She takes a step closer, reaching for me, and I crumble in her arms as the tears fall in earnest. I can barely make out their whispered words through my sobs.

"I don't know. We were talking and then she started crying," Henry says.

"What did you say?" Maggie says accusatorially.

"I was looking out for her."

Maggie runs her hand over my back and helps me stand before taking me upstairs and getting me settled in bed. She lies with with me until I'm so tired I fall asleep.

CHAPTER 14

Matt

I take the long way home from Zoey's, knowing Gianna is back at my place and will have questions I'm not sure how to answer. Sharing a meal with Zoey in a restaurant just the two of us was nice. I was so relaxed with her, and I thought everything was going well until Melinda showed up and Zoey ran out of there like her ass was on fire. The second she said she was leaving, my stomach dropped. That was the last thing I wanted. I wanted her to stay. I wanted to share a dessert, maybe go for a walk together before I took her home. The more we sat there, the more I wished it was actually a date.

Melinda showing up was a stark reminder of the life I've lived of moving from girl to girl, just having fun with no commitments. That's not something I want with Zoey. I want to see if we could have something real. I enjoy spending time with her, more than I have any other woman I've met.

The way she ran out of there has me thinking she doesn't want any of that. It was as though Melinda was exactly what she was waiting for to get out of there, but then she said she had fun. This woman has me all over the place, and I've never been like this before.

When I arrive home, I quietly let myself in in case Gi is asleep. She's wrapped in a blanket on the couch with a bowl of ice cream and watching a movie. I shouldn't be surprised. Gi's always loved her late-night sweets.

She smiles at me and pauses the movie. "So, how was the date?" she asks.

"She cancelled."

She grabs her phone and checks the time. "So why are you just getting home?"

I grip the back of my neck and take a seat beside her. "Zoey was in the restaurant, too, and her date stood her up, so we ate dinner together."

Gi's quiet as she watches me and takes a bite of her ice cream. Silence fills the room, and I feel her mind moving a mile a minute. Unlike Liv, Gi's always been quiet and lets people stew, hoping that will get them to open up.

I shuffle in my seat, not sure what else to say.

After a few minutes, she takes pity and asks with a grin, "So, how was your date?"

"Not a date," I say emphatically.

"Did you share a meal together?"

"Yes."

"Did you enjoy conversation? Laugh?"

I roll my eyes. "A meal and conversation do not make a date, Gi. I've done that with Josh and the rest of the guys. Those weren't dates."

She nods, taking another bite of her ice cream. "True, but did you ever want anything more from them?"

"No, of course not."

"Okay, and did you want something more with Zoey?"

I open my mouth to say my usual no, but I close it, because I don't think I can lie about this anymore. As much as I know I shouldn't be pining after Zoey Williams and wanting more, I do.

Gi points her spoon at me. "See, date."

"Not if she doesn't think it was," I say, defeat and disappointment filling my voice.

"Do you know what she thought it was? Have you talked to her about it?"

I steal the spoon and take a bite of ice cream. "No, she kind of ran away near the end of the meal and I had to chase her down. I convinced her to let me drive her home, but it wasn't exactly an ideal end to the night."

We get into a routine of passing the spoon back and forth.

"Sounds like there was a reason she decided to make a run for it," Gi says.

"Yeah," I say, not wanting to go into detail about past trysts with my little sister.

She raises a brow at me, holding the spoon hostage until I give her more.

I sigh. "A girl I know showed up, talked about catching up."

Gi throws her head back with a laugh, and I shush her.

"Jayden's asleep in the next room," I say.

"Sorry."

We listen for a minute, and when we don't hear any noises, she continues.

"Men can be so obtuse," she muses.

"Really?" My tone is both frustrated and annoyed.

"Do you really think if Zoey was just your sister's best friend, or just your friend, she'd want to bail as soon as a woman, whom you've presumably slept with, shows up and starts talking about catching up?" When I say nothing, she shakes her head. "She obviously has some sort of feelings for you. She probably hasn't figured them all out yet, but she doesn't see you as just a friend."

Gianna's words give me hope. I know I have to approach all of this cautiously, though, because the last thing I want to do is hurt Zoey. She means too much to me for me to be the cause of any hurt she experiences. Zoey is first and foremost Liv's *and* my friend.

I need time to think about all of this, so I ask Gi, "How was Jayden tonight?"

She lights up at the question. "He was an absolute doll. My nephew is the cutest little thing! We played for a bit, and he took his bottle well. He was a little fussy when you first left and when I tried to put him down, but he eventually calmed down."

I'm not surprised about him being a bit fussy. Mom said the same thing when she had him, and it's probably because I spend so much time with him and if it's not me, it's usually Zo.

"You ate?" I ask.

She nods. "Yeah, I stole some of the KD you had in the cupboard."

Of course she did. The girls could live off KD mac and cheese if

Mom let them when we were kids, and not much has changed as they've grown up. "You know KD here is so much better than the stuff in the States. It never hit the same when I made it at school."

I chuckle. "What else did you miss?"

She hums. "Definitely Coke, oh and ketchup chips. Liv shipped me a few coffee crisps once because I was craving them during exams. She threw in some Kinder Surprise eggs, too, not sure how those made it through customs." She laughs.

"I don't even make your list," I joke.

She rolls her eyes at me. "Of course I missed you. I missed everyone. I'm just talking food right now."

She takes her bowl into the kitchen and loads it in the dishwasher, and I know I should let her get some sleep. I head to my bedroom, stopping to ask, "You sticking around for breakfast?"

She shakes her head. "No, I have plans with Em."

I nod. "Okay, well, sleep well. Thanks for hanging out with Jayden tonight."

"Of course. I'm glad I'm home now and can spend more time with my niece and nephew." She smiles.

"We're glad you're home, too."

I close my bedroom door, stopping beside Jayden's crib to stare at my perfect little boy bundled in his sleep sack. I want nothing more than to reach in and brush my finger over his cheek, but I don't because I don't want to wake him. I quietly change and slip into bed, my mind wandering to how to handle things with Zoey.

It's Sunday, and we have a game today. While I love playing and seeing the guys, I don't usually look forward to games as much as I am tonight. Zo should be there, and I'm hoping I can pull her aside so we can talk about last night. I want to clear the air, if not to see where this could go, to at least make sure things aren't awkward with us going forward.

When I get to the rink, she's not there. I sit and talk with Liv, but my eyes are constantly scanning, waiting for her to turn the corner. I'm the last one not in the dressing room, and I ask Liv, "Where's Zo?"

She raises a brow quickly before schooling her expression. "She texted and said she couldn't come today."

Disappointment fills me.

"The girls and I've got Jayden, if you're going to play."

"Thanks, guys."

"Let me see that adorable little munchkin," Hannah says as reaches into the car seat and tickles his tummy.

I leave them and head into the dressing room to get ready for the game. Conversation is loud around me, but I can't find it in me to participate. I can't help but feel like I'm the reason Zoey didn't come today. This was the last thing I wanted. This is exactly why I've always said she was off limits. Not only do I know she's not one for just a fling, but mixing these kinds of relationships leads to messy situations.

Josh nudges my leg, and I look at him. He gives me an expectant look, and I know I must have missed his question.

"Hmm?"

"Any luck on the house hunting front?"

"Nope. I haven't looked too much, to be honest. I know I need to. It's just kinda slipped through the cracks."

"My realtor said he'd have a bunch of listings to me by end of day tomorrow. I'll send those over as soon as I have them," Caleb says.

I nod. "Thanks, man."

We finish getting ready and head out to the ice. Not seeing Zoey with the girls is weird. I find myself constantly looking for her smile or to see her bouncing Jayden. My head isn't in the game at all. I end up turning the puck over in the first period, allowing the other team to get on a breakaway. Thankfully, Mac stops it and steers the puck to the corner where we gather it. We win the game by one goal, no thanks to me. I change as quickly as possible and gather Jayden, saying goodbye to Liv before heading home. I need to call Zoey.

Once I get Jayden down, I settle on the couch and pull up Zoey's contact. I stare at her picture. It's one of her at Josh and Liv's wedding last year. She looks absolutely stunning. She's smiling brightly, her hair is perfectly curled, and her makeup is done in a way that highlights all of her best features. I've always known she's beautiful, but staring at this picture has me realizing that over the last year and a half, I've noticed so much more about her. I've looked forward to spending time with her. I'd invite her over even if we weren't trying to find ways to push Josh and Liv together. I wanted her company.

I drop my head back as it hits me all at once. I've slowly been falling for Zoey. Every time we'd spend time together, she'd leave me wanting to see her more. She had me falling for her with every interaction.

I finally press the call button and hold the phone to my ear. It rings several times, and just when I think it's going to go to voicemail, she answers.

"Hello."

A relieved smile spreads across my face. "Hey, Zo."

"Hey, Matt."

Silence fills the line, and I know I have to be the one to break it.

"I missed seeing you tonight."

I hear the rustling of sheets before she answers. "I'm sorry I couldn't make it."

"You okay?" I ask.

"Yeah, we just did family dinner tonight."

I know she's fairly close to her brothers, and if they all wanted to do dinner, she wouldn't miss it, but why didn't she tell me before?

"How was it?"

A little hmph comes through the line. "It was dinner with my five brothers. It was—I don't know that fun is the word—entertaining for sure."

I laugh. "I'm not sure how you grew up with five older brothers. I'm not sure I could have handled more siblings beyond Liv and Gi."

"I guess it helped being the youngest. John and Riley are the closest to my age, Kai, Ezra, and Henry are all quite a bit older, so we didn't have the same type of relationship. It was a lot more of them taking care of me when I was young, and by the time I was a pre-teen and teenager, they were moving out."

I nod, even though she can't see me. "At least you have the support system."

She makes a noise of frustration. "It would be great if my brothers would see that I'm a grown woman and can take care of myself."

I weigh my words carefully. On one hand, I can see why her

brothers are protective, I'm protective of Olivia and Gianna and always will be, but I can also see how she wants them to acknowledge her accomplishments and that she can take care of herself.

"You know they do it out of love, right? Big brothers just want to support and take care of their younger sisters."

She scoffs. "So, you've told Liv and Gi who they can and cannot date?" she asks.

Jealousy hits me, and I clear my throat to push the feeling down. "No, but I've told them when I haven't particularly liked someone they were dating." She doesn't say anything, and the next words leave my mouth without any thought. "Who did they tell you not to date?"

She sighs. "No one. It doesn't matter. It's not like it's going to happen anyway."

The jealousy grows. She's over there pinning after some man, and all I want to do is drive over there and kiss her so she stops thinking about him. But I know I need to be a good friend. I need show her that things aren't weird with us, even if I can't stop thinking about kissing her.

"Why won't it happen?"

"I'm not his type." Her answer is short and sure, but I don't know how she wouldn't be any man's type. She's heaven and sin all wrapped in one beautiful package, and I know that without even having touched her. I bite my lip, holding back the groan that wants to leave me as I think about what her moans would sound like if I ran my finger up the inside of her thigh until my finger dusted over her panties.

"How do you know that?" I ask.

She huffs, sounding frustrated. "I just know, Matthew."

The sound of her saying my full name only makes me harder. I don't want to push her anymore, so I say, "So, about last night. I wanted to clear the air."

"We're all good, Matt. It's fine," she says flippantly.

"No, Zo, it's not fine. You shouldn't have felt like you needed to leave when Melinda showed up. I should have made sure you knew I wanted to finish our meal and spend time with you. It never even once occurred to me to leave with Melinda. I wanted to stay. With you."

"Thank you." Her voice comes out soft, and I wish I was with her right now to wrap my arms around her and pull in tight.

"No person should make you feel like you need to leave like you did last night. I'm sorry, Zo."

"It's fine, Matt. I accept your apology." She yawns before she says, "I should head to bed so I can meet you at the rink tomorrow morning."

Knowing she's still going to be there tomorrow makes excitement radiate through me.

"Sleep well, Zo. I'll see you tomorrow."

She yawns again. "You, too."

CHAPTER 15

Zoey

I have no idea what it's going to be like seeing Matt this morning after everything that happened this weekend. After my breakdown on Saturday, Henry called a family dinner so we were all under the same roof. We haven't done that in a while, and it was nice to see everyone all in one place, but as always, the boys found different ways to push each other's buttons. If Maggie wasn't there, I wouldn't have been surprised if they had started throwing dinner rolls at each other.

During dinner, it really hit me that I need to figure out what I want to do with my life. I don't want to be living with my brother in five or ten years or be sitting around the table listening to my brothers talk about their latest accomplishments when I've done nothing.

I do my best to plaster on a smile as I enter the rink and make my way towards where I know Matt will be. He's bouncing Jayden when I round the corner, and they both light up when they see me. That is single-handedly the best feeling in the world, watching someone be excited to see you. I just wish Matt wanted to see me for reasons more than just our friendship.

Jayden reaches for me as I approach, and I take him from Matt. He babbles at me like he's got the most interesting story in the world to tell me.

"Oh really? That sounds so fun," I say to him, and Matt smiles at me.

"Thanks for coming."

I nod. "Of course. This little guy seems super awake today."

He chuckles. "Little man got a lot of sleep last night. He was rearing to go this morning as soon as he woke up."

I tickle his tummy. "Sounds like we've got to work some energy out of you, little man."

He giggles, and little spit bubbles form at the corner of his mouth.

"I've got to go check on the kids," Matt says and pauses before leaning down and kissing my cheek, whispering, "I'll see you after," across my skin. Goosebumps erupt down my neck and arms.

I watch as Matt makes his way to the dressing room before I dig into the diaper bag and pull out some stimulation toys to play with Jayden. He is bubbly and full of energy this morning. Thank God for the coffee Matt brought me, because I'm not sure I'd be able to keep up with him without it.

My stomach is growling by the time Matt finishes coaching and we head to breakfast. I love that we have a routine, something that's just ours. No one else knows about Matt's coaching, or that every Monday and Wednesday morning I get to spend time with Jayden and then share breakfast with Matt. It's all ours.

I'm surprised Maggie's home when I walk in the front door and find her sitting at the kitchen island. She smiles at me as I walk past her to the coffee maker and pour myself a cup.

"Early morning," she says.

"Yeah, just ran out and met a friend."

She gives me a look that tells me she suspects it was more, but thankfully, doesn't push. I pull out the stool beside her and take a seat, wondering how to go about what I want to talk to her about.

She finishes something on her computer and closes it, turning to face me and giving me her full attention.

"What's up?" she asks. Maggie has always been good at telling when I've got something on my mind. She was someone I turned to a lot in my later teen years.

"How did you finally settle on what you wanted to do?" I ask.

"You mean working with the foundation?" she asks, and I nod.

"Well, I always enjoyed charity work growing up. My parents and I often volunteered around the holidays. As I got older, giving back to those in need when I was so fortunate was something that interested me. I did the research on what types of degrees I could get to work with non-profits and settled on a business degree. Are you not looking forward to being a lawyer?"

I've only told Matt I'm not sure I want to be a lawyer. Admitting it to Maggie, which also means admitting it to Henry, makes me feel like a failure, and shame wants to overtake me. My skin feels itchy, and I suddenly feel extremely warm. I pull at the neckline of my shirt and take a deep breath, but it doesn't seem to help.

Maggie grabs my free hand and squeezes. It pulls me back from the panic that wants to take over.

"It's okay if you don't," she says softly. "You're allowed to change your mind."

Her words have tears gathering behind my eyes.

"I don't want to disappoint my brothers." My words come out soft and barely there, but I know she heard them when she squeezes my hand again.

"Oh, sweetie, you won't disappoint them by changing your mind. Your brothers just want you to be happy."

I wipe at a stray tear. "They all did so much to take care of me as a kid and support me. I know none of them wanted to be taking care of their baby sister as teenagers, but they were stuck with me. I want them to be proud of me after they sacrificed so much." I tip my head back, willing the rest of the tears not to fall.

"They would never say that." Maggie stands and rounds the island, pulling some cookies and sweets out from the cabinet before settling back beside me and pushing them towards me. "When Henry and I were first getting serious, he talked to me about your guys' childhood. He told me all about taking care of you and the boys, and all the responsibility he took on. Yes, he admits it was stressful and a lot for someone his age, but he's also talked about how much he loved watching you all grow up and become the people you are today. How he's grateful to have played a role in you all finding yourselves. I don't think he'd go back and change a thing. I bet Kai, Ezra, Riley, and John would all say the same thing. You guys are family. I know you would each do anything for your siblings, and I got to experience that when you five embraced me when Henry proposed. Henry's biggest wish for you and your brothers is to live your best lives and be happy. That's how he believes he'll know he's succeeded in raising you guys."

I grab one of Maggie's homemade chocolate chip cookies and take a bite, letting her words sink in. I'm so grateful to Maggie for being there to support Henry when he's spent his whole life taking care of everyone else. She's taken on the same role with all of us, being an older sister to my brothers and me.

"I feel so lost. I've just spent all this time getting a degree, and now I don't even know what to do with it. The thought of being a lawyer doesn't make me happy."

"And that's okay. What's important is how you go forward. You need to find what does make you happy. And you don't have to do that right this second. You're young and still have plenty of time. You're welcome to stay here as long as you'd like. I quite enjoy having someone else in the house and having another girl around."

"I love you, Mags."

"I love you, too, Zo."

I hug her, and when we pull apart, she grabs the sweets and I follow her into the living room, where she pulls out some blankets and puts on a movie. We sit together much like we did when I was a kid.

"Is she okay?" Henry's voice wakes me up.

"Yeah," Maggie answers. "It was just an eventful day."

"What happened?" Henry sounds worried.

"Let her tell you when she's ready, but she's okay. I think she could use some time with her big brother, though." Bless Maggie for letting me be the one to tell Henry.

"I'm worried about her."

"Why?"

He sighs. "I'm so glad to have her here. I've missed seeing her, and when she was in her own place, it was so hard for us to find time to see each other, but I know things aren't right if she is giving up the independence and freedom she had living on her own. Plus, she's been leaving early some mornings, like out the door before I'm out of the shower, and other days she's coming home super late. She doesn't seem happy."

I feel so weird lying here and listening to their conversation, but I'm not sure what to do and it's about me.

"Honey, she's twenty-six. She's living her life, and I know how protective you are of your siblings, especially her, but you have to remember they're adults now, too. They don't need you to worry about them all the time. They need you to just be there for them."

He lets out a deep breath and says, "I know."

Silence fills the room, and I decide this is the time to let them know I'm awake. I stretch and make noises, and they turn to me.

Henry smiles. "Well hello, sleepyhead. Have a good nap?"

I yawn and rub my eyes. "Yeah."

"Good. Mags and I were talking and we were thinking of ordering takeout for dinner. You good with Indian?"

I nod. "Sounds good. You know what I like."

"Butter chicken and garlic naan. Gotcha."

He pulls his phone out and orders while Maggie brings me a cup of tea. "Thanks," I say as she hands me the cup.

"You're welcome." She looks over her shoulder at Henry and drops her voice. "You should talk to him."

I smile at her. Of course, she knew I was awake.

"I will."

The timer in the kitchen goes off, and she quickly makes her way to the oven, where she pulls out a tray of cupcakes.

"Want to help frost them?" she asks, and I'm immediately off the couch and joining her. Decorating cakes, cupcakes, and cookies was something we did a lot when I was younger. None of the boys were interested in sweets, except eating them, so it was something for just the two of us.

Henry joins us in the kitchen, letting us know dinner will be here in thirty minutes. He comes behind us, wrapping an arm over each of our shoulders. "Look at my girls." He kisses both our cheeks. "I missed seeing you guys do this together."

I smile at them both. "Me, too."

Maggie and I finish decorating the cupcakes just in time for dinner to be delivered. While we finish cleaning up, Henry gets everything set up in the dining room. We talk and laugh while we enjoy dinner. Once we're all finished, I take a long sip of my wine and turn to Henry. He sobers when he sees my expression.

"What's wrong, Zo?"

I take a deep breath and say, "I don't want to be a lawyer."

He looks shocked for a second, and then he relaxes back into his seat. "Okay. Do you know what you do want to do?"

I spin my wine glass between my fingers and dip my head. "No."

He nods. "That's okay, Zoey. You don't have to have everything figured out right now. Part of being an adult is figuring it out."

"You're not disappointed?" I ask.

Shock fills his expression, and he shakes his head. "Of course not. Why would you think that?"

"Because you did so much to help make sure I got into a top school and was able to get my degree. You sacrificed so much when we were younger, and now I'm throwing away a degree that took a lot of time and money."

"Oh, Zo. I'm not disappointed." He reaches out and takes my hand. "You're my little sister. Everything I did for you and the boys was a sacrifice I was willing to make. And you're not throwing away your degree. You gained experience. Just because you don't want to be a lawyer doesn't mean you won't put your degree to good use. Take some time to figure out what you want to do. You're welcome to stay here as long as you'd like."

I push out of my chair and wrap my arms around my brother, and his immediately come around me, holding me to him tightly.

"You're the best big brother. I love you."

"I love you, too, Zoey."

He gives me one more squeeze, and we separate.

"Now, I think I'd love one of those delicious cupcakes in the kitchen," Henry says.

I nod and grab the plate full of them and bring them to the table. I feel so much better having had that conversation with Maggie and Henry. Nothing is fixed. I still have no idea what I want to do, and I still feel lost because of it, but I'm not worried about disappointing him now.

We enjoy a night in before Henry and Maggie call it a night. I follow not long behind them, curling up with a book before falling asleep.

CHAPTER 16

Matt

I rub my eyes as I try to wake myself up this morning. Jayden has been unusually fussy the last two nights and hasn't been sleeping, which in turn means I haven't been sleeping. It's Saturday and we have plans at my parents for a family brunch, which I've never been so grateful for. As much as I love my son, doing this solo is not the easiest thing, and being able to pass him off to Mom or Gianna for an hour will be amazing. I make sure to pack extra clothes as he's been drooling over everything. I've lost count of how many times a day I'm wiping his hands off because he keeps sticking them in his mouth.

He fusses in the car and nothing seems to make him feel better, but there isn't much I can do when he's in the back and I'm driving. As I'm pulling up outside my parents' place, my phone dings with a notification. It's one of the sports reporting apps I have, and I go to close it out when Josh's name appears in the brief summary on my screen. Shocked, I open the article.

NHL Commissioner and Board of Governors approve the sale of the Vancouver Cyclone.

In today's NHL news, the sale of the Vancouver Cyclone to Joshua Lincoln of Lincoln Enterprises has been approved by the NHL Commissioner and the Board of Governors. The sale of the team for the amount of $1.5 billion marks the change of an era in the Vancouver hockey market.

I sit and stare at my phone, not able to read any more. My best friend bought our favourite hockey team and never said anything to me about it. My sister never said anything about it. I go through the motions of gathering Jayden and our things and making our way into the house. The door is unlocked, so we walk straight in. Gianna spots us and has Jayden out of my arms before I can even say hi.

I move into the living room. Josh and Liv are already here, and Mom is holding Cate. I kiss Mom on the cheek and shake Dad's hand before turning to my sister and best friend.

"Any news you'd like to share?" I ask.

Josh grabs the back of his neck as he mutters, "Shit."

Mom looks between the two of us, confusion written all over her face. "What's wrong?"

"Oh, just that my best friend and sister are keeping secrets from me."

Liv holds up her hand. "Wait a second. We couldn't say anything. Not until the contract was signed and it was all official."

"So, I had to read about it in a news article on my phone?"

"We were hoping we could beat the news and tell you guys today. We're sorry you found out this way," Liv says.

I sit across from them, still dumbstruck. "One point five billion," I say.

"Yeah," Josh says.

"Holy shit."

"Yeah."

"One point five billion for what?" Mom asks.

"Josh just bought the Vancouver Cyclone for that much," I say.

You could hear a pin drop in the room it's so quiet.

"You're shitting me," Dad says.

I pass him my phone with the article pulled up.

"Holy shit."

"I was hoping to be the one to tell you guys. It's all been pretty hush-hush. I found out from a buddy the Baldwin family was looking to sell the team, and I put in an offer. We went back and forth for a little bit before we finally settled on a number. I was hoping they'd wait until Monday to do the announcement, but I guess not."

"I can't believe you're the owner of our favourite team," I say.

"Trust me, I couldn't believe it either," Liv says. "I also can't wrap my head around that much money."

I laugh. "You married into that much money."

She shrugs. "It's never really come up. I married Josh for Josh, not his money."

"I know you didn't. I'm still in shock, that's so much money."

"Congrats, son," Dad says and shakes Josh's hand.

"Thanks. And once everything goes through, I'd love for us to all go to a game together."

"Oh, that would be so much fun," Mom says.

We all hug and shake hands before following Mom into the kitchen, where we all settle at the table for brunch. I do my best to try to keep Jayden's fussing to a minimum, but he doesn't seem to stop. I have Jayden on my chest as I rub his back and Liv comes up behind me, sticking her finger in his mouth. She walks to the freezer and comes back with a blue rubber ring and hands it to Jayden over my shoulder.

"Your boy is teething," she says before taking her seat again.

Jayden calms down a little as he sticks the ring in his mouth and sucks on it. The tension slowly leaves me as I watch him relax bit by bit.

"Thank you," I say.

"Of course. Cate was a big fusser when she was teething. She'll be getting her upper teeth soon, and I just hope this round isn't as bad as the last one."

"I thought I had another month or two before he started. I was wondering why he hasn't been sleeping well the last few nights and just thought it was a phase."

Liv shrugs as she takes a bite of bacon. "All babies go through it at different times. Jayden's in the right age range at five months, a little on the early side of it, but still in range. He'll get his bottom teeth first and not long after, his top ones should come in. Cate loved those rings. I bought several and rotated through them. Baby Tylenol really helped her sleep."

"Thanks. I'll try those."

"You can always call me if you have any questions."

"I will."

I make a note to stop at the store on my way home and grab some things for Jayden before our game tonight. Mom, Dad, and Gi offer to take both Jayden and Cate for the day and we can pick them up in the morning. Mom assures me before I leave she has teething toys and baby Tylenol for Jayden and that he'll be fine. She promises to call should anything come up.

As much as I hate to leave Jayden, especially when he's like this, I trust Mom and I know I need to take help while I have it.

When I get home, I quickly pick up before settling on the couch and looking around. I can't remember the last time I had hours to myself with no plans and no kid. Jayden's been with me for a month now, and it's amazing how much he's changed my life. I pull up a show and get lost in it until it's time to head to the rink.

We're playing the worst team in our league tonight, so I expect the game won't be too intense. We end up winning 5-2.

Once we're dressed, we meet the girls upstairs in the restaurant. I haven't had a chance to talk to Zoey, because she only arrived just before puck drop. When I see an empty seat beside her, I make a beeline for it. She smiles at me as I pull out the chair and take a seat before she continues her conversation with Hannah.

"I don't know," Zoey says.

"Come on. You can't let one guy standing you up stop you from any other dates."

My stomach feels like it's bottoming out. Hannah is trying to set her up with someone. I order a beer from the waitress, trying to hide that I'm solely focused on Zoey and Hannah's conversation.

"It's not that—" Zoey starts, and Hannah sits straighter.

"Oh, do you have your eyes on someone?" Hannah's enthusiastic voice carries down the table, and I feel eyes move our way.

Zoey swats at her arm. "No, and can you keep your voice down?"

Hannah relaxes back in her chair, and I take a sip of my beer.

"You know you can tell me, right?" Hannah asks.

"I know." Zoey's eyes move around the table, lingering on me for a few seconds longer than anyone else. "I don't have my eyes on someone." Her voice sounds pained as she says it, as if she doesn't believe the words but there's a reasoning behind why she won't admit the truth. The notion that Zoey is pining over someone is like a stab to the gut. The idea that I've spent so much time being stupid and may have lost any potential chance I could have had with her is devastating. But until she actually says the words she's interested in someone, I have to do something.

"Let me set you up on one date. If you don't like the guy, you don't have to see him again," Hannah persists.

Zoey sighs. "Fine. One date, but I pick the date, time, and place."

"Sounds like a plan."

I listen intently as Zoey and Hannah talk about the details of Zoey's date. I need to make a plan to stop her from going on it.

CHAPTER 17

Zoey

I'm not excited about this date at all. While I get ready and take in the outfit I chose, I question if I should just cancel and stay in tonight. I chose a Wednesday night, thinking it put less pressure on it over a Friday or Saturday night. A week night says *it's just dinner, and I don't plan to be out late.* A Friday or Saturday night says *I'm open to more than dinner and don't need to be home early.*

I let out a breath, resolved to go because I promised Hannah I would. I grab my bag and head downstairs. Luckily, Henry and Maggie are out tonight, so I don't need to explain where I'm going. The restaurant I picked is only a fifteen minute drive away. I've been there several times before, so hopefully the familiarity will help me relax.

I give the hostess my name, and she tells me my date is already here. Points for being on time. She leads me to our table, and I take in the man seated there. He's not much older than me, and his dark-brown hair is styled perfectly. Even sitting, I can tell his suit is perfectly tailored to fit him. I can tell he prides himself on his appearance.

The hostess leaves, and I take a seat across from him.

"You must be Zoey," he says. There's something in his tone that rubs me the wrong way, but I push it aside.

"I am, and you're Charles."

He adjusts the watch on his wrist, pulling my attention to it before he reaches his hand out. I shake it.

"It's a pleasure to meet you, Zoey."

"Likewise."

He looks around the restaurant, his gaze moving over everything. "This place is—charming." There it is again, that tone that feels akin sandpaper on my skin.

"It's one of my favourite local spots," I say.

He nods, not offering anything else.

We look at the menus in silence, though I already know what I'm getting. I decided well before I left the house, so there was one less thing to make me anxious.

Charles closes his menu and places it in front of him, folding his hands together on top of it. Our server comes and takes our orders, and then Charles's focus comes to me.

"Hannah tells me you went to law school."

I take a sip of my water, putting off answering. "I did."

"Law school is a worthy pursuit." The way he says worthy pisses me off, like he doesn't think it's good enough for him.

"Hannah didn't tell me much about you. I'm assuming you work in the hospital."

As soon as the conversation moves to him, his entire demeanour changes. He straightens slightly. "I'm a surgeon. Cardiothoracics. Top of my department."

Pompous much? Who needs to tell someone they're on a first date with they're the top of their department?

"Must be challenging but rewarding work. Holding someone's life in your hands."

"It is. There's nothing like the feeling when you first cut open a patient and know you're what stands between them and death. You know, cardiothoracics is the toughest specialty. Your heart is one organ you can't live without."

Gag. The ego on this man knows no bounds, apparently. Why does he think this is what I want to talk about on a first date? Our food is delivered, and he continues to talk about himself. I would give anything for a fake emergency right now so I could get as far away from this date as possible. As if someone above could hear my prayer, I hear my name being called just before Matt, with Jayden strapped to his chest, is standing beside me. My heart rate picks up. He's a sight for sore eyes.

"Hey, Zo."

"Matt," I breathe out.

"How are you?"

Before I can even answer, Charles speaks up. "Hello. Can't you see we're kind of on a date right now?"

It takes everything in me not to roll my eyes. This is probably the worst first date I've ever been on.

Matt turns and offers his hand to Charles. "Hey, man. I'm Matt, Zoey's friend."

Charles shakes it but looks obviously pissed off as his eyes bounce between the two of us. "Charles, I'm her date."

Matt looks at me, and I plead with my eyes for him to give me some reason to leave. Anything. He nods slightly, and I hope that means he understands.

"Sorry. My sister sent me to collect Zoey. Something about flooding at Zoey's place."

I plaster on a look of shock. "Oh, no. Did she say what happened?"

Matt shakes his head, and I see the mirth in his eyes. He's enjoying this. "No, just said I should get you over there as soon as possible."

Jayden starts reaching for me, and I can't help the smile that stretches across my face.

"Hey, little munchkin."

He giggles as I boop his nose.

"We should probably get going," I say.

"You're not even done eating," Charles protests.

"I need to go check on my place."

He sighs.

"Thanks for tonight," I say before grabbing my stuff and following Matt out of the restaurant.

I'm so grateful to be away from that date that I don't notice I've blindly followed Matt to his car instead of heading to mine. Once he gets Jayden settled in the car seat, he turns to face me.

"Thanks for that save," I say. I'm not sure what I would have done if he hadn't of shown up. I was close to sneaking out of the window in the bathroom. But how did Matt know to save me?

He nods, shoving his hands in his pocket. "Of course."

"How did you know where I was?"

He leans against the car and crosses his arms over his chest as though protecting himself. "I heard you and Hannah set it up after the game on Saturday."

"So, you decided to follow me?" What the hell is going on right now?

He shakes his head. "No. I only got here a few minutes before I interrupted. I wasn't going to come. But I was sitting at home with Jayden and something kept eating at me, telling me I needed to be here. When I saw you from across the restaurant, I could tell you wanted to be anywhere but at that table with him."

I cross my arms over my chest, matching his position, except mines one of defiance. "So, you thought I couldn't take care of myself on a date and you needed to be my saviour?"

"No. It wasn't that."

I push. "Then what was it? What could possibly have you driving out to this restaurant when I'm on a date instead of relaxing at home with Jayden?"

He doesn't say anything, just stares me down. My skin heats as he holds eye contact.

"Matt."

He continues to stare, and it's like I can feel him under my skin now. Goosebumps scatter across my arms and up my neck as I hold back a shiver.

"Matthew," I say exasperated.

He throws his arms out to the side as he finally breaks. "I didn't want you to go on the date," he shouts, and I take a step back.

Pain travels through me. He crashed my date because he didn't want me to go.

"Why?" I ask, my voice pained. "Why would you not want me to go out and find someone who could make me happy? What's so wrong with me going on a date?"

He takes two steps closer to me, leaning down until his lips are beside my ear. "I think you know why."

Oh.

I stop myself from reaching out and clutching the front of Matt's jacket. I revel in the heat that radiates off him and close my eyes as his breath dances over my cheek and neck, and this time I don't hold back the shiver that travels through me. His heat disappears, and I open my eyes to see him back at his car.

"Did you drive?"

His question takes me by surprise. It's like he's done a complete one eighty. I guess I read too much into this. I feel like I'm experiencing whiplash. My emotions are all over the place, and right now, I want to process them with crying. I hold back my tears as I nod.

"You parked close?"

I nod and clear my throat. "I'm just a couple cars down."

It's his turn to nod.

"Text me when you get home."

I shake my head. "I'll be fine."

"Bug. Text me when you get home."

That nickname. That damned fucking nickname tears at my walls, and I know I have to leave now if I don't want him to see me crying. I turn quickly and make my way to my car, as soon as the door closes, the tears start to fall, and I bury my face in my hands.

I let myself get my hopes up only for Matt to pull away and be cold.

When I've finally gathered myself, I make the drive home, quietly sneaking into the house so I don't have to face Henry and Maggie. I do text Matt, because the last thing I want to deal with tonight is him calling to check on me.

I curl up in bed and wonder why the hell I did this to myself.

I wake up Thursday morning determined to do something about figuring out what I want to do with my life. Maggie's working from home today, and I help her with some of her paperwork. She tells me about a gala they're planning to raise money for the food bank before the holidays.

We work all day, and I realize I'm actually enjoying helping Maggie with this. She tells me I can help her out whenever I'd like. They're always looking for help around the holidays. Around dinner, I head upstairs quickly and change before I leave to meet the girls for one of our girls' nights.

We agreed to meet at the Clover, a bar we've frequented for years. I'm the first to arrive and order a drink and snag us a booth in the back corner. The girls slowly trickle in until the table is full and we're ordering appetizers to share.

"A month and a half until you head back to Willow Valley. You excited?" Liz asks Hannah.

Hannah beams. "Yeah. Grayson's mom and I have been talking and making plans. Dad's committed to going with us. It's going to be so nice to have all of our family in the same place for the holidays. I never thought I'd get that."

"It's your and Grayson's first Christmas together. That's got to be exciting," Liz adds.

"We're excited to start our own traditions. Liv, what are you guys planning for Cate's first Christmas?"

"Josh and I got her a baby's first Christmas ornament like I got when I was a baby. We want to give her one every year. We're doing Christmas Eve at my parents' like usual and Josh's family is joining. We want Christmas Day to be just us at home. Nice and relaxed."

"That sounds nice," I say. "I'll be spending the holidays with my rowdy brothers, but it should be fun. Henry and Maggie are hosting again, so I won't have to go far." I laugh.

"So, you'll be able to sleep in until they come kick your ass out of bed, then," Liv says.

"How was your date?" Liz asks, and I roll my eyes.

I turn and face Hannah. "I'm not sure what I did to make you think that horrible man would make a good date, but please, whatever it is, I'm sorry." I place my hands in front of me in a prayer position. "I'm sorry. Please, never again."

Hannah and Liv exchange a quick look before they look at me.

"What happened?" Hannah asks.

I shake my head. "How could you not know that man has an ego bigger than his head?"

She shrugs. "I don't spend a lot of time with him. I more relay test results and patient status than actually talk to him."

I throw up my hands. "And you thought that was enough criteria to set me up?"

"He seemed nice enough. I was just trying to help."

I scoff. It sounds annoyed, but it's to cover my hurt. "Do I really seem so desperate that I'll date anyone?"

Liz immediately reaches for my hand. "Zo, none of us think you're desperate. We all just know you'd like to be in a loving relationship and no one can fault you for that, especially these two when they have that already."

Bailey nods. "I think we sometimes overlook things when we aren't looking at someone as a possibility to be a romantic partner. I'm sure that's exactly what happened with Hannah." Her gaze moves to her, and Hannah nods enthusiastically.

"That's probably exactly what happened."

I slump back in the booth. "Why does this feel so hopeless? First Liv's guy stands me up and then Hannah's guy was a dud. Maybe I should take a break from dating. I need to focus on figuring out what I want to do with my career. Maybe this is all a sign I should focus on me for a while."

"Focusing on yourself is always good, and who knows, maybe Mr. Right will just fall into your lap when you're not even looking," Hannah says.

"Let's circle back to figuring out your career," Liz starts. "Do you not want to be a lawyer? You passed the bar and have the pick of almost any job you want." Her confusion is evident in her voice. She's right, I could have the pick of almost any job. I passed my classes with stellar marks, I got a great reference from the lawyer I articled under, and I passed the bar in the top five percent of my group. I'm good at it, but knowing my stuff doesn't mean I'll enjoy doing it for the rest of my life.

I run my finger over the rim of my glass. "I've decided I don't want to be a lawyer. I'm not sure what I want to do, but I told Henry, and he and Maggie said I can stay with them as long as I want while I figure it out. I've been helping Maggie with some foundation work. She's throwing a gala to raise money for some local food banks."

"Oh, Josh got an invite to that. It looks like they're doing amazing work. He RSVP'd for the two of us. We're going to make a weekend of it, drop Cate off with his parents."

Bailey faces Liv now. "Caleb mentioned Josh bought the Cyclone. That's insane. I can't even fathom that amount of money."

Liv's cheeks pinken. "The team is tanking. They haven't pieced together a solid season in years, and the previous owners were looking to offload the team. As soon as Josh caught wind of it, he jumped straight on it. He talked to me about it, wanting my opinion, but I kept telling him it's his money, he should do what he wanted. No matter what I said, he kept pushing that it was ours and he wanted my opinion. I don't know the first thing about owning a sports team. I told him I trust his judgement and he's the one who's going to have to run the damn thing."

"How many people get to say they own a sports team?" I muse.

Liv shakes her head. "I don't know, but I do know I plan on going to a few more games now."

Conversation moves fluidly, and when we call it a night, I'm more set on focusing on myself and enjoying what I do have rather than forcing dates.

CHAPTER 18

Matt

Zoey nearly had me breaking my resolve entirely yesterday. When she confronted me about why I crashed her date, she managed to pull out of me that I didn't want her to go, but I stopped short of telling her it was because I wanted to be the one she was going on a date with. She was so mad when we went our separate ways, and all I wanted to do was pull her in close and kiss her. I wanted to show her what I couldn't tell her.

I guess her texting when she got home was at least a positive sign that she wasn't icing me out totally. It's taken everything in me not to blow up her phone all day. My resolve breaks at the end of the night when I'm lying on the couch, torn between calling her and going to bed. Calling her wins out. I need to hear her voice.

Anxiety fills me as the phone rings. Just when I think it's going to voicemail, she answers, and it's like a weight has been lifted off me.

"Hello."

"Hey, Zo."

"Is everything okay?" I can hear a tinge of worry in her voice mixed with what sounds like the little lisp that comes out when she's been drinking.

"Yeah. I just wanted to talk to you. Have you been drinking?"

She hiccups through the line. "It was girls' night."

Well, that explains it. "Did you have fun?"

"Of course. A night with my girls is always fun."

"Mmmhhh. And how'd you get home?"

"Uber. You don't have to check up on me, Matt. I'm perfectly capable of taking care of myself. I've done it for years."

She's right, but I want to check on her. I want to know she's okay and having fun. Just because she's taken care of herself for so long on her own doesn't mean she should have to. But all of that is too much to drop on her during a half-drunk, late-night phone call.

"I know you can take care of yourself, but I care about you."

The sound of sheets rustling travels through the phone as she makes a contented sigh. "I care about you, too."

She yawns, and I know she's going to be out in minutes. I debate staying on the phone to listen to her fall asleep to have that small connection to her or hanging up and settling for calling her tomorrow. The rational side of me wins out, and I say goodnight before hanging up and moving to my own bed.

The entirety of Friday is spent trying to calm Jayden while he teethes. He is constantly in pain, and it hurts me to see him like this. The teething toys Liv recommended have been a lifesaver. He uses them constantly. From the research I've done, he could be like this for up to another week, but I'm hoping it dies down in the next few days.

I pack plenty of his toys in his diaper bag and lots of burp clothes, because he's been drooling like crazy. Liv seems to have the magic touch with Jayden right now, so I'm hoping she can help him during our game tonight.

As soon as we get to the rink, I search out Liv, hoping I can spot Zoey as well. When I get to the bleachers for our game, I only see Liv, and as much as I love my sister, I can't help the disappointment that runs through me. She smiles when she spots Jayden and me, and I join her. She's reaching for Jayden before I even have a chance to sit. Cate is sleeping in her car seat beside Liv, and it always amazes me how these kids can sleep anywhere, no matter how loud it is.

"How's he doing?" she asks.

"He seems to be doing better, but he's been inconsolable without the teething toys."

She nods. "Sounds like Cate during that time, too. Once the teeth actually broke through, she calmed down a ton. Hopefully, Jayden's the same way."

The sound of familiar voices makes its way towards us just before I hear a laugh I'll never forget. I quickly turn to face them, and there's no stopping the smile that spreads across my face when I see Zoey. When she spots me, her smile is genuine, but it's nowhere near as big as it's been in the past. I mentally slap myself for making things awkward between us. That's the last thing in the world I wanted. Her, Hannah, Liz, and Bailey join Liv and me, lost in their conversation. Liv joins in, and I know there's no way I'm breaking into their conversation to pull Zoey away, so I resign myself to trying after the game.

The entire game, I steal glances at Zoey, hoping she's watching me. Nothing has made me feel better than having her eyes on me. But every time I look towards her, she's either playing with Jayden or deep in conversation with one of the girls. Jealousy creeps up on me. I know I shouldn't feel jealous of my infant son, but he's getting all of her undivided attention, and I want it. I want her to look at me. I want her to talk and laugh with me.

When the game's over, I change quickly, hoping to catch Zo before she leaves. As I'm rushing up the stairs towards the restaurant, Zoey comes out and stops in her tracks for a second before rushing past me, saying a quick goodbye. I call her name, quickly pivot, and rush down the stairs to meet her at the bottom.

"Where are you going like your ass is on fire?" I ask, hoping I've added enough levity to my voice that it doesn't sound like an attack.

She avoids looking at me. "I just have some things to do. I'll see you later."

She moves to walk away, but I capture her wrist, and it's like a bolt of lightning hits me. She must feel it, too, because both of our eyes are locked on where I'm holding her. I trail my eyes up her arm, watching as her breathing picks up and then up to her face. Her lips are slightly parted, and it's as if all she can do is stare at that one spot.

"Zo?"

"Hmmm?"

I chuckle at her flustered-ness, and she quickly removes her arm from my grasp.

"I'm taking Jayden to a little pop-up fair tomorrow. I was wondering if you'd join us?" Hope fills my voice, and she worries her lip between her teeth. I can see her hesitance. "Please. It will be fun. We can play some of those totally rigged carnival games, and I'll try to win you something cool. Plus, they'll have all the great fair food."

She seems to have some internal conversation before she finally nods and looks up at me. "Sure. Sounds fun."

Her yes has me as excited as a kid in a candy store. The little kid in me wants to jump in place and punch his fists, but I hold that all back and grin at her.

"Great. Meet at my place at 11 a.m.?"

"See you then," she says before rushing out of the rink.

I stare after her until she's out of sight and head to the restaurant. Liv is rocking Jayden's car seat while Hannah bounces Cate and makes faces at her as she giggles. I walk up behind Hannah and start making faces at Cate, too, and she flaps her arms as she laughs. I reach for her and take her from Hannah.

"Now aren't you the cutest little girl," I say as I play eat her tummy. Her laugh is infectious. "How was Jayden?" I ask Liv.

"He was good. He seemed to be in a bit more pain towards the end of the game, so I gave him some baby Tylenol, and he fell asleep pretty quickly afterwards."

"That's good. Thanks for hanging with him, Liv. It means a lot that you'll watch him so I can still play."

"Of course. I know how much playing means to you, and I love spending time with my adorable little nephew." She runs her finger over his cheek and smiles at him.

"I'm thinking I should get him home and in bed. I want to make sure he's well rested for tomorrow."

She raises a brow at me. "Fun plans?"

"We're going to the fair, and I plan on tasting all of the food."

Liv laughs and shakes her head. "Well, have fun."

I nod and lean down, kissing her cheek before grabbing Jayden and heading to my car, stopping to say bye to the guys as they make their way up the stairs.

CHAPTER 19

Matt

This isn't even officially a date, so why the hell am I standing in my bathroom staring at my reflection as I change into my fourth shirt trying to figure out which one I should wear to the fair? I finally settle on a forest-green one and quickly slip on socks and shoes as I finish making sure I have everything we'll need packed in Jayden's bag. I make sure to bring the wearable baby carrier, because my son often prefers that over his stroller or car seat.

A knock at the front door has my heart racing, and I wipe my now clammy hands down the legs of my jeans.

Okay, Matt. It's just Zoey. You've hung out hundreds of times, it's nothing new. Except Zoey isn't just Zoey. She's Zoey. The girl you've decided to all of a sudden develop feelings for.

She knocks again, and I quickly move to open the door for her. I take her in. She's wearing black converse and black leggings with a purple V-neck tee that gives just a tease of what she has underneath.

"You ready?" she asks, breaking me from my haze of gawking.

I clear my throat. "Yeah, just let me grab a few more things and we're good to go."

It's been an unseasonably warm fall so far, with temps landing around fifteen degrees in the sun during the day. I pack jackets for Jayden and me just in case it cools down or we end up in the shade. Throwing everything into the diaper bag, I grab Jayden's car seat and we leave the apartment.

The fair is a bit of a drive, so I decide to make a stop before we make our way out there. Zoey seems lost in her phone as I pull up to the drive through and order. It isn't until I try to hand her a venti peppermint mocha that she looks up at me. I give it a small shake. Realizing it's for her, she lights up with a smile, and I count that as a small win. She accepts the coffee and takes a quick sip, melting into her seat.

"Thank you," she says.

I chuckle. "Of course. I know you need your morning sugar to function."

She takes another sip and shakes her head. "I did have some before I left the house, but it's always appreciated."

I take a sip of my double-double, and we make our way out of downtown Vancouver and towards the fair. We're lucky to find parking in the lot nearby. There are cars everywhere as families and couples mill about. I get Jayden settled in the stroller, and we make our way to the ticket booth. Zoey tries to buy a ticket, but I stop her. I invited her out, no way in hell am I making her pay. She tries again, and I pull her card from her hand and shove it in my back pocket before tapping my card. She grumbles about being able to pay for herself, but I just grin at her and we make our way inside.

Nostalgia hits me as we stand at the entrance. To the right there are lines and lines of food trucks. To the left is every carnival game you could imagine, and in the centre there are a variety of rides, mainly aimed at a younger demographic. When I was a kid, we made a few trips a year to Playland, the local amusement park that operates in the summer. Liv, Gi, and I would ride the rides until one or all of us got sick and we had to leave. We'd compete against each other in the carnival games, seeing who could win the biggest prize. By the time we left the park, we were so exhausted we'd all pass out in the car and would only make it inside so far as our beds before we'd pass right back out. The three of us went the summer before Gianna left for Stanford, but we haven't been back as a group since.

Zoey makes a little noise of excitement beside me, and I look down at her as she stares wide-eyed at the food trucks. I can't help but laugh.

"See something you like, Bug?"

She turns her excited eyes towards me as she raises up on her toes and does a little bounce. "Yes! How could you not tell me they'd have deep-fried Oreos?"

Of course, the first things she spots is something sweet.

"Okay, sounds like we're getting those. We doing poutine first or those?"

She drops flat on her feet and lets out a little huff. "I guess I'll be an adult and get poutine first."

She leads the way down the row of food trucks, stopping every once in a while to read a menu board. I don't think anything could wipe the excitement from her face right now. When we finally get to the poutine stall, she reaches out and grabs my arm, and I know she's excited about what she sees.

"They have mac and cheese poutine," she says under her breathe.

I lean down and whisper in her ear, "With bacon."

She nods, decision made, and orders one. I step beside her and order a regular one, quickly tapping my card before she has a chance to ask for her card back or to pull out another one. She rolls her eyes at me as I hand her her food and drink, and we make our way towards some picnic tables set up in a patch of grass nearby.

The moan she makes when she takes her first bite goes straight to my dick, and I adjust myself awkwardly on the bench. Each bite she takes, her moans become more sinful, and it takes all my strength not to snap.

When she's finished, she scoops every last drop of cheese sauce from the boat with her fork before she slowly licks it off. I have to look away to stop from thinking about what else I'd like to watch her lick with that much enthusiasm.

As soon as she puts the fork down, I'm up off the bench, taking our garbage to the nearest garbage can.

Get yourself together, man. You cannot be acting like a horny teenager in public. Especially not with Zoey.

When I join Zoey and Jayden again, I clap my hands and rub them together. "Okay. Now that we've eaten, what's first? Rides or games?"

She ponders it for a few seconds before she finally settles on rides. We move through the crowd of people, seeing what they have before settling on the teacup ride, deciding not to spin the cup once inside. Jayden's strapped to my chest and smiling like crazy. It's no thrilling rollercoaster like I would go on by myself, but seeing him having fun is worth it.

Zoey spots the bumper cars, and Jayden and I watch as she dominates. As soon as she steps off, beaming from ear to ear, Jayden reaches for her. She immediately takes him from me, and we continue our way around the fair. We hit up a few more rides before Zoey says she's ready for that deep-fried Oreo and leads the way to the stand. I grab one for her and a beaver tail for myself before we make our way towards the games. At the end of the row of stalls I see a giant stuffed animal I know I need to win for Zoey, no questions asked. As we slowly make our way through different games, my eyes keep finding that stall, making sure that prize is still there.

When we finally arrive, I hold back a groan as I see what the game is. I may be athletic enough and I know I'm good at hockey, but baseball was never my forte. Of course, this stupid game is knocking over glass bottles with a baseball.

I hand the attendant enough cash for three rounds. The first round, I only manage to knock off the top bottle, same with the second. The third time, I get two more bottles, but I still have three more to go to win. I hand them more cash and feel Zoey shaking her head beside me.

Three more rounds and three more fails.

"Matt, we can move on. Let's find another one."

I shake my head. I've got to win this for her.

I hand the attendant more cash, and this time I knock down all the bottles on the second round and instinctively punch the air in triumph.

"Which prize do you want?" the bored teenager asks.

I point directly to the prize I've been eyeing, and they pull it down for me. I hand it directly to Zoey, and her eyes bounce between the giant stuffed ladybug and me.

"It's a ladybug," she says, stating the obvious.

"It is." I grin at her.

"You remembered." Disbelief fills her voice.

"Of course, I remembered, Bug. How could I forget?"

Growing up, Liv and Zoey played in our yard a lot. Mom was a huge fan of gardening, and we had all types of flowers in both the front and backyard. One summer when the girls were probably seven or eight, we had several lovelinesses of ladybugs all over. Zoey was fascinated by them, and Mom told her about how they bring good luck. She became obsessed with them. She started wearing ladybug earrings and necklaces. Liv even got her a charm bracelet with a ladybug for Christmas one year when they were kids. As she's grown up, she's stopped wearing them. I'm not entirely sure as to why, but I'll never forget the little girl who would lie in the grass and watch the ladybugs for hours.

She clutches the stuffed animal as if her life depends on it. The look in her eyes has me wanting to lean down and kiss her, but instead, I lead us towards the carousel. I make sure Jayden is secured properly, and we get on. I follow Zoey as she makes her way to a bright-blue horse, and I grab the pink one beside her. The music starts and the horses start moving around as they slowly move up and down. If I'm not checking on Jayden, my eyes are glued to Zoey. She sneaks a few peeks our way, too, and her soft smile means everything to me.

When the ride finishes, we make our way out, and Zoey comes to stand beside me. She leans into me, staring at Jayden, who stares right back at her. I can't take my eyes off of her, though. My heart races as I take in the way her lashes flutter as she rests her head on my shoulder. I take a chance and link my fingers with hers, and when she accepts and smiles up at me, I swear my heart stops. We stand there for a few minutes, her at my side as she stares at Jayden and I stare at her, our fingers interlocked, and I soak in how perfect today has been so far. It's more than I had hoped for.

CHAPTER 20

Zoey

I haven't been excited about holding hands with a boy since I was in high school, but when Matthew Carter slipped his hand in mine and entwined our fingers, there was no stopping the giddy feeling that went through me. For all I know, it was just a friendly gesture as I leaned into his side to get a good look at Jayden, but the fact that he initiated it was everything.

As Matt drives us back to the city, I stare out the window, hiding the smile I can't fight. Today has been amazing. Trying new foods, riding the rides, and playing stupid fair games that are really just a grab for money was exactly what I needed to take my mind off everything. The highlight of it all was when Matt kept playing the stupid ball toss game, determined to win, and when he finally did, he got me that adorable stuffed ladybug. I was obsessed as a kid. After Mrs. Carter told me about them bringing good luck, I hoped if I spent enough time with them maybe they'd bring me enough luck that my parents would be home more often and when they were home, they'd play with me. I was in high school when I finally gave up hope that the ladybugs would bring me luck. I all but abandoned my love for them. I stopped wearing my ladybug jewellery and stopped lying in the grass beside the Carters' garden and watching them. By then, I knew my parents wouldn't change and hoping they would was more energy than it was worth. I had my brothers and Liv, and that's all I needed.

Matt winning that stuffed animal for me reminded a little of the joy they used to bring me.

"I had fun today," Matt says, breaking me from my fog.

I offer him a smile. "Me, too. I never got to go to the fair as a kid."

He looks at me, a little shocked. "Never?"

I shake my head and play with my hands in my lap. "Never. We didn't have the money growing up. Henry, Kai, and Ezra all made sure I didn't have to work as a teenager so I could focus on school and get to do a few extracurriculars, but there wasn't any money for those things."

I'm not sure Matt knows the extent of what my childhood was like. I'm pretty sure Henry had told his parents the gist of things when I was a kid because I was spending so much time at their house, and over the years, I've told Liv more and more and she has the whole picture now, but not many people know just how bad things with my parents were. I haven't spoken to either of them in years. In fact, I'm not even sure if they're alive, and as horrible as it is to say, I'm not sure I really care either way. They were never there for me growing up. They never attended school concerts, bandaged me up when I fell and scraped my knees, or even attended any of my graduations. My brothers and the Carters are the ones who were there for all of that.

"Well, we can't have that anymore. It's decided, next summer, you and I are hitting Playland, the PNE, too." Matt becomes more enthusiastic as he continues. "We'll get season passes and go as often as possible. We'll ride the rollercoasters and the flume. We'll try every food they have and play all the games. We'll hit everything."

His excitement is contagious, and I can't wait for us to do all of it.

"I'm sure Liv would love to join us," I say, and I swear I feel disappointment radiate off him at my words.

"I'm sure she would." His voice doesn't hold the same genuine excitement it had before.

As we enter the city, I watch as Matt starts tapping his thumb on the steering wheel, slowly increasing in speed before he finally says, "So, I was thinking about ordering some food in and watching movies. Jayden will probably crash for hours. Do you..." He looks over at me before looking back at the road. "Do you want to join me?" There's a hint of vulnerability to his voice, like me saying no would genuinely disappoint him.

I don't want our great day to end yet, so I say, "Only if we order from that Indian place down the street from you."

He laughs, and his shoulders relax. "Sounds like a plan."

After we finish getting Jayden settled in his crib and everything brought in, we settle on the couch and my phone buzzes.

HANNAH

Grayson's working night shift tonight. Want to come over for drinks and movies?

I look up at Matt, who's pouring us drinks in the kitchen while he orders food over the phone, and smile.

ZOEY

Have plans tonight. Thanks though.

HANNAH

Plans? The girls didn't mention anything

ZOEY

I'm not with the girls.

Hannah's name and face fill my screen as she attempts to video call, and I immediately decline it. She tries again, and I decline it. She messages the group chat instead.

HANNAH

Zoey says she has plans tonight but is refusing to accept my video call

LIV

Zo, are you on a date? What happened to taking time for yourself?

BAILEY

Are you okay? Please don't tell me someone else got your phone and that's why you're not answering.

ZOEY

I'm fine. I'm not in a place I can answer the phone.

HANNAH

So secret date.

ZOEY

No, not a secret date.

Matt brings our drinks over and sets them on the coffee table before he pulls out a blanket and spreads it on the couch.

ZOEY

Got to go.

I only catch a glimpse of Liv's name on the screen before I lock my phone and put it face down on the table. Matt grabs the remote and settles on the couch, but instead of sitting on the far end, he sits in the middle, right beside me.

He grins and asks, "*Star Wars* marathon?"

Oh, he's good. He knows there's no way I'm saying no to that. He kicks up his feet on the table, crosses his ankles and plays *Episode I*. There's no way we're pausing in the middle of a movie, so we eat our dinner on the couch, playing the next movie as soon as it finishes. When we hit the halfway point in *Episode III*, I feel myself getting tired, all the excitement of the day finally hitting. I relax further into the couch cushions and find myself leaning towards Matt. His arm goes around the back of the couch, and it's like my body takes that as a sign to curl up into his side. I question it for a minute, until his arm drops around me and his thumb moves slowly up and down my arm.

A contented sigh leaves me as I get more comfortable, relaxing into Matt. I force my eyes to stay open until the end of the movie, not wanting to miss anything no matter how many times I've seen the movie.

The credits roll, and we sit and watch them. My eyes are getting heavier as the words scroll up the screen. Matt tucks my hair behind my ear, and I smile, revelling in his delicate touch as my eyes close.

"You can take my bed," he says, and I just rub my face against his side. "Jayden will probably wake you up in the morning, but I think he will here, too." He chuckles. He runs his hand over my hair, and it only lulls me to sleep more. "I'll take the couch."

"No." I didn't think I was awake enough to answer as quickly as

I do. I rub my eyes and yawn. "I'm not stealing your bed. I'll sleep on the couch."

"I'm not letting you sleep on the couch."

I push up from my position and stretch. When I face him, I can tell he's being his usual stubborn self, and I don't have the energy to fight him. "Fine, we'll behave like adults and sleep in the same bed."

I watch the wheels turn in his head before he finally nods, pushing up from the couch and making his way to his bedroom, opening the door quietly. He comes back out with a pair of shorts and a black T-shirt.

"You can wear these to sleep. Those should be more comfortable."

I take them from him and head to the washroom and quickly change before meeting him in his room.

"What side should I take?" I ask.

He points to one side, and I move and settle under the blankets. Matt's scent envelops me, and it's intoxicating. I pull the blankets up, hoping to smell them and not look like a total creeper.

Matt gets in beside me, and I kind of hate the distance between us. I was enjoying being curled up in his side as I slept on the couch. Now I'm all alone on my side of the bed, far from where I want to be. I shuffle a little closer to the middle, and I swear I feel Matt do the same. I toss and turn for a few minutes, but ultimately fall asleep, too tired to keep my eyes open any longer.

CHAPTER 21

Matt

What the hell, why am I so hot? I'm sweating through my pyjamas, and something is wrapped around me.

The events of last night hit me.

Zoey is wrapped around me.

My eyes fly open. Zoey Williams is wrapped around me, in my bed, and I'm sporting morning wood. *Of fucking course.* As much as I absolutely love her this close and in my bed, I need to slide out so I can deal with my situation before Jayden wakes up, which I know will be any minute now. I'm surprised he hasn't woken me up yet.

I go to lift her leg, but she clamps it down and tightens her arm around me. This woman has me so torn. On one hand, I want to stay with her and just enjoy this, because who knows if this will ever happen again, but the last thing I want to do is freak her out when she wakes up and finds me hard.

My rational brain wins out, and after some finagling, I manage to slide out and make it to the bathroom. I lean over the bathroom counter.

Okay, get your shit together, Matt. Zoey only slept over last night because there was no way you were letting her drive home with how tired she was. It was nothing more. She only cuddled you last night because she was probably cold, and you were right there. It doesn't matter that you've never enjoyed cuddling but wanted to stay in her arms.

Jayden starts making noises, and I take a look at myself in the mirror and give my head a shake. I open the bathroom door and make my way to Jayden, but I stop in my tracks when I see Zoey standing beside his crib. Last night, I never took in how good she looks in my clothes. My shorts come almost past her knees and my shirt swallows her, giving her no shape, but damn is she gorgeous. She's pulled her messy hair into a bun on top of her head, showing off her face and bright smile as she bounces Jayden and talks to him.

"Didn't we have a long sleep? Do we think we're ready for a new nappy and some breakfast?" She presses her face into his tummy, and he giggles. Watching them together like this has me wishing we could do this every morning.

She turns and smiles when she sees me. "Good morning."

I smile back. "Good morning. Did Jayden wake you up?"

She looks at him with the softest expression. "He did, but what a great way to wake up to this adorable little one. I was just going to change him and make him a bottle."

I reach for him. "Why don't I change him?"

She laughs. "Sounds good, because I think he left a present in there for you. I'll get his bottle ready."

I take him from her, kissing his cheek and, without thinking, kiss hers as well. I swear she blushes, but she's around me before I have the chance to confirm my suspicion.

When I come out of the bedroom with Jayden, Zoey is sitting cross-legged on the couch with a bottle between her legs. I join her, and instead of handing me the bottle, she takes Jayden from me and starts feeding him. I stare at them, not sure what I'm supposed to do. For the last almost two months, I've done it all, the changing, the feedings, playing with and entertaining him, and I love it all. I love bonding with my son, but you never realize how much work it is until you're the one doing it.

"Breakfast?" I ask, and Zoey nods.

I rummage through the fridge, pull out some eggs and bacon, and find a box of pancake mix in the cabinet, and whip it all together, bringing Zoey a plate when it's all done. She puts Jayden in the Jolly Jumper, and we dig in.

"So, what do you say about finishing that *Star Wars* marathon?"

"I have no change of clothes," she says.

I grin. "I think you look perfectly fine in what you're wearing."

She looks down at my old Vancouver Cyclone shirt and basketball shorts. "Matt, they're your clothes."

I nod. "I know, and you look great in them."

I never thought I'd get off on seeing a woman wearing my clothes, but I guess, much like cuddling, it's something I only enjoy with Zoey. This time I do catch her blush as she tries to hide her face by tucking a piece of hair that's fallen from her bun behind her ear.

"What do you say, Zo? We doing this thing?"

She nods, and I can barely contain my excitement. I pull up *Solo,* because if we're doing a marathon, we're doing this right way and watching them all in chronological order. Having her so far away is annoying. Last night when she curled up into my side, it felt so natural, like that was where she was supposed to be. We split our time between watching the screen and making faces or dancing toys in front of Jayden. His favourite one is the blue stuffed elephant Zoey bought him.

When the screen fills with colour, he becomes so fascinated with it, making squealing sounds and shaking his arms as he bounces when explosion sounds fill the room. We spend the entire day together, playing with Jayden and watching movies. We only make it through *Episode VI* before we decide to call it a night.

"Do you want to crash another night so we can finish this marathon tomorrow?" I ask as she yawns and stretches her arms above her.

She shakes her head. "I should probably get home. I'm sure Henry is going to be wondering where I've been the last thirty-six hours."

I don't blame him. If Liv or Gi lived with me and they didn't come home, I'd be wondering where they are. Worried about whether they're safe or not.

I walk her to the door, wanting to be close to her as long as possible. As she reaches for the door, something in me snaps, and I hold the door closed and stare down at her. Her expression is shocked. Her beautiful brown eyes are wide as they look back at me. She sucks in a breath as I push a stray strand of hair behind her ear.

"Let me take you out on a date." It comes out sounding like a demand, but really it's a plea. I've never wanted to spend this much time with a woman, but with Zoey, I can't get enough. I want to see if maybe we could be more.

"A date?" She practically squeaks out the words.

I nod and grin. "Yeah, Zo, a date. You and me, maybe some dinner and conversation."

"With me?"

My grin widens. "Yes, Zoey. I want to take you out on a date."

She is far from her usual confident self right now, and it only adds to my ego that I have this effect on her. She bites her lip and nods slightly before she pulls her shoulders back and I see a little shine of her confidence. "Yeah, I'll go on a date with you."

"Good. I'll text you the details." She nods again, and I lean down and kiss her cheek. "Text me when you get home."

I open the door for her and watch as she makes her way down the hall to the elevator, looking over her shoulder with a slight blush as she presses the button. As soon as she's inside, I close the door and do a little fist pump, because I just scored a date with Zoey fucking Williams.

I text Gianna right away.

MATT

Can I drop Jayden off with you on Friday for a sleepover?

GI

Sounds good. I'm sure Mom will be happy to have him in the house.

MATT

Thanks. Does 4 p.m. work?

GI

Yup.

With babysitting covered, I get to work picking a restaurant. I call and make a reservation, and when Zoey texts that she's home, I tell her I'll pick her up at 5:30 p.m. on Friday.

CHAPTER 22

Zoey

Holy shit.

How I manage to make it back to Henry's without completely freaking out, I have no idea. I still haven't wrapped my head around the fact that Matthew Carter just asked me out on a date. Like a legit date.

When I get home, Henry makes a comment about me being back, but thankfully doesn't ask any questions about where I've been. As soon as I'm upstairs, I throw myself on my bed, squealing into my pillow before rolling over and composing myself long enough to send Matt a text that I'm home. I'm right back to squealing when he texts me the details for our date on Friday.

I'm not sure how I make it through Monday and Wednesday morning, being so close to him and not completely freaking out about our upcoming date. I spend all week thinking about what the hell I'm going to wear. I finally settle on a black skirt and maroon blouse paired with some knee-high black boots and a black jacket. I keep my hair a more natural wave and don't do much makeup. This is Matt; he's seen me when I've been sicker than a dog. I don't want tonight to come across as me trying too hard.

I check myself out in the floor-length mirror in my bedroom, and I look hot, if I do say so myself. This outfit accentuates all my favourite parts of my body, and these boots make my legs look fucking amazing. I check the time, and it's still a whole forty-five minutes before Matt said he'd pick me up, but I'm so nervous and excited that I couldn't help getting ready. I settle in the chair in the corner of my room and grab a book, trying to read, but it's pointless. I keep reading the same page over and over or just staring at it as my mind thinks of all the different ways tonight could go.

Tonight is important. If this goes well, it could be the start of something. If it goes bad, it could ruin everything. It could ruin our friendship, and it could ruin my friendship with Liv.

Ten minutes before he's supposed to be here, I make my way downstairs. I don't want him knocking and Henry answering the door, or Maggie, for that matter. She and Henry tell each other everything. So if she answers, Henry would then know Matt was picking me up for a date.

As soon as his headlights hit the front of the house, I'm out the door and Matt's getting out of the car.

"I was going to come to the door to get you," he says, raising a brow.

I smile. "I know, but Henry's home."

A flash of disappointment fills his face before he nods. "Of course."

I meet him at the front of the car, and he walks around it with me, opening the passenger door for me.

"You look gorgeous," he says before leaning in and kissing my cheek.

I take him in, his button-down blue shirt, dark jeans, and dress shoes. He's shaved the scruff that had been growing since Jayden came into his life. "You don't look so bad yourself."

I swear I see the tips of his ears turn pink at the compliment, and I do a little mental happy dance.

I slide in, and he closes the door before rounding the car and pulling out of the driveway. I fiddle with my hands in my lap, feeling more nervous than I thought. I don't know why. It's not like we haven't been friends for years and known each other longer, but something about Matt wanting to go on a real date has me worried I'm going to screw this up somehow.

Other than the music Matt has playing, the drive is silent. When we get to the restaurant, I immediately recognize it as one of the top date spots in the city. They're well rated for their comfortable atmosphere and good food. It's not fancy, but seems to be a place to help people relax and enjoy their time with the people they're sharing a meal with. You can't just walk into this place and get a table. You've got to make a reservation and even at that, those can be hard to come by.

I follow Matt inside, and he gives his name to the hostess, who eyes him before offering him a flirty smile and leading us to our table. He pulls out my chair for me, and I take a seat, ducking my head to hide my smile. Matt takes a seat across from me, and we browse the menu. In the past, we'd usually fill this time with conversation, discussing what we're considering getting. Today is silent, and I hate it. I surprise myself when I practically slam the menu down on the table.

"I hate this," I say.

He looks at me, shocked. "The restaurant?"

I shake my head. "No. This." I motion between us. "We're never like this. We talk and laugh and have a good time. I hate the quiet."

He reaches across the table and takes my hand, running his thumb over the back of it. "I do, too. Nothing between us really has to change. We're going to enjoy a meal together the way we have countless times in the past. I just may hold your hand a little more while we do it."

"And if this all goes wrong and blows up in our faces? What happens to us? To me and Liv?"

He gives my hand a squeeze. "We're going to take this one step at a time. Just know that I respect you, and I respect your relationship with Liv. We won't let anything that happens between us affect your relationship."

Sincerity is written all over his face. I know he means everything he just said. I squeeze his hand back and relax a little. I pick up the menu again and scan it, my eyes catching on potato skins. I drop the menu enough that my eyes can peer over the top and stare at Matt. He grins at me, and at the same time we say, "Potato skins." I can't help the laugh that leaves me.

We agree to share the potato skins as an appetizer and order a steak and burger and split them. We slip into easy conversation like normal, and a thrill goes through me when Matt takes my hand again, running his thumb slowly over my knuckles and then up the back of my hand.

I completely lose track of time. It isn't until I watch the table beside us stand and grab their jackets and I realize it's not the same couple that arrived just after us that I check my phone and see we've been sitting here for nearly three and a half hours.

"Holy shit," I say.

"What? Is everything okay?" Matt's on high alert, and knowing he's worried for me makes my heart race a little.

I nod. "Yeah, everything's fine. It's just that we've been here for three and a half hours. We should probably give them their table back."

Matt seems to think for a minute before nodding and asking the waitress for our bill. When she comes back, he pays and we gather our stuff, heading out of the restaurant, but instead of heading to the car, Matt stops me. "Walk with me?" he asks.

I intertwine my fingers with his, and he smiles at me before walking down the block. The silence between us as we walk isn't awkward this time, but more comfortable. Like we just want to spend time with one another and don't need to talk. I spot a park on the other side of the street and pull Matt with me as I make my way towards it. He follows, and we hurry across the street before I bring us to the swings.

"I loved the swings as a kid," I say, sitting in one of them. "I always felt so free when I was on one, trying to see how high I could go."

Matt circles the swing so he's at my back and grabs the chains, pulling the swing back slightly before giving it a push. I tip my head back and giggle as he pushes me again. The breeze blows through my hair, and I close my eyes, reveling in the feeling. After a few minutes, Matt slows the swing, and I look at him over my shoulder. His eyes hood as he looks down at me, and I suck in a breath.

He leans down and pauses, silently asking my permission, and I nod. When his lips meet mine, my eyes close, and I swear I can see fireworks. The kiss is soft and slow at first, but becomes more exploring, and I lean into Matt. His hand comes to my face, and he strokes my cheek with his thumb. I let him take control. I don't often let men take control away from me, but with Matt, I feel a sense of safety, like I won't lose everything if I give him control.

I try to twist to face him more, and the swing rocks. We break apart, both working to catch our breath, and my hand instinctively comes up and touches my mouth.

Holy shit. Holy shit. Holy shit. I just kissed Matthew Carter.

I quickly turn and face forward, my cheeks heating the more I think about it. Matt rounds the swing and stops in front of me, tipping my head back with his fingers under my chin.

"Please don't tell me you regret letting me kiss you," he says, his voice laced with so much vulnerability.

I quickly shake my head. "Not at all," I breathe out.

He grins. "Good, because I'd very much like to do that again."

I grin back. "Me, too."

He leans in closer and dusts his lips over mine before stepping back and offering me his hand. I take it, and we walk back towards the car, but I'm not ready for tonight to end. Even if we don't kiss again, I want to spend more time with him.

When we get to the car and he pulls open the passenger door, I turn and face him. "We still have some movies to finish in our *Star Wars* marathon. How about we watch some tonight?"

His face lights up, as though he didn't want to end the night either. "That sounds like a perfect plan."

I slide into the car, extremely pleased with myself, and Matt drives us back to his place.

CHAPTER 23

Matt

I've never gone on a date where the end goal wasn't sex. I've taken women out, but they always knew they weren't getting a relationship out of it. With Zoey, it's all different. Do I want to sleep with her? Of course. I'd be idiot to see how gorgeous she is and not want to. But if she never wanted that, or made me wait an entire year for it, I'd be okay with that, because it's her. Kissing her in the park was not the plan, but when I saw how carefree she was and she laughed as I pushed her on the swing, I couldn't stop myself. It wasn't an overly explicit kiss, but it was hands down the best one I've ever had.

When we stepped out of the restaurant, I knew I wasn't ready for the night to end. I was not ready to just drive her home and drop her off, so I suggested a walk. When she later asked about watching another *Star Wars* movie, I knew she felt the same way.

I'm itching to hold her hand as I drive, but I hold back, not wanting to dive into anything too quickly. I need to make sure we take all of this at Zoey's pace.

Inside my apartment, Zoey takes off her boots, and I watch as she undoes the zipper, slowly exposing more of her legs. I can't seem to take my eyes off it. When she looks up at me, she smirks, knowing exactly how enrapturing she is. I clear my throat and head to the kitchen.

"Popcorn?" I call.

"Of course. We can't watch a movie without snacks."

I shake my head with a smile. Of course. I do know this about Zoey, I don't think I've ever seen her watch anything without either eating a meal or snacks. She settles on the couch, and I put the popcorn oil and kernels in a pot on the stove.

When I notice her pull at her skirt as she adjusts herself on the couch, I head into my room and grab the same clothes I gave her the last time she was here and hand them to her. I tip my head towards the washroom. "Put these on, you'll be more comfortable."

She offers me a relieved smile and heads to change. By the time she's out, the popcorn is done and I'm salting it. I settle at the end of the couch, and when she tries to make her way to the other side, I grab her wrist and shake my head.

"You are going to sit right beside me and share this bowl of popcorn."

She raises a brow. "Now, who said anything about sharing? I may just eat the whole thing myself."

I raise a brow back. "Oh really? You may have to fight me for it."

She takes a step closer and lowers herself in front of me. "Oh, I could take you in a fight, Carter."

She reaches into the bowl and grabs a large handful and shoves it into her mouth, a few kernels missing and falling down her shirt. She pulls it away from her chest and grabs them before tossing them into her mouth, and I shake my head. It's something I've seen all the girls do before, they've all become very comfortable in the group and have no qualms about eating anything that lands on or between their boobs.

She plops beside me and pulls a blanket off the back of the couch, which has only found residence there since Zoey started coming over a year and a half ago. The girl is always cold and is always in need of a blanket when she's sitting still, so I left one out for her. Plus, the look of joy on her face when she gets all bundled under it and does a happy dance in her seat is worth it.

I press play on the movie, and we settle in. Once the popcorn is finished, I put the bowl on the coffee table. Zoey leans into my side, and I wrap an arm around her. My thumb hooks under the fabric of the sleeve of her T-shirt, and I run it up and down her arm, loving the feel of her soft skin.

When the movie finishes, she looks up at me with hopeful eyes as she asks, "Next one?"

Who am I to say no to a request like that? Pressing play, I hold her tighter into my side.

It's 2:30 a.m. by the time we finish the movie, and I'm yawning, beat from the day. Zoey is yawning beside me, and I know there's no way I'm taking her home tonight.

I kiss the top of her head and say, "We should head to bed."

She nods against me as she yawns again. I get up and offer her a hand, and she takes it, following me into the bedroom. She climbs into the same side as last time, and when I climb in this time she doesn't stay on her side, she curls into my side, resting her head on my shoulder. I run my hand through her hair, allowing it to sink in that I have Zoey Williams in my bed, consciously cuddling me, and there's nowhere else I'd rather be. She drifts off quickly, and I'm reminded that the girl snores, and not some cute soft snore, but in the shake the walls of the house kind of way. Luckily I've always been able to sleep through anything and can drift off.

When I wake up in the morning, I don't even bother hiding the fact that I'm hard. There is no way I'm getting out of this bed, or out of Zoey's arms, until I absolutely have to. She nuzzles into my side and lets out a contented sigh, only solidifying my decision. I grab my phone and quickly send a text to Gi asking if I can push back picking up Jayden, and she tells me Mom was hoping to keep him for the day and offered to keep for the night again if that helped. I agree, hoping I can get Zoey to stick around a little longer this morning.

I brush back some of her hair that's covered her face and smile as I take in her peaceful expression. Her eyes flutter, and she smiles up at me when she closes them again, protesting waking up.

"Morning."

"Not yet," she mumbles.

I chuckle.

She cracks one eye and asks, "What time is it?"

"Nine a.m."

She nuzzles deeper into my side. "What time do you have to pick up Jayden?"

"Mom offered to keep him for the day and do another sleepover."

"So more sleep," she says with a smile.

I chuckle again. "You can, but I don't think I'll be falling asleep again."

She huffs. "So breakfast."

I laugh so hard my body shakes, and Zoey makes a face at me, making me laugh even harder. "Bug, when it comes to you, I know I must feed you first thing in the morning and give you plenty of sugar if you're to function normally."

"Well, I'm glad you've learned that. So, what are you feeding me?"

I stare at the ceiling, running my fingers through her hair.

"What do you want? I have everything to make pancakes, or French toast, or omelettes. I have hash browns in the freezer and bacon, and of course, coffee and some flavoured creamer."

When I look back at her she's grinning like crazy. "Did you say pancakes, hash browns, bacon, and eggs?"

I nod, and she's throwing the covers off and sliding out of bed as I laugh and follow her.

She turns the coffee pot on as soon as she's in the kitchen, and I start gathering the ingredients. She grabs a baking sheet and wire racks and gets to work laying the bacon out while I whip up the pancakes. We work perfectly in sync. I've never cooked with a woman. I've never let one stay the night. Sleepovers imply the possibility of doing something the next morning, and I never wanted to give women that hope. That's why most of the time I'd go back to her place, that way I could dip out when I wanted to. Cooking with Zoey feels natural, as though we've been doing this for years.

When we finish, we head to the dining table, and Zoey wastes no time digging in. We eat in relative silence and after a few minutes, I pull her chair closer to mine. That gets her to stop and look at me. Her brows furrow in confusion for a second before she smiles at me. She's right handed, so I can't take her closest hand, so I settle with a hand on her knee, stroking my thumb across the outside of it. She bites her lip and ducks her head as she gives it a slight shake and continues to eat.

When we finish, we take our plates into the kitchen.

Zoey's hands land on my chest as a playful look takes over her expression. "So, what do you say about a second date?"

I grin back at her. "I'd say I'd love one."

"And what about right now? Wanna binge the rest of the movies?" I can feel the excitement radiating off of her.

"Sounds like the perfect plan."

She bounces up on her tiptoes, placing a chaste kiss on my lips, and bounces towards the couch, and I'm left staring dumbfounded at her. She just kissed me casually, as if it wasn't the first times she's done it, and God, I hope it's not the last.

I join her, and she curls into my side. I wrap an arm around her, pulling her in close and playing the movie. Zoey and I are both people who don't enjoy talking a lot during movies; we like to settle in and enjoy them. It's one of the things I love about spending time with her.

We decide to do snacks for lunch instead of making something and eat them while we watch. When the final movie finishes, we sit there with Zoey tucked into my side and my hand running through her hair, neither of us wanting to be the first to pull away.

She eventually pulls back, looking up at me. "Any plans tonight?"

I shake my head. "No, I'm completely free."

She gnaws her lip as if deeply contemplating something, and I can tell the second she makes her decision. Her fingers dance up my arm slowly as she asks, "Would you say the fair and *Star Wars* binge was our first date?"

I quirk a brow at her. "Do you want it to be our first date?"

Her eyes hood as she sits up on her knees. "Well, if it was, that would make this our third date."

I know for a fact she's thinking something mischievous right now, and if I say no, I may just lose out on experiencing something amazing. I swallow and nod. "Yeah, we can call it our first date."

She grins. "Good, then I won't feel so bad about doing this." She swings her leg over mine and straddles me, wrapping her arms around my neck and leaning in until her lips dust over my jaw. She places gentle kisses up my jaw until she reaches my ear and whispers, "Do you want me to stop?"

"No." My voice is strained, because I was not expecting this at all.

She pulls my earlobe between her teeth, and I groan, trying not to toss my head back. She rolls her hips against me, and my hands immediately find her hips, holding tightly. Zoey is entirely in control right now, and it's fucking hot.

She moves to the other side of my jaw, repeating the same movements, and then she's kissing me. She puts everything on the table with this kiss as she takes control. When she licks my lips, seeking entrance, I give it to her, my tongue meeting hers stroke for stroke. I'm hard as a rock in my shorts, and she grinds against my erection, causing me to groan into her mouth and tighten my grip on her hips.

Our kiss is hot and heavy. I eventually break it, kissing her jaw and neck in the same way she was doing to me earlier. She leans back, giving me better access. My stupid T-shirt has her covered almost to her neck, and I want nothing more than to take it off and throw it as far away as I can.

My hand skates under the hem of the shirt and dusts over her skin. Her grip on my shoulders tightens as my hands skate further up. She grinds against me again as a soft little hum escapes her. I kiss her again, trying to take control, but she won't give it up.

She pulls back, panting. "Wait."

My hands pull away from her as my chest heaves.

"No sex. We can make out, but I'm not going to be another notch in your bedpost. I'm not jumping into sex."

She doesn't really believe that's all she'd be, does she?

I cup her cheek. The look on her face is strong but reserved, like she's ready to protect herself no matter the blow. "Zoey, I will one hundred percent respect that. We'll do this all at your pace, however fast or slow that is. But you also need to know you could never, and I mean never, be just another notch in my bedpost. You mean way too much to me for that to ever be the case."

She stares at me for a minute then nods. "Okay. I believe you."

My hands slip into her hair and grab a good fistful, and she mewls.

"Can I kiss you again?" The words are barely out before her lips are on mine and she's devouring me like she can't get enough.

I keep asking myself, why Zoey? Why is Zoey kissing me? Why is Zoey the only woman I've ever thought I'd never get enough of kissing? I want to consume her. I want this kiss to be her only thought, to be the thing that distracts her in the middle of the day because she craves it so much. I want to be her every thought like she's become mine.

We sit on the couch, exploring each other's mouths as our hands roam, never crossing that line. When we finally separate and come up for air, she grins at me.

"I can say you've at least learned a thing or two from all the experience you've gathered."

I grip her hips tightly. "I don't think we should be talking about any of that experience when you were just grinding yourself on me like the needy girl you are."

Her eyes shine, and she leans forward, whispering in my ear, "You haven't seen just how needy I am."

This time, I do drop my head back as I groan. All I can picture right now is her riding my dick on this couch as she tells me over and over that she's so needy for me.

She must know just how she's affecting me, because she slides off my lap and heads towards the bathroom, calling over her shoulder, "I'm going to grab a quick shower."

Great, that will hopefully give me enough time to pull myself together.

CHAPTER 24

Zoey

When I come out of the shower wrapped in a towel, Matt is perched on the edge of his bed with head in his hands. When he looks up at me, a pained look crosses his face.

"Fucking hell, Zo."

I walk closer to him, stepping between his legs, satisfied by the reaction I get from him. His hands find my hips as his eyes slowly trace up my body until he meets my gaze.

"You're killing me. You're such a fucking tease."

I lean over him, dusting my lips over his, and when he goes to kiss me, I pull back. "I promise it will all be worth the wait."

"You're worth everything, Zo."

His words hit me, and I stare at him before tightening the towel around myself and taking a step back. "We should get some sleep," I say, and Matt nods, handing me a fresh set of his clothes to change into.

He heads to the shower and leaves me to lie in his bed as the heaviness of his words really sink in. Saying that I'm worth everything is a huge declaration, one I was not expecting, but it also makes me think maybe he's ready to step away from his playboy ways. I'm not going to just have sex with him. If he wants it, he has to earn it. Prove to me this isn't just some quick fuck.

Even without us having sex, I know there's a conversation I need to have. I grab my phone, sending a quick text before settling back under the covers.

When he comes out of the shower, he's already changed into pyjamas. He climbs into bed beside me, and I curl into his side, flinging a leg over his as his fingers run through my hair. Despite everything going through my mind, being this close to Matt and the feeling of his fingers in my hair have me drifting off quickly.

I'm the first to wake up this morning, and I take the opportunity to take Matt in. He looks so peaceful with a small smile as he sleeps. He must have gotten hot at some point in the middle of the night, because he's now shirtless under me. I allow my eyes to eat up every inch of him.

Matt's fit. Not in a ripped with a six-pack kind of way, but rather one that tells you he takes care of himself and exercises, but also enjoys having fun and doesn't count his calories and carbs. He's got a softness to his stomach I absolutely love.

As my eyes travel farther down, I see his erection. I noticed it yesterday, too, but didn't want to say anything. This morning, I find myself staring at it unabashedly. As much as I want to make him work for sex, I also really want to know what it would be like to be with Matt.

"Zo, you can't stare at it like that. That's so unfair."

I look up at him through my lashes. "Like what?"

He rolls us, and I giggle as he hovers over me. I squeeze my legs together, fighting the ache growing between them. "Like you want to know what it would be like to have my cock in your mouth or how good it would feel to have it stretching your tight little cunt as I take you fast and hard."

"And what if I was thinking how good it would be to have you handcuffed to this bed as I rode your face and cock until I come so hard I can't walk after?"

He drops his head to my shoulder and groans.

I reach between us and run a finger over his shorts-clad cock, and his hips jerk. "You might want to go take care of your problem."

He pushes up until he's hovering over me again, raising a brow. "Did you really just tell me to go jerk off?"

I nod. "Yup, because I'm not helping." I lean up and kiss him before sliding out from under him and heading towards the kitchen, stopping just before I leave his room and look over my shoulder. "Just make sure it's my name you say when you finish."

I prep the coffee pot and turn it on before grabbing eggs out of the fridge and getting to work on making some breakfast. As I'm taking the eggs off the stove, I hear Matt call my name, and the grin that splits across my face is so wide my cheeks hurt.

When Matt emerges from his room, he's got a shit-eating grin on his face and he cages me against the counter.

"How was it?" I ask.

He reaches up and runs his thumb over my bottom lip. "Not as good as it would have been if it was your pretty little mouth wrapped around my cock, or if I got to see just how wet you were for me."

His lips find my neck, and I lean to the side, granting him more access as I squeeze my thighs again.

"Just know all your teasing is going to make it all the more sweeter when I actually get to fuck you and watch you come undone as you call my name over and over. And you best beware that when I finally get to have you, it won't be a one-time thing. And when I'm done with you, I'll have you begging for more, and I may just tease you the same way, making you wait until you can have more."

I swallow and pull my shoulders back. "Oh, Matthew, once you get a taste, you won't be holding out on me."

He grips my jaw and looks me in the eye. His gaze is molten. "Is that a threat?"

I go up on my tiptoes and whisper over his lips, "A promise."

His lips meet mine in a bruising kiss, and I kiss him back just as fervently. His hands find my ass, and he lifts me onto the counter. I wrap my legs around his hips, pulling him in closer. I run my hands over his naked chest, enjoying the way he reacts to my touch.

His lips leave mine and nip at my jaw. "Fuck, you're going to make me need a cold shower."

"Good," I murmur.

His thumb finds my bare skin under the hem of his T-shirt I'm wearing, and I reach between us, grabbing the hem. I pull it over my head and drop it on the floor beside him. "We're not having sex, but I need your lips on me."

"Fuck." He groans before his lips find the tops of my breasts as he lathers them with kisses.

"Matt."

He doesn't stop. His hands join in his efforts, cupping my breasts and rolling my nipples through the lace of my bra.

"Yes," I moan.

"You're a fucking gorgeous sight," he says.

I roll my hips and grind against him, and he rolls his into me. The moan that leaves me is absolutely feral. It only seems to spur him on as he does it again, but now his mouth has found my nipple through my bra and his tongue is flicking it and his teeth are pulling at it gently. His right hand continues to roll my other nipple, and my hand comes to his hair.

"Yes, Matt. Yes."

He grins against me as he pushes his erection into my centre, somehow finding the spot that aches for him the most. When I grip his arm and my nails dig in, it's like he takes that as his signal to not be gentle with me. He bites my nipple, and I fall back on the counter, panting. He grips my hips and pulls me further to the edge of the counter. His hand finds my hair as he pulls me up against him and kisses me. He kisses me as though he's trying to consume me, and fuck if I don't let him. I'm wrung so tight that I hand him complete control.

"Matt," I pant. "I want to come."

He pulls back and grins. "Do you think you deserve to come?"

I need to come so badly that I'm not putting up with bullshit right now. My chest is still heaving as I say, "You can either help me, or you can stand there and watch as I get myself off." My hand snakes down my stomach and between my legs, but he grips my wrist stopping my movements.

"Don't you even think about it. I got you here, I'll be the one to make you come," he grits.

"Then make me come."

His mouth latches onto my nipple again, and he pinches the other as he rolls his hips into me. My eyes are trying to roll into the back of head, because holy hell, I feel Matt everywhere.

He removes his mouth from my nipple and looks at me. "Can you be a good girl and come like this?"

I bite my lip and nod. He leans forward, his teeth grabbing my nipple as he holds eye contact with me, and pulls. I'm sent over the edge, my arms that were holding me up nearly giving out. I call out his name as my orgasm tears through me.

Oh my God. I don't think I've ever come while still fully clothed on my lower half.

When I've finally collected myself and can sit up on my own, Matt's looking at me with a devilish grin. I just gave him a ton of control and power, but I'm not letting him keep all of it. With a matching grin, I reach between us and grip him through his shorts, giving him a long stroke. His grin falls away as he leans forward, bracing himself against the counter on each side of me.

I lean in until my lips are by his ear and whisper, "Are you going to be a good boy and come for me?"

He drops his head to my shoulder, and I tighten my grip. "Whatever you want, Zoey."

I grin at the feeling of power and control I have right now. Matt bucks into my hand, bringing himself closer to the edge as he moans into my shoulder.

"Come for me, Matt. Come in your shorts like a good boy."

Two more strokes, and he's groaning, "Fuck," nice and loud into my shoulder as his knees try to give out, sending me over the moon with pleasure. I just brought Matthew Carter to his fucking knees.

When he finally catches his breath, he takes me by surprise and kisses me like I'm the air he needs to survive. I take from him as much as I give. The kiss eventually goes from hungry to more intimate, and my skin feels like tiny little needles are under it as it heats. Matt strokes my jaw with his thumb as he places soft little pecks on my lips.

When he pulls back, he stares into my eyes, his expression soft, but there's something else I can't pinpoint. I lean my face into his hand as he continues to stroke my cheek.

He clears his throat and says, "I, uh, I should go shower and change."

I nod. "Breakfast is done when you get back."

He nods, and I watch his back as he makes his way into the

bedroom. My heart is racing as I duck my head. What the hell just happened? I never planned for this. A heavy make out session, maybe. Letting Matt make me come and making him come, no. No matter how much I think about it, I can't find any part of me that regrets it, though. He respected my boundary of not taking it any further, and that only goes to make me feel safer with him.

I shuffle off the counter and grab the food and take it to the dining table. When Matt joins me again, as soon as he sits down, he pulls my chair closer same as he did yesterday and runs his thumb over my knee. The little touches from Matt have butterflies filling my stomach in a way I've never experienced. I've been in relationships before, but never had I felt this way especially so early in a relationship. I don't even know what Matt and I are, but I do know I want to explore it. I want to see what this could grow into. I also know I need to be clear with Matt about what I'm looking for.

When I finish my food, I push my plate forward and turn to face him, adjusting myself so I'm sitting with legs crossed under me. Matt places his fork on his plate and gives me his full attention.

"What's up?" he asks, and I raise a brow. He gestures at me. "I can tell you want to talk about something, so what's up?"

"I know I probably should have said something before we"—I look to the kitchen, feeling my cheeks heat, and then back at him—"did what we did, but I need to be clear with you."

"We're exclusive," he says, and my jaw drops before I quickly recover, closing my mouth and giving my head a shake. "Zo, I know you're not one for a fling, and that's not what I want with you. I wouldn't have asked you out if I wasn't serious about giving this a shot. About seeing what we can be. So, yes, you and I are exclusive. Is that all you wanted to talk about?"

He picks up his fork and takes another bite of eggs while I continue to stare at him, not sure how he was able to read my mind like that, but also noticing how the butterflies grow because he was able to do that so easily.

"Ummm, yeah."

"Good." He grabs both of our plates and pushes up from his chair, placing a chaste kiss on my lips. "Thanks for breakfast," he says before he makes his way into the kitchen.

"I should change and head out, you've got to leave soon to grab Jayden."

"I'll give you ride home."

"I'm not going home."

He turns and raises a brow.

"I'm heading to Liv's."

"Okay, I can still drop you off on my way to my parents. If you need a ride after, just let me know and I'll pick you up."

I shake my head, even though the corner of my lips turns up. "I can get myself home."

He walks towards me, stopping in front of my chair and tipping my head back with his fingers under my chin. "I know you can, but I also know your car is at Henry's and I want to make sure you get home safe."

He kisses me, and I smile against his lips.

"I'll be fine."

"Call me anyways."

"Okay."

One last peck and then he steps back, allowing me to get up. I head into his bedroom and change into the clothes I wore on our date and throw my hair up into a ponytail. When I head back into the living room, Matt stares at me as I make my way to the front door and slip my boots on and zip them up. When I finish and face him, he wraps his arms around my waist and pulls me into him, my hands finding his chest.

"Did I tell you how fucking good you look in this?"

I nod and grin. "You did."

"Good, I'm going to say it again, you look hot in this."

"Why thank you. We should get going."

"I wish we had more time." He pouts.

I chuckle. "Matt, we're going to see each other in the morning."

"Not soon enough, Bug."

I pat his chest. "You're a big boy, you'll survive."

I step out of his arms and grab my purse, and he sticks out his lip. All I can do is laugh as I open the door and head for the elevators. Matt eventually follows me and locks the front door.

CHAPTER 25

Zoey

I buzz Liv's apartment, and she lets me in. I ride the elevator up, tapping my foot as it hits me as to why I'm here, dressed the way I am. When the elevator arrives on her floor, I make my way to her front door and take a deep breath before knocking. She answers almost immediately.

She eyes me then turns and makes her way towards the kitchen, and without a word, grabs down a wine glass and pours a glass of white and passes it to me before pouring herself some orange juice. "Okay, what's up?"

"You realize it's like nine in the morning, right?"

She nods. "Yes, but you texted me last night asking to meet today, and you just showed up like"—she motions her hand up and down in front of me—"this. I know something's up, and from the look on your face and the seriousness of your text, I'm guessing it calls for some booze. As much as I wish I could join you in this..." She motions between her boobs, because she's breastfeeding. "Don't worry, Josh is with Cate right now."

"God damn, you and Matt," I mutter.

"Hmmm?"

"Nothing. Let's sit."

We grab our glasses and move to the couch in the living room and settle in.

"So, the reason I wanted to talk is I need to let you know that Matt and I are dating." I bite my bottom lip as I watch her.

"That's it?"

I nod, and she tips her head back and laughs. Just when I think she's done laughing, she laughs harder. When she does stop, she looks at me and then starts laughing again, and I take a large sip of my wine. This is not the reaction I thought I'd get.

"You made it sound like it was going to be a big deal. I've already told you I don't care if you and Matt date. In fact, I kinda love that you could one day be my sister-in-law."

I throw up my hand. "Whoa, you're putting the cart before the horse. Matt and I have only gone on one date, two if you want to call the weekend two."

"So, you spent the night?"

I roll my eyes. "Nothing happened. We only slept, but it was too late for me to leave Friday night after our movie ended and the same last night."

She almost chokes on her drink. "You spent two nights at his apartment?"

I shrug. "Yeah, it's nothing I haven't done before."

She stares at me. "But let me guess, this time you shared his bed instead of sleeping on the couch."

My cheeks heat, and Liv smiles as she shakes her head.

"Of course you did." She adjusts herself so she faces me fully and crosses her legs under herself. "So, tell me about the date. Where did he take you?"

Remembering Friday night, really this entire weekend, has me grinning like a fool. I tell her about dinner and our stop in the park before we went back to his place to continue our *Star Wars* marathon. I watch every little expression that crosses Liv's face, trying to fully gage what she's thinking, but she doesn't say anything during my retelling of the weekend.

When I finish, she pats my leg and says, "I'm happy for you."

"Thanks, Liv. I don't want anything to be weird or awkward with us. I love you too much for that, but..." I take a deep breath, mustering the strength to say this out loud. "I have actual feelings for your brother and really want to see what this can be. I want more dates and to see if what started as a genuine friendship can be more."

Liv takes my hand. "I know, Zo. I trust you and I trust him. I know you two wouldn't have crossed any lines unless you were sure you genuinely wanted this. I'm happy for the both of you. You deserve each other in every positive way. I know you'll take care of and support each other, and that's all I've ever wished for you two."

I wipe away a tear that escapes, and Liv's face fills with over exaggerated shock. "Did I just make Zoey Williams cry?"

I swat at her. "Yes, you brat. You went and said all those nice things. How am I supposed to not cry?"

She puts her glass down, and I follow as she pulls me into a hug. "I love you, Zo."

"I love you, too."

As we separate, Josh comes down the hall with Cate. I immediately do grabby hands at him, and he hands her to me.

"Gives Aunty Zo a whole new meaning," Liv says, and Josh tilts his head at her. "Oh, just Matt and Zo dating, so..."

"Matt's dating?" Josh asks skeptically.

Liv nods with the largest smile on her face. "Yup," she says, popping the P. "Him and Zoey are dating."

Josh sits beside Liv on the couch, and she leans into him. "I didn't think he was there yet. I knew he'd eventually date, I just figured he'd wait until he was in his mid-thirties for some reason. He was enjoying his bachelor lifestyle."

I shrug. "I don't know what changed his mind. But we've agreed we're dating and we're exclusive."

Liv is still grinning. "It was you. That's what changed his mind."

I shake my head. "Nope. Not me. No way I could make him change his ways like that." There's nothing I could have done to make the perpetual playboy decide he wanted a monogamous relationship. Saying that gives me way too much power, and as much as I like having power when it comes to our relationship, that is too much. It puts too much pressure on me. On our relationship.

Liv, seeming to read the slight panic that's going through me right now, drops the subject. "How about breakfast?"

I shake my head. "I'm good. I ate with Matt before he dropped me off. But I'll stick around and spend time with you and"—I lean down and blow raspberries on Cate's cheek, and she giggles—"my adorable niece."

"Sounds like a plan."

Josh seems to take that as his cue, because he gets up and heads to the kitchen. Liv and I slip into normal conversation, and I'm beyond relieved there's zero awkwardness between us. As much as someone may say they're okay with you dating their sibling, you can never truly know how much they mean it. And I know Liv doesn't really say things she doesn't mean, but the hypothetical of your brother and best friend dating versus the reality are very different, and she may change her mind when she sees us together. While we talk, she feeds Cate.

She and Josh settle at the dining table and eat their breakfast. I take Cate and play with her on the living room floor. As I play with her, I see the similarities between her and Jayden. Cate definitely has a lot of Josh, but I can see Liv, and she does little things that immediately make me think of Liv, and Jayden does the same thing. I'm sure when these two grow up, they'll be very similar.

When Liv and Josh finish breakfast, Josh takes Cate and says they have a daddy-daughter date planned for the day before grabbing the diaper bag and stroller and leaving the apartment.

"Did you just kick your husband out?" I ask.

She shakes her head. "No, Josh is very serious about daddy-daughter dates. He's tried to work less during the week, but it's hard when he's so needed and he just bought the team, so he dedicates his weekends to time for us and with Cate."

"He's a good dad."

She nods. "A very good dad. I'm lucky to have him."

"You're both lucky."

We settle on the couch, and Liv tosses me a blanket before pulling up a romcom and pressing play. We make it through three movies before Josh comes home, and I figure I should head home. I shoot Matt a text, letting him know I'm just going to catch the train home. I don't want him to have to get Jayden ready and into the car when I'm perfectly capable of getting myself home. He texts me to wait, but I tell him I'm fine.

When I enter the living room again, Liv is on the phone, and she's staring right at me with a grin so big I'm sure her face hurts. That look tells me everything I need to know.

"He didn't," I say when she hangs up, and she nods.

"I've been given strict instructions to not let you leave until Matt gets here to take you home."

"I'm a grown-ass woman. I can get myself home."

"Matt said it's dark and he's taking you home."

I roll my eyes. "I'm leaving. I love you, and I'll see you later." I turn to the front door, and Josh steps in front of it. "Josh, could you please let me go."

His eyes dart over my shoulder and back to me. "Sorry, Liv said you're staying."

I look over my shoulder at her and scowl. "Seriously?"

She shrugs.

"You've got him so pussy whipped he's not letting me leave?"

She shrugs again, and I shake my head.

I turn and start to head down the hallway towards the washroom. When Josh starts to move away from the door, I turn and try to beat him to the door, but it's no use. "Fucking hockey player," I mutter.

It's no use. I settle at the end of the couch and cross my arms like a toddler, and at this point, I don't give a fuck. I'm being locked in my best friend's apartment because her brother won't let me take the train home. The same train I've taken for years, all because it's fucking dark. Stupid daylight savings.

Liv's phone rings, and she answers and presses a button and I know Matt's here. I'm not happy with him right now. Matt knocks on the front door, and Josh answers, letting him in.

He's got Jayden in his car seat in hand, and when he spots me he asks, "What did I say this morning, Bug?"

I turn and face him, not leaving the couch. "Nope. You're not going to Bug me right now. I'm pissed. I'm a big girl, I can get myself home. I told you not to come get me."

Liv meets Matt and takes the car seat from him, and he walks towards me. There's something in his expression that goes straight between my legs, but I fight it. I'm not backing down on this. When he's in front of me, he leans over me on the couch. As I look up at him, his expression softens.

"Do you trust me?" he asks, and I nod. "Do you believe that I care about you?"

I nod again.

"Do you believe I'll do everything I can to make sure you're safe and taken care of?"

That's a big question, but I somehow know deep in my bones it's true. I nod.

"Then I'm not going to let you take the train home in the dark when I'm perfectly capable of coming to pick you up and make sure you get there safely."

"But Jayden..." I whisper.

"He loves car rides, and I'm sure it will put him right to sleep on the way home."

"But—"

He shakes his head, cutting me off. "Bug, let me take care of you. I know you're independent, and I love that about you, but I need you to let me do this for you. I need you to let me make sure you're safe." His voice and eyes are pleading, as if being able to do this for me is important to him.

"Okay," I finally say, and he releases a breath and his shoulders relax.

"I care about you, Zoey.

I reach up and cup his face, and he leans into my touch. "I care about you, too, Matthew."

He turns and kisses my palm. "Let's get you home."

He pushes up to stand and offers me his hand. He looks over my shoulder, and I follow his gaze to Liv with Jayden's car seat on the kitchen counter and her pretending like she's not constantly peaking over at us.

"She knows," I say, and Matt looks back at me. "I came over to tell her. She's one hundred percent okay with us and was actually quite happy when I told her."

He grins at me before taking my chin between his thumb and forefinger. "I'm glad, because I really want to do this." He leans forward and kisses me. It's soft and intimate and leaves me wanting more when he pulls away. I shake my head at him despite my smile.

He takes my hand, and I follow him into the kitchen.

"Okay, little man," Matt says as we reach Liv and Jayden.

I poke my head in front of Jayden, and he starts babbling and kicking his feet and shaking his arms like crazy.

"Hey, munchkin."

He babbles more.

"Oh really? You had tons of fun with Aunty Gi and Grandma and Grampa!"

"Yup, you should see all the toys they bought for him. This kid is spoiled," Matt says.

Liv laughs. "You don't get to complain one bit. You did the same to me when Cate was born. We're all just making up for lost time."

A solemn look takes over Matt's face. "I know."

Liv reaches out and grabs her brother's arm. "We don't blame you for any of this. We all just want to connect with him. He's your son, and he's family."

Matt nods, and I hug his arm and lean into his side. "He is also just an adorable little one, too." I pinch Jayden's cheek, and he squeals. "Who could help spoiling this cutie patootie?"

I feel Matt shake his head, and he grabs the handle of the car seat. "Time to get you two home," he says before turning to Liv. "Thanks, Liv."

"No thanks needed."

A quick kiss on her cheek and wave at Josh, who's leaning against the entry to the kitchen, and he makes his way to the front door. I say my goodbyes and follow Matt.

When Matt pulls up in front of Henry's, he quickly rounds the car and opens my door for me, but he blocks me in. "Let me pick you up in the morning." It's a mix of a demand and a plea.

"Matt, it's just easier to meet you there then after breakfast I can come back here."

"I can drop you off after, it's fine."

"It's not exactly on your way home."

"I know, but it means I can spend more time with you."

My eyes widen. Matt is coming on very strong right now, especially after having only one date. I don't know what I'm supposed to do.

He cups my face. "I should have asked you out earlier, that was my fault, but now I'm going to enjoy all the time I can get with you, and if that means driving a little out of my way so I can drop you off, then I'll do it."

Those damn butterflies take off again, and I can't say no to him right now.

"Okay. Just text me when you're on your way."

His grin is blinding. "I will."

He helps me out of the car and pulls me into him before kissing me in a much different way than he did at Liv's. I wrap my arms around his neck as he wraps his around my waist and holds me against him. After a few minutes, he peppers a few pecks on my lips and whispers, "I'll see you in the morning, Bug."

"See you in the morning."

I look over my shoulder twice on my way to the front door, smiling from ear to ear the whole way. Henry and Maggie aren't home when I walk in, and I jog up to my bedroom before quickly grabbing a shower and changing into some lazy lounge clothes.

CHAPTER 26

Matt

After breakfast I drop Zoey off at home and then meet the guys at Caleb's. I'm the last to arrive, and I let myself in and find them in the kitchen where Caleb is pouring the guys each a cup of coffee. He holds the pot out to me in offer, and I shake my head. Caleb being who he is, gets right to business.

"So, here are all the listings my realtor sent over. There's about twenty, he said a lot of people are selling right now. Hopefully, everyone can find something in this stack."

We each grab one off the stack and browse, passing them around when we're done.

"There are a couple open houses in about an hour or so, and then the others he said, if we're interested, he can schedule some private showings."

We all nod.

"Which ones have open houses today?" I ask.

Jayden starts to fuss in his carrier on my chest, and I start to pace.

Caleb picks out a few listings and puts them in a stack. "These ones."

I take them from him and thumb through them. There are a few I'm seriously interested in. In fact, almost all the ones I want to see are in this stack.

"Sounds good." I hand the stack to Josh. "You going to pick up Liv to come to the open houses?"

He shakes his head. "I'll take videos and stuff for her if I think she'll like them, and then we can schedule another appointment. You bringing Zoey?"

I stop in my spot and stare at him while the guys all stare at me.

"Why would he be taking Zoey to look at houses?" Grayson asks.

"Because they're dating," Josh says.

"Matt's actually dating?" Grayson asks incredulously.

"Yeah, I am. And who the fuck are you to say anything? You're the one who was sleeping with anything that walked and then married the girl who couldn't stand you."

He points his finger at me. "You're wrong. I wasn't sleeping with anything that walked."

I laugh, and Josh and Caleb just stare at him.

"I hadn't been with anyone for almost two years before I married Hannah."

"What do you mean?" Caleb asks. "You were collecting numbers the whole time."

Grayson shakes his head. "You thought I was. I wasn't. After my first date with Hannah, I never touched another woman."

"Fuck," I say. "You were in love with her the whole time."

He looks at me completely unashamed. "I was."

Josh claps him on the shoulder. "I know how that feels. I'm glad you guys worked it out in the end."

Grayson chuckles. "I'm just glad mine wasn't almost an entire decade like yours."

"Touché," Josh says. "Let's circle back, though, are you inviting Zoey?"

I shake my head. "That's a great way to scare her off. *Hey, Zoey. I know we've only gone on one date, but do you want to go house hunting with me?* That is probably the worst thing I could do right now."

Grayson shrugs. "I don't know. She knows you've got a kid, so if you guys are serious, it's basically an instant family. Maybe house hunting won't scare her."

"He's right about her knowing about Jayden. Getting into a relationship with someone who's a parent isn't something most people do on a whim. There's a lot of thought that goes into it," Caleb says.

"And what made you decide to date Bailey even though she had Charlie?"

He smiles. "She made me feel like the risk was worth it. I felt something with her I'd never felt before, and Charlie was just so strong. She had seen so much for a young kid, and was so resilient and happy despite it all. Finding them is by far the best thing that's happened in my life. If I hadn't found them, I wouldn't be growing my family. When I say it's a big deal to date a single parent, I just mean that Zoey thought this out. She didn't just randomly decide and agree to go out with you. She knows if you guys get serious, it's an instant family. So, if you're looking for a house for the long term, maybe taking her with won't scare the crap out of her."

Caleb's coming in with the heavy shit this morning. I grip the back of my neck. "I may already know what she wants in a house."

That surprises them all.

"How do you know that already if you guys just started dating?" Grayson asks.

"We've been friends for a while. Zoey's been coming over to my place ever since Liv and Drew broke up. We worked together in trying to get Josh and Liv to finally tell each other they had feelings, and Zoey occasionally likes to watch home makeover shows and has told me several times about what she hates and what she loves in those houses."

Josh shakes his head. "Why am I not surprised Zoey was involved?"

"Oh, you can't get pissy about it. You married Liv. You have a daughter together."

He holds up his hands. "Not pissy at all. Just should have guessed."

"We should probably get going," Caleb says, and we gather our stuff and head out to our cars. Caleb takes Josh and Grayson, but I don't want to deal with moving the car seat and I don't think the guys would all fit with the car seat in my car, so I drive on my own.

With Jayden strapped to my chest, we walk into the first open house together, and it's nice. The front door opens into an entryway with stairs on the right and a sitting room on the left. We walk further in, and it opens into a large open space.

The kitchen with an island and dining area are on the left, and a large living room with a built-in fireplace is on the right. I walk into the kitchen first, checking the appliances and cabinets. From there, I can see that between the sitting room and kitchen is a dining room. And there's a door off the living room that leads to an office space.

I head upstairs next. This is a five bed, four and a half bath house, with all five of the bedrooms located on the second floor. There are four full baths up here, and the half bath is on the main floor.

Walking into the master bedroom, I take everything in. It's got a large walk-in closet and an ensuite. There are two sets of bedrooms connected with Jack-and-Jill bathrooms and another bath beside the stairs. There's a spacious area at the end of the hall that looks over the backyard and would be perfect to set up a play space. I can see these rooms filled with kids and hear Zoey laughing as she plays with them or see her downstairs curled up with a book in front of the fire.

If I had my way, and I knew I would get this house, I wouldn't go to any of the other open houses. It has everything Zoey has said she'd love to have in a home, and all I care about is the space and that she's happy.

I find the guys gathered in the master suit, and they all look at me when I walk in.

"And?" Josh asks.

"I like it. You?"

"It doesn't feel like Liv's style."

I nod and look at Grayson.

"Too much space. We're not planning on having kids, so we don't need this many bedrooms. How many kids are you planning on having?" he asks.

I shrug. "I don't know, but I want something we can grow in. If it's too big down the line, we can always sell, easier than trying to go bigger later."

Grayson grins and runs his hand down his face as he shakes his head.

"What?"

"You're just saying we. Sounds like you're factoring Zoey into this all."

"I am. I should have asked her out earlier. I'm all in with Zoey."

"After a single date?" Josh asks.

"Yes. After a single date. It's not like I haven't spent hours and hours with her before. Zoey's made me want to stop the endless cycle of women. Her and Jayden have me seriously looking at settling down. I'm not saying I'm going to get down on one knee and propose to her tomorrow. I'm not insane. But I am saying that if I'm taking this seriously, that means factoring her into my future plans. Thinking about what she wants and needs."

The guys nod, and we make our way downstairs. I grab one of the realtors' cards as we head to the cars and off to the next open house. I don't love any of the next houses the way I did the first one. Something about it felt right.

After the open houses, I contact a realtor and we put in an initial offer on the place.

CHAPTER 27

Zoey

I spend so much of my week helping Maggie with getting ready for the gala that I don't see Matt except for our usual Monday and Wednesday mornings. On Friday night, Liv texts and asks me to come over Saturday morning. She'll have breakfast and wants to talk. I tell her I'll be there but spend all night anxious about what she wants to talk about. Liv should know better than to text me that far in advance with an *I want to talk*.

I don't sleep well at all. I'm constantly tossing and turning and even waking up with anxiety. When I finally say fuck it and get out of bed, I throw on some sweats and a comfy shirt and hoodie before grabbing my keys and purse and leaving. If Liv's going to give me anxiety, I'm showing up to her house butt-fuck early to get some answers.

When I pull up to the buzzer pad outside their place, it's 6:30 a.m. Liv doesn't answer the first time, so I buzz a second time and she finally answers.

"Yeah?" her groggy voice comes through the speakers.

"Let me in."

"Zo?"

"Yeah, now let me in."

A sound comes through, and the gate opens. I park quickly and dart to catch an elevator. When I get to their door, Liv is pulling it open before I have a chance to knock.

"What's going on?" she asks, rubbing her eyes.

"Ummm, you texted me last night you wanted to talk this morning."

She stops rubbing her eyes, and they widen. "Oh, fuck." She fully takes me in and wraps her arms around herself. "I'm so sorry, Zo. It was late, and I wasn't thinking. Everything's all good. We're all good."

Some of the tension leaves me, but it won't all leave until I know what's going on.

"Have you eaten anything or had any coffee?" she asks, and I shake my head.

She turns on her feet, and I follow her to the kitchen, where she turns the coffee pot on and starts grabbing ingredients out of the fridge. When the coffee's done, she pours me a cup and adds a healthy dose of flavoured creamer before handing it to me.

"So, really it's both Josh and I who wanted to talk to you. He's still in bed. Cate wasn't feeling well last night, and he stayed up with her."

I nod and watch as she makes her way around the kitchen, making us breakfast. I hear Cate through the baby monitor and collect her from her crib and bring her with me back into the kitchen.

When Liv spots us, she smiles. "Does your Aunty Zo got you?" she says to Cate, and I adjust her on my hip.

"I do. This little girl looks a little snotty." I grab a tissue and give her nose a wipe.

"Yeah, I think she's getting some kinda cold. Josh was standing in the bathroom with the shower on high heat at one point last night. I don't know how he troopered through the whole night, but he did."

Cate's quiet as we sit and watch Liv cook, but she holds on to me pretty tight. When Liv finishes, she plates everything and heads to wake up Josh. He offers me a smile and a good morning when he sees me, but beelines over to take his daughter from me.

"How is my baby girl feeling this morning? Are we feeling better?"

That girl lights up when she's in her daddy's arms. She's still snotty and I can tell she doesn't have her usual energy, but she's happy to be in her daddy's arms. I hand him the tissue from earlier, and he gives her nose a wipe. We eat our breakfast before Josh finally turns to me and starts.

"So, Olivia mentioned you're considering a career change." My eyes flick to her, and Josh steps in. "She only mentioned something because I was telling her about a position I was considering creating and she thought you might be a great fit."

That piques my interest, and Liv's forgiven for spilling that secret.

"I'm looking to create a position that would have someone working with both my company and the Cyclone. In taking over the team, I'm wanting the organization to be more involved in the community and more involved in giving back to the people who have supported the team. I'm looking for someone who can plan and run fundraisers and community outreach events for both organizations. You'd work pretty independent of any other management, reporting directly to me and my VP. As this is a new position, I'm wanting someone who is proactive and can take the lead in coming up with ideas and drumming up interest. Olivia mentioned you've been working with your sister-in-law with the planning of the gala for food banks in the area that's coming up just before Christmas. That with your legal background, I think you'd the perfect person for the position."

I stare at them, dumbfounded. I'm sure not how to wrap my head around this. I've just been offered a position with one of the largest companies in the city and with an NHL team. I'm not into sports, but I know what a big deal that is.

Josh leans forward, resting his arms on the table. "You don't have to accept right away. I know this is a big deal and something you'll want to think over. I'm having my HR department draft a contract, and they'll send it your way to review. If you have any issues with it, please let me know. And know I won't be upset or offended if you don't want the job, but I do agree with Liv that you'd be a great fit."

"I don't know what to say."

Liv reaches forward and squeezes my hand. "Like Josh said, you don't have to say anything right now. When he first mentioned it to me, I immediately thought of you. We wanted to talk to you about it right away, because if you're not interested, he'll need to get the position posted, but it's yours if you want it."

I sit back in my chair, and my mind continues to go a million miles a minute. "I'll review the contract and get back to you as quickly as possible."

"Thanks, Zoey," Josh says. Cate begins to fuss, and he stands and takes her from Liv and paces with her.

"No, thank you."

My first thought now is I want to tell Matt. I want to share this with him. I won't make any decisions until I read the contract, but my gut instinct is to take it. Even if it's something I only do for a short time, it will be great for my resume, and it will also be an opportunity to help people. If I'm given complete control, like Josh said, I'd be able to help people like my parents. That hits me like a ton of bricks. I never thought I'd be able to do that, and I may have just had the most amazing opportunity dropped in my lap.

I stand and hug Liv, squeezing her tight and whispering, "Thank you," before I head to my car then head straight to Matt's.

Someone recognizes me and lets me into the building, even though I know they shouldn't, and I jog towards the elevator, excitedly hitting the up button. When I get to Matt's door, I stop myself from banging on it like a fool and knock at a respectable volume.

Matt opens the door with a look of confusion, but when he sees me, he lights up. "Hey, Bug."

"Hey."

We stare at each other for a second before he reaches for my hand and pulls inside, closing the door behind me.

"I missed you," he whispers as he wraps his arms around my waist and mine come up and around his neck.

"Me, too."

He leans down to kiss me, and I feel like a giddy schoolgirl when his lips meet mine. He kisses me lazily, like he's not looking for anything more from me than this kiss right here, and that means everything. He's proving over and over that he's respecting my boundaries.

When he breaks the kiss, he rests his forehead on mine and asks, "What's up? I'm sure you didn't come here just to kiss me."

I grin up at him. "And what if I did?"

He grins right back. "That would make me a very happy man."

"Well, as much as I would do that, I didn't today."

Matt takes my hand, and I follow him to the couch. He sits in the corner and pulls me down beside him, and I instinctively curl into his side as his hand comes to my hair and he runs his fingers through it.

"So, ah, Josh offered me a job."

His fingers only pause for a second before they continue making their way through my hair. "What kind of job?"

The excitement is radiating through me all over again. "It's a new position. It's one that would be in charge of community outreach and fundraising. I would be working with both Josh's company and the Cyclone. I'd be able to put my law degree to work with my understanding of contracts, and"—I sit up and turn to look at him —"I'd also be able to help make a difference in the community."

"That sounds amazing, Bug. I'm so happy for you."

I lean back into his side, wanting to open up to him some more, but not sure if I can do it while looking at him. "I think I'd want to do something to help people like my parents. People who are victims of addiction. I wasn't able to help them when I was a kid. Really, I didn't notice much of it back then. Henry and the boys kept me pretty well guarded from all of that until I was in high school." I take a deep breath, fighting my tears, and lean into Matt more when he starts massaging my scalp. "Maybe we can do something for children of people with addiction, ones who don't have family the same way I did who were there to protect me."

Matt kisses the top of my head and holds his lips there. "You're so strong, Bug," he whispers against my hair, and his words break a dam I didn't know I was holding together with every last piece of my will. It crumbles, and my tears fall.

"I missed them so much as a kid. I was always wondering why Mommy and Daddy didn't love me, why they didn't want to spend time with me. I loved my brothers, I still do, but it was never the same. I was the youngest, so I always wondered what I did to make them never want to be home. I got to see how much your parents love Liv and you and Gi, and all I wanted was that love from my parents."

Matt pulls me in tighter.

"As I got older, I realized it wasn't my fault, but it always felt like something was missing. Like I'd never be complete until my parents loved me."

"Oh, Bug. I'm so sorry you went through that. I'm sorry I never knew you were experiencing all of that. You need to know you're so loved in the world. You have so many people in your corner."

A sob leaves me, and he whispers, "Come here."

I move and straddle his lap as he wraps his arms around my waist and holds me so tight it's as though he's willing all my fragile little pieces to stay together. I cry into his shoulder, allowing all of this pain to leave me. I can't remember the last time I cried about my parents. It was probably after my high school graduation. I wasn't surprised when they didn't show up for my college or law school graduations. After high school I built this wall to avoid any disappointment and hurt when it comes to them, but it seems as if it only held for so long.

Matt whispers, "You're so strong," and, "I've got you," into my ear as he rubs a hand up and down my back. After a few minutes, my crying stops and I just hold him, taking comfort in his arms.

When I hear Jayden through the baby monitor, I'm immediately off his lap and making my way to Matt's bedroom. "I need baby cuddles," I say, and Matt nods.

The joy on Jayden's face when I lean over his crib helps to slowly patch that wall. I make a face as I pick him up, and he giggles. I smell his diaper right away and quickly change him before we join Matt.

"Someone left a little gift when I grabbed him, but he's all taken care of now and I think we're ready for some nom-noms."

Before heading to the living room, I grab a jar of puree out of the cabinet. I give him a partial bottle before I get him settled in his highchair and feed him a few bites. He seems to really love mushy peas, not sure why because that just sounds gross, but you do you, boo.

When he's done and I've burped him, we join Matt on the couch who's been watching us this whole time. Matt walks his fingers up Jayden's tummy, and he giggles.

"You're so good with him," Matt muses.

"He makes it so easy. If only all kids were as easy as him."

Matt nods slightly. "Do you want kids?"

I smile. "One day, yeah. I'd love a house full of them. I may have had crappy parents, but I loved growing up with my brothers." I turn to face him. "Do you want more kids?"

"I did before." He tucks a piece of hair behind my ear. "But with you? One hundred percent. As many as you want."

I blush. "A little forward and early to be asking me to give you kids," I joke.

He grins and shakes his head a little, like he thinks I'm funny. "I'm all in, Zo. I'm not holding anything back. I'm not asking for them now. I just want you to know I'm on the same page."

"You, Matthew James Carter, are surprising me."

He strokes my cheek, and Jayden reaches for his hand. We both chuckle before his attention returns to me.

"Only in good ways, I hope."

I nod. "Only in good ways."

He places a soft kiss on my lips and takes Jayden from me before lying on the ground with him. I didn't plan to spend my entire day with them, but that's exactly what I find myself doing. Playing games and laughing with these two boys who are slowly changing my life.

CHAPTER 28

Matt

I drop Jayden off with my mom Saturday morning. She wanted to take both Jayden and Cate for the weekend. She loves being a grandma and having both Dad and Gi at home means it's been pretty easy for her to handle them both. I'm never going to complain if Mom wants to take Jayden. It gives me time to feel a little more human and hopefully get some one-on-one time with Zoey.

I texted her last night asking if I could pick her up this morning. She's waiting outside when I pull up to the house. I get out and meet her at the front of the car, kissing her before I open the passenger door for her. I got to see her for a brief time on Monday and Wednesday morning, but she couldn't stay late because she had promised to help Maggie with the gala, so I reluctantly had to drop her off right after breakfast. I never realized how much I could miss a person until Zoey. Of course, I missed Gianna when she went to school in California, but that was different in a way. I love my sisters, but I don't need to spend every day with them. With Zoey, I want to spend all my free time with her. Even if we're doing meaningless tasks, I want to be in the same room as her.

She's so enthralled with the story she's telling me she doesn't even notice I'm driving us into Caleb's neighbourhood. I pull into the driveway of the house and turn the car off, and she finally notices where we are.

"Where are we?" she asks, confused.

"Come with me," I say and get out of the car.

She meets me at the front, and I take her hand, walking up to the house. I fish a key out of my front pocket and unlock the front door. Zoey doesn't say anything as I lead her inside. I take her straight to the kitchen and watch as her eyes widen and she spins in a small circle in the middle of the open space.

"Whose is this?" she asks.

"Mine."

She stops and stares at me. "What do you mean it's yours?"

"I mean, I came to an open house a couple weeks ago with the guys, put in an offer the same day, and the sellers accepted. They were trying to sell so they could move to the interior of BC. They wanted to be there before Christmas, so we were able to do a quick closing, and as of 5 p.m. last night, this place is mine."

"It's gorgeous."

I walk up behind her and wrap my arms around her, resting my chin on top of her head as she leans into me. I point towards the dining room. "There's enough space in there for a large table to host big group dinners. The kitchen has tons of space. There's a walk-in pantry beside the fridge." I turn us to face the living room. "There's a nice office space through that door and the fireplace has been serviced and is good to go." I grab her hand and lead her up the stairs to the open space that overlooks the backyard. "This is a great place for toys, and I could build a play set for Jayden in the backyard." I excitedly take her through the rooms, pointing things out to her, ending in the master bedroom. I had a new bed delivered and set up early this morning, and it sits in the middle of the room. They were nice enough to put the new bedding I bought from them on it, too.

"I wanted you to be the first person I showed this place to," I say.

She turns and faces me. "It's amazing. There's so much space and the backyard is amazing for Jayden. It must be nice for you to know you'll get your room back, too. I know you love Jayden, but having him in your room must not be the greatest."

I pull her into me. "It will be nice."

Her arms wrap around my neck. "I see you were very proactive about getting a bed set up in here."

I grin. "I wanted an upgrade. You should feel it, it's gonna be the best sleep of your life."

She raises a brow. "Of *my* life?"

"Oh, Bug, you've got to know I plan to have you spending many nights in that bed."

Her fingers play with the hair at the base of my skull as her eyes take on a mischievous glint. "And how exactly do you see me spending my nights in that bed?" She smirks, and it goes right to my cock.

"I was thinking some nights would be my head between your thighs, some would be you riding my cock, definitely have to have you on all fours as I fuck you from behind."

She pretends to ponder that for a second, with her finger on her chin. "I don't know, do you think you've earned all of that?"

I stare at her, my expression a mix of serious and playful. "And how do I earn that?" I release my hold on her and take several steps back, giving her plenty of space. "Tell me what you want, Zo. Tell me what you need. Do I need to drop to my knees to earn just a little taste of you?"

Her skin is flushed now, and her breathing has quickened. I'm hard as a rock thinking about where this could go. I've never been submissive in any way in the bedroom. Giving up control means handing someone complete trust, and you can't do that in one-night stands. I wholeheartedly trust Zoey, and I know she understands that when I drop to my knees and her eyes widen as her pupils dilate.

"Should I crawl to you and beg for a taste of your pussy?"

She visibly swallows, and I take pleasure in her nod. I drop to my hands and slowly crawl across the floor. Her breathing accelerates the closer I get.

When I stop in front of her, I slowly drag my hands up the outside of her legs.

"Zoey, I want you. I *need* you."

She bites her bottom lip, and I continue to slowly drag my hands up her legs.

"I want to peel these jeans off you and see what pretty pair of panties you have waiting for me before I help you out of those and taste your perfect cunt."

Her head falls back as a small moan leaves her. When she looks back down at me, my eyes are waiting for hers. My fingers move to the button of her jeans, and I wait for an answer. She nods, and I slip the button through the hole and pull the zipper down, taking my time as the sound of the zipper opening fills the room. My heart rate and breathing increases as I slowly pull her jeans down. I savour each inch of skin I expose, inhaling sharply when I see the deep-red lace panties she's wearing. I've seen Zoey in bikinis before, but this is much different. I'm the one who gets the pleasure of revealing all her skin. I'm the one who's going to get to taste what she's got underneath these sexy-as-sin panties.

I lean forward and place gentle kisses on her thighs. When I've got her jeans to her ankles, I help her lift each foot and gently slide them off. I sit back on my heels, my eyes raking up her legs slowly and up to her face, taking her in. She's fucking gorgeous standing in front of me in a T-shirt and lace panties. Holding eye contact, she slowly pulls her shirt over her head, revealing the matching bra that's holding her gorgeous tits. I lick my lips. This woman has me absolutely ravenous.

I reach for the waist band of her panties and ask, "May I?"

Her responding, "Yes," is breathy and such a turn on.

I pull them down her legs, helping her step out of them before encouraging her to spread her legs for me, and she does. I grab her right foot and place my lips on her ankle, taking my time as I drag them up her leg and watch goosebumps erupt over her flesh. When I drag my lips across her hips, a whispered, "Oh, God," escapes her.

I grin up at her. "Are you wet for me, Bug? When my fingers play with your pretty little cunt, will they find you weeping for me?"

"Yes."

"Have I finally earned the right to taste and fuck you?"

"Yes, please, yes. Please, Matthew."

I groan at her use of my full name. My fingers find her centre, and she's fucking soaked. I push two fingers inside, and her pussy willingly accepts every inch of them. I crook them towards her G-spot, and she drops her head back as her hips buck.

"Fuck," she moans.

"Do you like that, Zo? Do you like it when I finger-fuck this perfect pussy?"

"Yes," she moans.

I pull my fingers out, and now she's moaning, "No," as her head comes forward and she looks at me. I stick my fingers in my mouth, making a show of how much I'm enjoying having her taste on my tongue.

"You taste like the perfect mix of heaven and sin, and I could die a happy man with your taste on my tongue." I lean forward, looking up at her. "But now I'm going to taste you direct from the source."

My tongue slowly tastes her, and the groan that leaves me is feral. She's the best thing I've ever tasted. As my tongue works faster, her legs begin to quiver. I suck her clit into my mouth, and her hand finds my hair, holding it tight. I don't mind the little bit of pain it causes; it only goes to show how much she's enjoying my face between her legs.

My fingers join in, and she leans back, bracing herself on the edge of the bed.

"Don't you fucking come, Zoey. Don't you dare fucking come. When I finally get you to shatter, it will be with me balls deep inside you."

She shakes her head, her grip on my hair tightening. "Matt, I need to come. I'm gonna come."

I slow my fingers inside her. "Should I stop?"

"No, please no." She's panting as her hips buck, trying to get more from my fingers.

"Are you going to be my good girl and not come?"

She looks down at me with the most desperate look I've ever seen. "Matthew," she whines. "I want to come. I *need* to come."

I remove my fingers, and she whines as I suck them off and stand. I reach behind her and deftly undo her bra, letting it fall to the ground. Cupping her breasts, I run my thumbs over her hardened nipples. "You have the most perfect tits."

She bites her bottom lip as she tips her head back and leans against the bed more. I lean down and wrap my lips around her nipple, using my tongue to flick over it before sucking on it.

"Ahhh, Matt."

I grin against her skin before moving to her other nipple, doing the same. She's perfectly on edge, her legs can barely hold her up anymore.

"On the bed," I demand, and she quickly scrambles onto it. She watches as I slowly remove my shirt and then my jeans and boxer briefs, grabbing my wallet out of my pocket and retrieving one of the condoms I stashed in there. I hold eye contact with her as I rip it open and slowly roll it down my cock before climbing between her legs. I slowly kiss up her stomach and between her breasts until I'm hovering over her.

"Are you sure?" I ask, and she cups my face.

"Yes. Please, Matthew. Fuck me."

Reaching between us, I grip my cock and run it between her folds before playing with her clit.

She grips my arm, her nails digging in. "I said fuck me."

"With pleasure," I groan as I push inside her. She's fucking tight, and I dip my head between her neck and shoulder as I wait for her to adjust. "Breathe for me, baby."

She nods, and I feel her breath against my shoulder. She relaxes, and I push in further.

"You're doing so well," I praise, and she relaxes even more. I push the rest of the way in and hold myself up and stare down at her. "Fuck," is all I manage before my lips are on hers and I'm kissing her. Our tongues fight for control, and I give her more in this kiss than I've ever given anyone. If Zoey wanted to destroy me, I'd let her. I'll let her do whatever the fuck she wants to me as long as she gives me a small slice of herself that only I get to experience.

Her legs come up and wrap around me, and I pull out slowly before thrusting back inside her. She moans into my mouth, and I devour it. I start out slowly, letting her fully adjust to me before I pick up the pace and truly fuck her. She claws at my back the faster I go. She moans, "Yes," into my mouth, and it only drives me on. I slowly pick up the pace and fuck her harder.

I break the kiss, panting, my lungs burning, and I try to get air, but I can't stop. I need her to come. I need to watch her fall over the edge all because of me. I feel her tighten around me, and I trap her bottom lip between my teeth, giving it a slight pull before releasing it.

"Come for me, Zo. Come on my cock."

That seems to be all she was waiting for, because she explodes around me as her eyes pinch shut, her back arches, and her nails dig into my biceps. She's fucking gorgeous when she comes. A true sight to behold.

I do everything I can to draw her orgasm out longer, enjoying watching her give me everything. It's not until she's spent that I give myself permission to finish. A few long thrusts and I'm emptying myself into the condom.

I hold myself over her as I try to ingrain every part of this image in my mind forever.

I roll off her and pull her with me, kissing her softly. I tuck some of her now sweaty hair behind her ear, and I can't wipe my grin away as I stare at her.

"That was amazing," I say.

She nods against my shoulder. "That it was."

"Stay with me here tonight."

She lifts her head and looks at me. "Here?"

I nod. "I want you here for the first night I spend in this house."

"What about clothes?"

"I have a bag in the car."

"Food? Entertainment?"

"Take-out." I roll her so she's on her back again, and she giggles. It's one of my favourite sounds. I kiss her cheek and down her neck. "And I think you're all I need to keep myself entertained."

She moans softly. "As much as that sounds fun, I'm not letting you completely destroy my pussy by fucking me all day and night."

"I can always eat it, too." I chuckle against her skin.

"You're good at that."

"We can find multiplayer games on our phones, or we can start a fire and bring blankets down and talk. We can find plenty that's not me fucking your brains out to keep us entertained." I nip her shoulder.

"Okay."

I climb off the bed and find the bag they left when they delivered the bed and pull out the towels I ordered. "How about a bath?"

Zoey pushes up and looks at me, raising a brow. When she spots the towels, she's clambering off the bed and into the en suite washroom, and I chuckle when I hear the water turn on. I follow her, and when the tub is full, I step into the water, helping her in next and pulling her against my chest.

She closes her eyes as I gently run the backs of my fingers up and down her arm and kiss her temple. She eventually falls asleep in my arms, and I just hold her, even after I'm pruney and the water goes cold. I let my mind wander to what we could make this house look like. How we could spend many more mornings or nights in this bath together, maybe with scented candles, bubbles, and the lights off. How she could leave her mark in every room in this house and how happy that would make me.

When her stomach grumbles, I slowly wake her up.

"Bug," I whisper as I kiss her temple. She stirs a little, but nothing, and I chuckle. "Bug," I say again, a little louder.

"Cold," she moans.

I laugh. "That's because the bath has gone cold.

Her eyes flutter open and widen when she looks down and sees we're still in the tub. She drops her head back and groans. "I fell asleep in the tub. You must be so uncomfortable."

I wrap my arms around her. "I'm fine. Your stomach grumbled, so I'm guessing you're hungry. I didn't bring my phone in here, so if we want to order food, we'll have to get out."

She nods and lets out a breath before using the edge of the tub to push herself up and grabbing a towel to wrap around herself. I do the same and pull the plug.

I unlock my phone and hand it to her. "Why don't you order us something while I go and grab those clothes out of my car."

She nods, and I kiss her nose before heading to the car.

CHAPTER 29

Zoey

I cross my legs as I sit on the edge of the bed and order us some comfort food. I don't want anything too fancy right now, and quite frankly I'm still waking up from that extremely relaxing nap I had in the tub with Matt. I can't believe he let me fall asleep and stayed in there with me. By the time he finally woke me up, the water was freezing and my hands and feet were pruney beyond belief.

I let the app auto pick the address based on GPS and hope it's right. Just as I'm about to lock the phone and put it aside, a text comes through.

HAZEL - RAINCITY PUB

How's my baby boy doing?

I stare at the message, not sure what the hell I'm supposed to do. I know I'm not supposed to respond, but every part of me wants to delete the message and pretend it never came through. The last thing I want is this woman to come back to town and try to take Jayden away from Matt, or even try to take Matt from me. She's the mother of his son. I know Matt was never in an actual relationship with her because he's never done the monogamous thing before, but would he try because she's the mother of his son?

I hear Matt jog up the stairs, and when he stops at the end of the bed and sees me, his grin drops.

"What's wrong?"

I clutch his phone tight in my hands. "Please don't be mad."

He drops the bag on the end of the bed and climbs on beside me. "Bug, what's up?"

I take a deep breath. I've never been one to back down, and I'm not going to now. Even if the answer hurts me. "When I finished ordering food, a text came through. It was Hazel asking how her baby boy was doing, and assuming you aren't into that kink"—I force a laugh—"I assume she means Jayden, and I wanted to delete the message. I didn't, it's still there, but I got angry and insecure and wanted you to not see it." I turn and face him more fully. "I don't want her to take Jayden from you, and I don't want her to take you from me. I only just got you, and you just got your son, and you love him so much, and you're such a good dad."

Matt's grinning at me like a fool while I'm over here having a mini freakout in nothing but a towel on his brand-new bed.

I give his arm a shove. "Why are you grinning at me like that?"

"Only just got me?"

I scoff. "That's what you pulled from that?"

He shrugs. "Right now, that's the only important thing I caught."

"What about her trying to take Jayden from you?"

He tucks a piece of hair behind my ear and strokes my cheek. "Bug, when she first dropped Jayden off, I made sure I got certified copies of her signing her rights away. The courts don't typically terminate parental rights in Canada, but I made sure there's a copy with a lawyer, with my parents, with Josh and Liv, with Caleb, with Grayson, and I have one. The original is in a safe deposit box. I wasn't risking her trying to take him away. I will fight her tooth and nail if she tries anything. But I love that you're so worried about that. I love that you care so much about Jayden."

"I love him," I whisper, and he kisses me softly.

"I know. And you're not losing me either."

I look up at him through my lashes.

"Zoey, you have me completely."

I hug him, and we fall back onto the bed. My stomach makes noise again.

Matt laughs. "My girl is hungry."

"Food's on the way."

He goes to roll away, and I tighten my hold on him. "Hold me for a bit longer," I beg, and his arm is immediately back around me and he kisses my forehead.

When the doorbell rings, I finally release him, and he slides off the bed, dropping his towel. I stare as he pulls on a pair of shorts, and he just shakes his head at me before jogging down the stairs. I grab a set of clothes out of the bag, loving how they smell like him and are so baggy on me. I meet him downstairs with the blankets from the bed, and we move in front of the fireplace. The sellers must have left their leftover wood, because there's a nice stack beside the fireplace that Matt uses to start a fire.

When he's done, I open the food and hand him his burger and take my chicken strips and we watch the fire crackle. When we finish, I stare at him, a fantasy filling my mind as the firelight flickers across his face. I crawl towards him, and desire fills his gaze.

"Ever fucked in front of the fire?" I ask.

He shakes his head.

"So, what do you say to me riding your cock right here?"

"Fuck yes," he moans.

I grin at him. "But first I'm going to ride your face."

I don't even have all my words out before he's ripping his shirt over his head and tossing it to the side. The second I'm close enough, his hand comes to the back of my head, and he fists my hair and pulls me in for a kiss. Kissing Matt is like fireworks every time. The second his lips find mine, my entire body lights up. Every sense is heightened, and I feel like I may just explode. It's a feeling I've never experienced before.

I straddle his lap, and he pulls my shirt over my head. I never put my bra back on after the bath, and he takes full advantage, his mouth wrapping around a nipple and pulling it with his teeth. I fall back, propping myself up with hands on his legs as I shove my chest into his face more. His hand comes up to my other breast, and he rolls and pulls my nipple. He's doing exactly what I want without me having to tell him a thing.

I grind my hips against him and moan as I feel how hard he is. I shuffle back, forcing him to release my breast, and shove my sweats down. He takes my cue and pushes his shorts down. He pops free, and I practically salivate at the sight of him. I didn't really get to take in how big he truly is earlier. It hit me like a ton of bricks when he stretched my pussy, though.

"Zo, baby, you can't stare at it like that and not do anything."

I grab hold of him and bring my mouth close to the tip, breathing over it lightly, enjoying the way it makes him shiver. I smirk at him and flatten my tongue as I lick him from base to tip, trying to wrap my head around how I'm supposed to fit this whole thing in my mouth. I tease the tip before wrapping my lips around him and slowly taking more of him. He gathers my hair into a ponytail, and I look up at him.

"You're doing so well, baby."

His praise only pushes me to try to take more. Tears gather at the corners of my eyes, and he wipes them away. "Relax your throat for me. You've got this."

I do as he says, and I fit more of him in my mouth.

"You look so good with your mouth full of my cock. So pretty crying as you take me."

My eyes roll to the back of my head, and my pussy pulses. I need something. My hand snakes between my legs, and my finger finds my clit, causing me to moan around him.

"Fuck, baby, you look so hot right now." He runs his hand down my back, and I love the feeling of him touching me. "Shuffle over, I want to watch you finger your cunt while you suck my cock."

I release him from my mouth, saliva dripping down my chin, and shuffle so I'm perpendicular to him then suck on the tip of his cock. He leans back on his hands and groans.

"You're such a mess right now. You're dripping down your thighs and drooling all over me."

I take more of him in my mouth than I have and remember to relax, trying to take all of him. He moans and mutters obscenities, and pride radiates through me. His thighs tense, and he begins to grow in my mouth, and I release him with a pop.

"Should I tell you not to come, like you did to me earlier?"

He's lying flat on the ground now, shaking his head. "No, make me come, Zo."

I give him a couple of pumps. "But won't the orgasm be so much better if my pussy is wrapped around your cock?"

"God, yes, but I just want to come."

I release him and shuffle closer to his head. "If you want to come, you're gonna eat."

"You're a fucking dream, Zo. Give me that pussy."

I straddle his face and lower myself until his tongue dips inside me, and I moan. Dropping forward, I grip his cock again and lick him, taking my time before taking him as deep in my mouth as I can and sucking. He bucks, and his grip on my hips tightens. I do it again and take great joy in his response.

"You don't come until I do," I tell him, and his fingers immediately join his efforts. It's a lot of work trying not to lose myself completely in the pleasure he's bringing me right now and remember to actually get him off. I feel my orgasm building. I'm close. Just as I'm about to fall over the edge, I release him from my mouth, and tremors rack my body. When the orgasm subsides, I take him again, rolling his balls, and he comes, filling my mouth. I swallow everything he gives me.

I roll off him and work to catch my breath. Matt crawls up my body, grinning, and kisses me, neither of us turned off by tasting ourselves. In fact, I think it spurs him on more as his tongues sweeps through my mouth.

He breaks the kiss and hovers over me. "You on birth control?"

I shake my head. "No, it fucks with me too much."

He nods and pushes up and runs to the stairs so quickly I'm surprised he doesn't trip. He comes back with a strip of condoms, already tearing one open and rolling it down his already hard cock. He lies back down and motions to me.

"Come ride my cock, baby."

I scramble towards him, straddling him as I lean down and kiss him. I reach between us and position him at my entrance before I slowly sink down. The stretch isn't as bad as it was this morning, but he's still bigger than I'm used to. When I've taken all of him, his hands find my hips as I roll mine.

"God damn, you look fucking perfect," he moans.

I fall forward, my hands landing on his chest as my hair creates a curtain around us. He bends his legs and thrusts up into me.

"*Fuck!*" I moan.

I'm wound tight, but I'm just not getting over the edge. I lean back, holding myself up on his legs.

"Play with my clit, and suck on my tits, Matt."

He doesn't hesitate. "Yes, ma'am."

Holy shit, that goes straight to my pussy. I enjoy giving instructions and being in charge, but I've never had someone say that to me before, and it does things to me.

"Fuck, you like that, baby. Your pussy just squeezed the hell of out me." He pulls my nipple between his teeth and increases the pressure on my clit. "Should I call you ma'am more?"

I squeeze him again.

"Will you make a mess of me if I do? Should I beg to come?"

Everything he's saying is getting me closer and closer.

"Do you like the way I suck your pretty tits, ma'am?"

Dammit, this shouldn't do it for me.

"Am I filling your pussy just the way you want me to, ma'am?"

I pull his hair, and it only spurs him on.

"Ma'am, I want to fill you with my cum."

I shatter, coming so hard I can't hold myself up any longer. Matt wraps his arms around me as he continues to fuck up into me. When the orgasm subsides, he asks, "Can I come, ma'am? Can I please come?"

I nod as another orgasm tears through me, and my vision darkens as little floaties fill it. I feel myself dripping between my thighs and onto him.

"Fuck yes, make a mess of me. You're so pretty when you come." He applies more pressure to my clit, extending my orgasm.

I'm out of breath and my mouth is so dry by the time I finally come down.

"Holy shit, you squirted," Matt exclaims.

"Huh?" My mind has barely returned to me, but after a second, it hits me what he said. "I've never done that before."

He kisses me hungrily. "I'm so fucking glad I'm the one that made you do that. I'm the only one that will make you do that." There's a prideful possessiveness to his voice that turns me on. Not one like he owns me, but like he's proud that I've chosen him. That I've given him this.

I delicately remove myself from his lap and offer him my hand. "We should shower and grab a towel to clean up this mess," I say.

We head upstairs, and while I hop in the shower, he goes back downstairs with a towel and brings back our clothes. I kiss him as I exit the shower and he hops in. We don't have any soap here so it's more of a rinse off and we'll have to shower tomorrow when we each get home.

We spend the rest of the day talking and playing games on our phones. We order takeout again for dinner, and when we call it a night, we curl up in his new bed, and I do truly have the best sleep of my life.

CHAPTER 30

Matt

I manage to convince Zoey to spend the majority of Sunday with me. We lay in bed and talked. We talked about what I'll do if Hazel does come back looking for Jayden. Zoey watched as I texted Hazel that any communication will need to go through my lawyer and gave her his details. I don't want to give her an inch and she then takes a mile, and it ends up biting me in the ass down the road. I'm not risking losing my son, not after I just got him. Jayden deserves consistency. He deserves a loving home, and I plan to do everything in my power to give that to him.

I day dream with Zoey. I tell her about how I want to fill the house with happy kids and hear laughter and running feet; how I want to see a big Christmas tree beside the fireplace and stockings hung. I don't expressly tell her that I'm thinking about all of that with her, but I hope she knows she's the only person I could think about any of that with. Lying in bed with her on my chest as I run my fingers through her hair feels right. It feels natural. Having her this close brings an overwhelming sense of calm to me. I spend every day worried about Jayden and whether I'm doing right by him. Am I raising him correctly? Am I giving him everything he needs? Those thoughts don't just magically disappear when I'm near her, but they don't feel like this weight that's going to crush me if I move the wrong way.

After dropping Zoey off at home, I head to my parents' to pick up Jayden. I tell them about the house I bought and that I'm moving in as soon as possible. When we were doing the open houses, the guys offered to help move when it came to that. I've been packing slowly since the open houses, putting everything I don't need in boxes. I've got a good amount done, and the guys are coming over on Wednesday night to move the furniture. Mom, Dad, and Gi say they'll come help as well, and I leave knowing I have a plan to get all of this done.

Jayden is beat by the time we get home. I'm sure Mom and Gi played with him like crazy, and having Cate there all weekend means he had a play buddy. I put him down and decide to pack a few more boxes. I grab my phone, stick a headphone in, and smile as I pull up Zoey's number. She picks up on the second ring.

"Hi." I can hear the smile in her voice.

"Hi."

We both let silence fill the line, like just knowing the other person is on the other end of it is comforting.

"How's my boy?" she asks, and I grin.

"Oh, I'm just fine."

"Haha, you know who I'm talking about."

I do, and I love that she just called him her boy. The bond those two have amazes me every day. Jayden's favourite toy is the blue stuffed elephant Zoey got him. He swings it from its ear or trunk when he's happy, and I constantly find the thing in his mouth.

"He's beat. He had plenty of fun with his cousin, his Aunt Gi, and Grandma and Grampa. I put him down as soon as we got home. What are you up to now?"

I hear shuffling through the line. "I'm in bed reading. You?"

Images of Zoey lying in bed in sexy pyjamas immediately fill my mind. "I'm packing, but I think the most important question is, what are you wearing?"

She laughs, and the sound fills me with joy. "How about you pack and after each finished box I'll describe something to you, and when you get five done, I just may let you listen to me as I play with my pussy and moan your name as I come."

I groan and brace myself on the counter. "You like to torture me, don't you, Bug?"

"I do, but know it's so much better when I get to do it in person and watch just how needy you get."

"I'll always need you," I say without thinking. Not wanting to freak her out, I move on. "So, I just have to pack a box and you'll describe in detail for me what you're wearing?"

"Uhuh."

I quickly move around the kitchen, packing foods I know I won't use in the next couple of days, and as soon as it's done, I say. "First box, done."

"Good boy," she purrs, and fuck, it goes straight to my cock. I've never enjoyed being called that. It always sounded too much like what you say to dogs. But coming from Zoey's mouth, it turns me on. "I'm wearing a red silk two-piece set. There's lace along the bottom hem of my shorts."

I wait, listening for more details and when nothing comes, I work on the next box, talking to her about random things and trying to keep myself sane. I tell her when the second box is done, and she praises me again.

"When I stand, these shorts barely cover my ass. If I were to bend over, you'd catch a glimpse of it."

"Fuck," I groan, and I swear I hear a slight chuckle from her.

I look at my cabinets and figure I have enough for probably one more box and start tossing it all in a box, barely paying attention to how it goes in. I have to stop myself from shouting "done" when I finish.

"The tank top dusts against my lower stomach, showing you a sliver of skin between its hem and my shorts."

I can picture her lying in bed as she lazily drags her finger over that exposed area, and dammit, I wish that was my finger, or better yet, my tongue.

I move into the living room and start throwing my movies and video games into a box, nothing organized and just haphazardly thrown in.

"The tank top is silk, but it's lace around my breasts. Only my nipples are covered by a tiny triangle of silk."

"Woman, you're killing me."

"One more box, and I'll make it worth your while."

Standing in the centre of my living room, I try to figure out what to pack next, and my eyes catch on the throw blankets I've grabbed over time for Zoey. Those will easily and quickly fill a box. I throw them in and plop myself on the couch.

"You really are a needy boy, aren't you, Matthew?"

"Fuck yes, Zoey. I need to hear you."

"I think you're missing something," she purrs.

"Please, Zoey. Please let me hear you come." I sound like a desperate fool, but I am, and I don't care if she knows it.

"Good boy. I'm taking my pyjamas off now and grabbing one of my trusted little helpers out of my drawer."

I moan.

"What would you to do to me if you were here, Matthew?"

That's a very easy question to answer. "I'd spread your legs nice and wide to get a look at your perfect pussy. Would I find you wet for me, Zo?"

"Soaked."

"I'd slowly fill you with two fingers as I watch your face. I love the look on your face when I fill you."

"Mmhmmm."

"I'd suck on your clit until your hand is in my hair." I'm as hard as a rock. I push my sweats and boxer briefs down and grip my cock, giving it a long stroke. "What are you doing right now, Zo?"

"I have two fingers in my pussy. I'm imaging they're yours. And a clit sucker on my clit, imagining it's your mouth."

"Is that how you'd want to come? Do you want to drown me in your cum?"

"Yes," she moans, and my hand picks up speed.

"Do you think I could get you to squirt all over my mouth? Would you make a mess for me to clean up?"

"Matt."

"Play with your nipples, baby. I want to hear you come."

"What are you doing, Matt? Tell me."

"My hand's around my cock, but it's no substitute for your perfect pussy."

She moans, and I move my hand quicker.

"*Fuck*, I can't wait to get my hands on you again. I want nothing more than to keep you tied to my bed until I've had my fill of you."

"I think I'll be the one doing the tying up."

Everything Zoey says turns me on. This woman has me wrapped around her little finger, and I'm not even mad about it. If she says jump, I'll ask how high.

"You can do whatever you want to me, Zoey, as long as I get to watch you come."

"I'm close, Matt. I'm so close."

"Come for me, baby."

I hear her shatter through the phone, my name on her lips, and it sends me over the edge. As I gather myself, I listen to her breathing return to normal and her satisfied hum.

"I miss you," I admit, and she chuckles.

"You saw me this morning."

"I know. I still miss you." I don't know why. I should be able to go a day without seeing her and be okay, but I'm not. I wish I could drive over there right now and slide into bed with her and pull her to my chest. I want to bury my nose in her hair as I fall asleep.

Her pause has me on the cusp of freaking out that I've just gone and put my foot in my mouth and screwed this all up, but she eventually whispers, "I miss you, too."

"I'll see you in the morning, though," I say, more as a reassurance to myself than anything.

"Bright eyed and bushy tailed."

It's my turn to laugh, because that's the exact opposite of what she'll be. "No, you won't, but that's okay because it's you. I should let you get some sleep. Sleep well, Bug."

"Sleep well, Matt."

I keep my headphone in, waiting to hear the click of the call ending, and smile when I realize just how long it takes her to actually end the call.

I head into the washroom and clean myself up before climbing into bed, looking forward to getting to see Zoey first thing in the morning.

CHAPTER 31

Zoey

When Matt told me a few days ago he'd be moving on Wednesday, I thought it was going to be some huge undertaking. I hated moving my apartment, and I didn't have furniture to move, but with everyone showing up to pitch in and all the vehicles available, we got everything out pretty quickly.

And of course, because it's moving day, Jayden's been extremely fussy. Even this morning when I met them at the rink, he wasn't acting like his normal self. He didn't want to be in his car seat at all while we were there and only wanted to be in the carrier on my chest. He slept quite a bit when we went to Matt's afterwards to do some final packing before everyone came over to help.

I'm upstairs stocking Jayden's change table when Matt's voice comes from downstairs. "Bug!"

I stop what I'm doing immediately and rush down stairs where Matt has Jayden strapped to his chest as he paces and rubs Jayden's back. Jayden is crying, his face red as he tries to communicate whatever he's feeling. Matt looks beyond stressed.

"What's up?"

Some of Matt's panic fades when he sees me. "Have you seen his elephant? He won't stop."

"I put him in my purse so we didn't lose him," I say as I walk around him to the kitchen island. I join Matt at his side with the stuffy and dance it for Jayden. He starts reaching for it, but when I give it to him, he drops it and reaches for me. I can't read Matt's expression, but he starts to hand Jayden to me, and I take him. Jayden doesn't stop crying, but he calms a little. I bounce him and coo that everything's alright, and slowly, he starts to calm down.

Matt's shoulders slump as he watches me and Jayden. "Thank you. Nothing was working."

Stress and anxiety are coming off Matt in waves, and I need to try to relax him. "I guess I just have that special touch with the Carter men," I joke.

That pulls a smile from him. "That you do."

"I've got him if you want to help everyone bring in the last of the stuff."

He nods and kisses my cheek before heading out the front door. I bend and grab the elephant before continuing to walk and soothe Jayden. He's starting to get stuffy and has some snot collecting below his nose. I look around for a towel or maybe some tissues and, of course, don't find any. Not sure how I'm supposed to find anything when it's all in boxes. I decide fuck it and pull at the sleeve of my long-sleeve shirt and wipe his nose. I'll wash it later.

Once everything is inside the house, Mrs. Carter tries to help unpack the kitchen, Matt and Josh head upstairs to set up Jayden's crib, and Gianna is behind them to unpack as much of Jayden's stuff as possible.

I sit on the couch that's been just pushed against a wall to be out of the way. Jayden's fully asleep right now, and I don't want to disturb him if I don't need to. Liv takes a seat beside me with Cate.

"He's very attached to you."

I smile at her. "I'm very attached to him."

"Which of them?" she asks.

I turn my head to face her, and she's got a serious expression. It has my mind racing, because my first instinct is to say both. I'm now so attached to both Matt and Jayden that I'm not sure I see my life without either of them. If you had asked me a few months ago if I saw myself as someone who would join a ready-made family, I'd have told you no, I wanted to build my own. But I feel about Jayden the same way I think I would my own children. I want to help give him the world. I want to be there to support him in every adventure he tries and to help pick him up every time he falls. I'm scared as hell about how much I care for this little guy and even more scared for how deeply I care for Matt. It's like he's managed to dig up all these feelings I've had all this time that were buried so deep I didn't even know I had them. I knew I had crushed on him, but this isn't just some crush. These are life is better, breathing is easier, feels like anything is possible feelings.

I can't look at Liv right now. I don't need her pushing and trying to get more out of me than I'm ready to admit right now. I need time.

"Both," I whisper, hoping it's enough to satisfy her for now. Of course, my best friend can read me. She reaches out and squeezes my arm but doesn't say anything. She scoots closer, and I lean into her, two babies asleep on us as we take in everyone moving around helping Matt get settled.

The guys and Gi come downstairs, and everyone gathers in the living room.

Matt takes a seat beside me and runs his hand over Jayden's back. "Thanks for all your help, guys. I appreciate it."

Everyone nods or says, "of course," and Matt shakes their hands and hugs them before everyone leaves.

"We should get this little one in his bed. He's out like a rock," I say, and Matt nods before following me upstairs.

The guys and Gi did really well getting Jayden's room set up as much as possible. I lay Jayden down in his crib and stare down at him for a minute, taking in his cuteness. He's a little snotty again, so I wipe his nose with my sleeve again before whispering, "Goodnight, little guy," and leaving his room.

Matt and I are silent as we make our way down the stairs and I grab my purse.

He wraps his arms around me and pulls me in close. "Is there any way I could convince you to spend the night with me?"

"I have some things to do in the morning with Maggie, and I don't have any clothes here."

"Maybe we should change that," he says, a soft smile on his lips.

"Which part? My plans with Maggie or the clothes?"

"The clothes. Why don't you bring some stuff here? The closet is plenty big enough, and I want you spend more time here."

"So, we're at the I have a drawer phase, then?"

He seems to contemplate his words for a minute before he asks, "Is that where you want us to be?"

Something about it sounds so right. Matt and I spent so much time as friends that when we moved into dating, it just felt natural. Now I constantly want to be around him. I've slept the best I have in a while when I've been in his bed. A drawer would be the next logical step.

I nod, and he grins like a freaking fool, but I love that he's that excited about my answer.

"So, the next time you come over, bring a bag. Bring as much as you want."

"Don't you know to never trust a girl with your closet," I tease.

"I'd let you take the whole thing if you wanted it."

The genuineness of his words hits me, and I fall even more for him. Matt's in this. He's not pushing me away or looking for an out. He's in it.

He smiles at me and shakes his head.

"What?" I ask.

He drags his teeth over his bottom lip. "Just something Liv said when she left today."

I chuckle softly knowing it could be anything when it comes to Liv. "What did she say?"

"She said you're taming me. Got me all domesticated and shit."

I grin up at him. "Well, I'm glad I'm the one taming you."

His smile matches mine. "Me, too."

He kisses me softly, and I hum against his lips as I lean into him. I fight the desire to stay wrapped in his arms.

"I should get home, but I'll talk to you tomorrow," I whisper, and he nods.

"Text me when you get home."

Matt doesn't release me until I agree, his protective side needing to know I'm safe.

I groan as my phone rings Friday morning. I roll over and see the time on the screen. It's only 6 a.m. Matt's name and picture fill the screen. I know Matt wouldn't be calling me this early if it wasn't important.

"What's wrong?" I answer.

"Jayden's sick. Like super sick. I have no idea what I'm doing." Matt is freaking out.

"Okay. He's going to be okay. Let me get up, and I'll be over as soon as I can."

"Thanks, Zo."

"Of course. Everything is going to be fine."

Matt sighs and says, "Okay."

I hang up and throw a few extra things in my partially packed bag I had sitting on my reading chair. I quickly change into some clothes and rush out of the house and over to Matt's.

CHAPTER 32

Zoey

When I finally get to Matt's, he looks like he's on the verge of a breakdown. Jayden is screaming at the top of his lungs, and I don't think Matt's slept a wink, which means Jayden probably hasn't either. The look of utter relief on his face when he sees me has my heart breaking and soaring at the same time. Breaking because he looks so lost and soaring because just seeing me can bring him relief when he needs it most.

Without thinking, I go on my tiptoes and kiss him before wrapping my arms around him and holding him. His entire body is rigid, like he's been wound so tight for so long he's not sure how to relax. When his arms do wrap around me, some of the tension leaves his body.

"He's going to be okay," I whisper, and he nods against me.

When we finally pull apart, I head into the living room where Jayden is in his jolly jumper. He looks so unhappy. As soon as he sees me, he's reaching for me. I pick him up and hold him close and can tell he has a slight fever. I ask Matt for the thermometer, and he brings it to me, telling me he took it earlier and it was one hundred and one degrees, so not in the hospital zone, but still warm. I take it again and get the same reading.

Matt sits on the couch with his head in his hands. I feel like he may break.

After a few minutes, he takes a deep breath and runs his hands through his hair. "He's blowing out almost every diaper. I've changed him a few times and gone through almost all of his clothes because if he didn't have a blowout, he's puked. It's been like this since 1 a.m. He woke up screaming, and I just haven't been able to get him to calm down."

I tilt my head to look at Jayden as I continue rubbing my hand over his back. "Are we sick, little man? We're gonna get you all better." I turn to Matt. "I've got him. Why don't you throw his dirty clothes in the wash? He seems congested, too, so I'm going to take him to the bathroom and turn the shower on."

He nods, and I head upstairs to one of the bathrooms and turn the shower on to high, waiting for the bathroom to fill with steam. After a few minutes, Jayden seems to calm a little, but he's still not feeling well. As we step out of the bathroom and Matt comes up the stairs, he pukes all down my front and starts crying.

"Oh, it's okay, baby."

"Shit, I'm sorry," Matt says, and I shake my head.

"It's fine. I brought clothes, they're in my bag in my car. My keys are in my purse, can you just grab the bag for me?"

He's jogging down the stairs before I even finish. I take Jayden into the kitchen to see if I can maybe get him to eat some puree so we can keep something in him. He's not happy when I put him in the highchair, but I need to reach into a cabinet to get his food.

When Matt comes back in, he pulls out a shirt and hands it to me. I take mine off, and he takes it from me before taking it into the laundry room. When Matt's done, he picks Jayden up from his highchair, and he calms a little, but he keeps reaching for me. It seems to crush Matt a little.

"Do you want me to leave? Maybe call Liv?" I ask.

"No," Matt rushes out. "I get it. When I was sick, I wanted my mom, too. I love my dad, but it wasn't the same."

I still for a second, the gravity of his words hitting me, and I'm surprised they don't make me want to run. In fact, they make me never want to leave.

I reach for Jayden, and Matt passes him. Jayden calms. "Okay, little man, can you eat a little bit for me?"

I offer him a bite of the pureed carrots, and he takes it. Thankfully, he eats a decent amount before he's had enough and refuses any more.

We're relaxing on the couch with him in my lap when he has a blowout. We spend the whole day doing everything we can to help Jayden. He takes naps on me, never wanting me to put him down, and Matt doesn't leave our side. I finally convince him to take a nap, too, but he does it on the couch. Matt was able to get the TV set up above the fireplace, so I watch movies while the boys sleep.

It's been crazy. I've managed to go through all the clothes I brought with me between the puke and baby poop. Standing in Matt's bedroom, I quickly strip out of my clothes and open his dresser drawers. I grab the first things I find, a pair of his boxer briefs and a T-shirt and throw them on. I pick up my gross clothes and rush them to the washing machine before taking a wailing Jayden from Matt.

Matt's eyes hungrily take me in as I sway Jayden, trying to calm him. Poor Jayden just can't seem to catch a break today. When he finally stops screaming, I feel the tension in the room slip away. My shoulders relax, and I watch as Matt exhales and leans against the wall.

"You look good in my clothes," he says, and my cheeks heat at the same time my stomach growls. It's been so long since I've eaten real food.

"I guess that's my sign to feed you some dinner," he says as he pushes off the wall outside the laundry room and makes his way to the kitchen.

While I'm pacing and rocking Jayden, the doorbell rings and I call out, "I'll get it."

Pulling open the front door, I'm stunned to see my five brothers standing on the other side. They're each holding canvas bags or a six-pack of beer, and Ezra is holding a bottle of red wine. Their eyes are huge as they take me in, and it hits me that I'm standing here holding a baby in a man's clothes.

"*Fuck. Shit,*" I hiss loudly.

"You okay, Bug? Please don't tell me he puked again or had another blowout. I'm not sure we have any more clean onesies," Matt calls, and I turn to watch him round the corner in nothing but a pair of basketball shorts. *Great.*

My brothers' eyes move to him and then back to me, bouncing a few times before they finally settle on me. I feel Matt approach before he offers his hand to my brothers, and they all shake it.

"Hey, guys. It's nice to see you. To what do we owe the pleasure?"

"Well, Zoey didn't show for family dinner," Henry says, his eyes never leaving me as mine bug out. *Fuck.* I had totally forgotten about our sibling dinner we planned with Maggie out of town.

I run my teeth over my bottom lip. "Sorry about that. It's been kinda crazy. How did you even find me?"

John holds his phone up, a giant grin spread across his face. "I guess it's a good thing Henry is Mr. Overprotective and made us all share our locations with the family. It was pretty easy to figure it out once we got on the street and saw your car."

I nod, not sure what else to say.

"You going to invite us in, or not?" Riley says as he lifts the bags in his hand. "We brought food."

"And booze," Kai says, holding up his six-pack.

Matt's hand finds the small of my back. "Yeah, of course. Please come in. I'll get the table set."

"No need, we'll figure it out," John says as he passes.

Henry and Ezra hover while Kai and Riley follow John. They step inside enough that I can close the door from the brisk wind outside.

"Why don't I take him," Matt says, reaching for Jayden, and I quickly turn, moving him out of reach.

"So help me God, Matthew, if you make him cry one more fucking time, I will have your balls." I'm exhausted and cannot deal with any more crying, or vomit, or shit. I don't know how Matt dealt with this for hours by himself this morning, but I'm so tired. I need Jayden to sleep and get better, and if he'll only do that while I hold him, then I'll hold him.

He holds his hands up and takes a step back. "Okay. I'm just going to find the others. Call me if you need me," he says, his eyes darting to Henry and Ezra before he leaves us.

I run a hand over Jayden's back, and he snuggles deeper into me.

Henry and Ezra are both quiet. They've always been this way, and it's one of the things I love most about them. They don't push or speak to fill the space. When Henry does speak, I know I'm in for a conversation I'm not sure I'm ready for.

"A baby." That's all he says, as if that's enough.

"Yup, this is a baby. Way to point out the obvious," I say, rolling my eyes.

"What's going on with the baby?" Henry asks.

"He's sick. He's puked and shit on almost every piece of clothing I brought and a ton of Matt's."

Jayden starts to make the noises he makes just before he goes into a crying fit, so I begin pacing and rubbing my hand over his back as I shush him.

"What are you doing here?" Ezra asks.

"I'm helping Matt. He called me this morning, freaking out about Jayden being sick. He's only calmed down when I've been holding him." I feel their eyes boring into me, tracking my movements in the entryway.

"But, why are you doing it?" Ezra pushes.

"Because he needed help, and I want to."

Both of them give me an as-if expression as Matt comes back to join us. "Hey, Bug, go grab some food, you need to eat."

Jayden fusses again, and I start bouncing him softly. "In a bit," I say.

"No, now, Bug. Even if that means I'm cutting up food and feeding you. You need to eat something."

My stomach growls again, and my mouth waters as the smell of baked pasta and cheese wafts out of the kitchen.

"Fine," I grumble and move in the direction of food, Matt and my brothers hot on my trail.

The dining table is full of food: lasagna, meatballs, salad, garlic bread, roast vegetables, and potatoes. We've always had to make a ton of food when we all eat together, because I swear my brothers can eat enough for an army. I settle in a chair, and Matt takes a seat beside me and starts making me a plate as Ezra and Henry grab a seat. I can honestly say this is not a situation I ever saw myself being in, sitting with Matt and a baby with my brothers at the dinner table.

As Matt places a piece of lasagna on the plate, I ask, "Who made the lasagna?"

"Henry," Kai says, and I nod, satisfied with the answer. The last time Riley was given the responsibility, it was like a giant mouthful of salt.

Supporting Jayden with my left arm, I take a bite of potatoes and moan. The table is full of awkward silence, like no one is sure what to say to start conversation.

"So, this is why you snuck out this morning," Henry finally says in his typical big brother way.

"I didn't realize moving in meant I was reporting to you. Was it really sneaking out?"

"You've seemed to be doing it a lot. Leaving and not saying goodbye. Out super early in the morning and sometimes not coming home for days."

"She's been up early? No way," Ezra says. "She was such a pain to get up for school, always fighting tooth and nail for five more minutes."

"She's been waking up as early as 5 a.m. and out the door before 6 a.m."

All five of my brothers are now staring at me, and I continue eating. I don't owe them an explanation. They're my brothers, not my keepers. It's also not my secret to tell, so I keep my mouth shut, but Matt says, "You can tell them, Bug."

I shake my head. "It's none of their business," I say loud enough they can hear me.

"You're our business, so how is it not?" Riley asks as he continues to shovel more food in his mouth.

"Careful, Ri. You might just choke if you keep eating like that." I look around the table at my brothers. "You guys don't tell me everything about your lives. Why am I required to do so?"

"You're our baby sister," Ezra tries to argue.

I look at John, who's been quiet. "Do they do this to you? Ask you all these questions about your life?"

He shakes his head.

"John's only three years older than me. Why don't you ask him this stuff?"

"Because he doesn't need protecting," Henry says, and my blood starts to boil as I remember our conversation in his kitchen.

"I don't need protecting anymore. I'm an adult, and I'm perfectly capable of deciding who I date and how I spend my time."

"So, you are dating him," Henry pushes.

"I am. I'm also the happiest I've been in a long time." Jayden starts to make noises, and I stand and pace. "You five were there for me as a kid, and I appreciate it endlessly. I know not everyone is as lucky as I was to have five brothers to look after me so I didn't end up in the system, but I'm an adult now. I just need you to support me."

Matt reaches for Jayden, but I don't give him over. While I'm helping him sleep, he's helping keep me calm right now. "Bug, why don't I take him to the other room so you guys can talk?"

I shake my head. "I've got him." My eyes are pleading, and he knows exactly what I mean.

"You're also here on a Friday night taking care of a baby that's not yours," Henry says, and it kind of hurts, because as much as I know Jayden isn't mine, he feels like mine and I want him to be.

"That's my choice. Do you really think I'd be here right now if I didn't want to be?"

Matt rubs my back as I pass him in my pacing, and Henry's attention turns to him. "So you've just dragged my sister into this? What's going on with the kid's mom?"

"He has a name," I interject. "It's Jayden."

Henry notices my tone, nods and returns to his questions. "What is going on with Jayden's mom? Are you just using my sister for a fun time?"

Matt shakes his head furiously. "I would never use Zoey for just a fun time. I respect her too much, and I know that between her and my sister I'd be a very unhappy man if I messed with her like that. Zoey is the only person who has made me want to settle down. I wasn't in any rush to stop having fun and settle down and start a family. Even before Jayden was dropped off, I found myself going out less to spend a night in with Zoey. So, even if Jayden wasn't dropped off, I think we'd be right here eventually."

I stop and stare at him. I never even stopped to realize Matt was spending a lot of weekends with me, and they weren't just when other plans fell through, he was consciously making plans with me.

"Why do you call her Bug?" Ezra asks thoughtfully.

"He called me that as a kid," I say off-handily before resuming my pacing.

"Okay, but why does he call you that now?"

Matt grips the back of his neck, his eyes flashing to me before his attention is focused on Ezra. "As a kid, I called her that because she loved ladybugs and it got a rise out of her. She'd turn this adorable shade of red and say, 'Don't call me that,' but she eventually got used to it, stopped complaining, and it faded. A few months ago, it hit me like a semi just how fucking lucky I am to have her in my life, even if at the time it was just as friends. Zoey makes me feel safe and comfortable, and just *me.* So Bug, like ladybugs, because she is the luck in my life."

I'm crying now. No one has talked about me like that so earnestly. Liv and the girls have always said nice things and helped build me up, but this is different. Matt makes me feel not only needed but wanted, like his life isn't the same without me, and I feel the same way.

Ezra and, surprisingly, Henry nod as though they get it, Riley, Kai, and John are more so focused on eating it's as though they're not even sure why they're here.

Matt looks over at me and is rushing out of his seat, taking my face in his hands. "Please don't cry.

"I don't want to cry," I whisper, and he kisses my nose.

"So why are you crying?"

"Because I never thought I could feel like this. I never thought I could feel so strongly about someone or that they'd feel the same about me. You make me feel seen and wanted."

Matt wipes away my tears, and I close my eyes as I lean into his touch. Jayden hasn't fussed in a bit, and I would love to put him down and see him get some good sleep, so I say, "I'm going to see if he'll be okay in his crib."

"I can take him," Matt offers, but I shake my head.

"I need a minute."

He nods, and I head upstairs.

CHAPTER 33

Matt

I watch Zoey make her way up the stairs. As soon as she's out of sight, I take my seat again. I met Zoey's brothers a few times growing up, but she's talked about them enough that as soon as they showed up, I knew who was who. And right now, I know I need to focus the majority of my attention on Henry and Ezra.

"I don't know how long she'll be up there for and I need to say this before she comes back down. I know you're protective of her. She's your younger sister, and you spent a lot of your life raising her. I get it, I have younger sisters. You guys helped her become the amazing, strong, independent woman she is now. I've told her I'm all in, and now I need you guys to know it, too. I want it all with Zoey. I want the life, the family, the memories. All of it. When she's ready, I want to marry her. It's too soon now. She needs time to let herself come to terms with how she feels about me and how I feel about her. But I will spend the rest of my life making sure she knows she's loved and supported." I sigh, knowing this next part will not be as easy for them to hear. "She told me about your parents."

The shock on all of their faces is visible.

"I need her to know she's in a safe space and loved unconditionally, and I'll always be there for her."

John, who hasn't said anything this entire time, finally says, "She said she's happy and even though she looks like a mess, she seems it."

I grimace a bit at the full realization of what they came into hitting me. "Yeah, I just moved, and Jayden's been sick. He's only wanted Zoey. Like in a cry his head off when she hands him to me kind of way."

Ezra chuckles. "Zoey was that way when she was sick as a kid. She only wanted me. It drove Henry up the wall, kept going on about how he was the one who did all these things for her and she just wanted to curl up in my bed and cuddle and sleep."

Henry grumbles something, and Ezra nudges him with his elbow. "When she didn't feel well, she never came to me. It was usually you or even Kai and Riley. She never wanted me." Henry seems genuinely upset by this.

"Have you ever asked her? I'm sure she'll shoot straight with you if you ask."

The man rolls his eyes at me. "No, I haven't asked my baby sister why she never wanted me when she was sick," he says as though it should be obvious.

"Because I didn't want to seem weak." Zoey's voice comes from the entrance to the dining room. "You were always the strongest of us all. You were kind of forced to be. I didn't want to seem any weaker by needing to cuddle you when I was sick."

Henry does his best to hide the pain, but I see it flash through his expression quickly.

"I know that's dumb now, that you wouldn't see it as weak, but I was a kid." Zoey rounds the table and hugs Henry from behind and kisses his cheek. "If it will make you feel better, the next time I'm sick, I'll climb into bed with you and snuggle."

He pats her arm. "I'll be perfectly fine, Zo."

"My bed is off limits, the number of times you got me sick from your cuddles was insane," Riley says.

"She was always patient X, she'd bring it home and then cuddle us and we'd all be sick by the end of it," Kai says.

She grins at them from Henry's shoulder. "You know you love me."

"Loving you doesn't mean we want your sick cuddles anymore, my bed's off limits, too" Ezra says, shaking his head.

Everyone else, including Henry, says, "Same."

"I forgot she'd pass those things around like free candy," Henry says, and they all laugh.

"That's fine, Bug. You've always got my bed." Now I get her smile, and I can't help but return it.

"Well, thank you. You are the superior cuddler."

John groans, and she shakes her head. Her stomach growls again and I look at her full plate of food. Grabbing it, I head into the kitchen and pop it into the microwave. When it beeps, I bring it back with me into the dining room.

"Come eat, Bug."

She rolls her eyes at me.

"You're hungry and you've been taking care of a sick baby all day. Come eat something."

She finally relents and takes a seat beside me and digs in. Everyone else has finished eating, but this girl prioritized Jayden, a baby who isn't biologically hers, because she was the only person he wanted. I tuck a stray piece of hair behind her ear and feel an overwhelming sense of love for her right now. As I stare at her, I wonder if I've bounced from woman to woman because I've spent the last twelve years in love with my sister's best friend, but had convinced myself I couldn't have her. Did a small piece of me always know this, but because she was always off limits, I subconsciously pushed it to the side so I didn't look into it too much?

I look around the table and know if her brothers weren't here, I'd be blurting the words out right now, but I want those three words to be said when it's just us. When I can not only tell her but also show her.

I've told her before I'm all in, but this is so much more. If I told someone I've caught myself getting pulled in by engagement ring ads and have browsed, getting a sense for what I know she'll absolutely hate and what she'd be more drawn to, they'd think I was crazy. It's like every part of my subconscious has been screaming at me for weeks, months, years, that I love her, but I was too dumb and stubborn to see it. Now that I've realized it, I don't know if I can convince her I'm worth taking a shot at forever with. I don't want to do *just for now* with her. I want everything. I can't wait to watch her grow our children and for us to fill this house with adorable kids.

Zoey looks up at me and raises a brow. "What?"

I shake my head and smile. "Nothing."

"Do I have something on my face?" She grabs a napkin and wipes it.

I shake my head again. "You look perfect."

"You know it's rude to lie," she says.

"Not a lie."

"Whatever."

I lean in close so only she hears me. "Zoey, I wouldn't lie to you. You look perfect. You look like you just spent the day being selfless and took care of a sick baby who has grown so attached to you and loves you so much that you're the only person he wanted. You look like when I called you worried out of my mind about my son being sick, you climbed out of bed and rushed over here. You look perfect."

She avoids saying anything by shovelling another bite into her mouth. I sit back, and her brothers all seem to be in their own conversations, Henry's eyes darting to Zo and I every once in a while.

"What do you want to do tonight, Zo?" I ask.

She looks at her brothers then back at me. "We were supposed to play board games tonight. We used to do it when I was a kid and our parents were having a bad night. Henry would round us all up, and we'd hide in his and Ezra's room and play all night until they went to bed. We've tried to put a fun spin on it as adults."

I brush my hand over the back of her head, hating that they had to do that as kids, but loving that she feels so comfortable telling me. "Board games it is." I turn and face the guys. "Did you guys bring games with you, or should I raid my collection?"

John grins and reaches beside him and plops a bag on the table. "Of course, we brought games. No way could we have a sibling dinner and not play."

"Okay, I'll just get this cleaned up and then we can play," I say, stacking plates.

Ezra pushes back in his seat and helps, following me into the kitchen.

As I start rinsing plates, Ezra says, "I know five older brothers can be a bit overwhelming, and trust me I know how Henry especially can be, but we just want to look out for Zo."

"I get it. I have two younger sisters, and while we may not have grown up the way you guys did, I've always wanted to protect them." I turn off the water and face him, crossing my arms over my chest. "I meant everything I said in there. I will do everything I can to take care of your sister."

Zoey pokes her head out of the dining room, a large grin spread across her face. "Come on, guys, we've got it set up."

I love seeing her like this. She has this way of being the reason people smile and laugh and enjoy themselves without even trying, just by being her. "Coming, Zo."

"I believe you," Ezra says before following Zoey to join their brothers. I quickly make Zoey a cup of tea, knowing she's going to want one soon, and join them. Thankfully, Jayden must have exhausted himself because he doesn't wake up, and we spend the entire night playing games.

CHAPTER 34

Zoey

Even though this was not the way I wanted to tell my brothers about dating Matt, I'm glad we had today. After spending the day with a sick Jayden, playing games with Matt and my brothers was exactly what I needed. I hope my brothers got to see just how happy I am with Matt.

As we finish our last game, I yawn, ready to climb into bed. We all pack up, and Matt and I follow the guys to the front door.

I hug each of them, and Henry asks, "Will I see you at home?"

I look over my shoulder at Matt and shake my head. "I want to be here when Jayden wakes up."

He nods after a few seconds and offers Matt his hand, and they shake. I hug Henry one last time before he follows the boys outside.

I close the door, and Matt's arms wrap around me and he kisses my cheek. "How are you feeling?"

I lean into him, loving being in his arms. "Tired."

He kisses my cheek again and says, "Well, let's get you in the shower and into bed."

I make my way upstairs while Matt makes sure all the doors and windows are locked and turns the lights off. Matt joins me in the shower as I rinse the shampoo out of my hair. He reaches for the conditioner and massages it into the ends of my hair.

"I'm grateful for you," he whispers, and my body warms. "You have done so much for me and Jayden, I'm not sure how I'll ever repay you."

I shake my head. "There's nothing to repay. I want to do it all. I love spending time with you both. I'm choosing all of it. I know I can say no if I'm not comfortable with anything."

His arms wrap around me, and he rests his chin on my shoulder. "I know, but I need you to know that I know I'm lucky to have you in my life, that you choose to be here and with me."

I lean back into him and close my eyes, loving being in his arms and the feeling of the warm water. I grin as I take his right hand and start moving it down my stomach. "You know how you can show me and help me sleep well tonight?"

His lips find my neck, and I lean my head to the side, granting him better access as he takes his hand back and moves it further down my stomach until he's cupping me between my legs. I'm wet already just thinking about how it's going to feel to have his fingers inside me.

"So wet for me, baby."

I nod.

His fingers dip inside me, and I moan as I roll my hips into his hand, seeking more. He nips my shoulder, and it only gets me going even more.

"So needy," he whispers.

"For you," I moan.

His fingers curl inside me, and I bite my lip. His free hand comes up, and his thumb rolls my lip out of my mouth.

"I want to hear you. I want to hear just how good I make you feel."

If he wants me to be vocal, I can be vocal. "Play with my clit."

When his thumb finds it, I moan loudly, and he steps into me further, pressing his erection into my ass.

"I love your sounds," he whispers into my neck between soft kisses.

"Mmhhhh," I moan as his fingers continue to work. "If you keep this up you'll get to hear me come."

"My favourite sound."

His fingers work faster as his free hand moves down to my breast and tweaks my nipple, causing me to thrust my chest into his hand, and he chuckles against my skin. "So responsive."

I reach between us and grab his cock, giving it a few strokes, and feel him stiffen behind me as his breathing accelerates. It's my turn to chuckle. "So responsive," I tease.

His fingers work faster, and he pinches my nipple harder, and it's almost become a competition to see who can make who come first.

I turn my head, and my other hand comes to his hair as my mouth seeks his. Our kiss is hot and passionate. I'm so close, my toes start to curl as Matt's hand leaves my breast and his arm wraps around my waist, holding me closer to him. My orgasm tears through me, my legs wanting to give out and Matt holding me up.

Between the sound of my orgasm and a couple more pumps of my hand, Matt comes, spilling himself all over my back. We both pant as we work to catch our breath. The second I feel like I can breathe normally again, I'm kissing him. When he breaks the kiss, he takes a step back and examines my back.

"Fuck," he groans.

I grin at him over my shoulder as he runs his hand down his face.

"You look so good painted in my cum. I need to do that more often."

I throw my head back and laugh. "Get your fill, because I'm going to wash this off now."

He shakes his head and grabs the removable shower head. "Let me."

I nod, and he gently washes me, taking his time as he rubs soap over every inch of me and then rinses the conditioner out. When he's done, he quickly washes himself as he stares at me like he's in awe that I'm here with him right now. He turns the water off and dries me off before himself and then pulls me into the bedroom. Just after we climb under the covers, Jayden's cries come through the baby monitor. I put on one of Matt's shirts and make my way into his room, Matt right behind me. I lean over Jayden's crib and smile at him. He reaches for me, and I pick him up, checking his temperature with a kiss on the forehead. He's much cooler than he was this morning.

"Seems like someone may be feeling better," I say. "I think someone may be a little hungry."

"I'll go make him a bottle," Matt says before kissing my cheek and leaving the room.

I take Jayden to the rocking chair in the corner and settle with him. The second Matt hands me the bottle, Jayden is reaching for it, and I can't help the smile that spreads across my face. He hasn't been this eager for a bottle all day, so I'm hoping this means he's feeling better.

Matt leans against the wall with his arms crossed over his chest as he watches us with the softest smile.

"Why don't you get some sleep? You've been up for hours," I say, and he shakes his head vehemently.

"No, I want to be with you two."

I shake my head, but the smile won't leave my face. When Jayden finishes his bottle, I burp him and quickly change his diaper before settling him back in his crib. Matt takes my hand, and I follow him back to bed, crawling under the covers and into his side.

As he runs his hand softly up and down my back, he says, "You're so good with him. I hope he grows up and realizes just how lucky we are to have you."

I rest my chin on his chest and look up at him. "I'm just as lucky to have you two."

He kisses my forehead, and I rest on his chest again, allowing the exhaustion of the day to finally catch up with me.

The next morning, I find Matt and Jayden downstairs with Jayden in his highchair with baby cereal and Matt at the stove cooking. I have no words to describe the joy I feel every time Jayden shows just how excited he is to see me like he does right now. I make my way over to him quickly and pepper his cheek with kisses as he squeals.

"So, it's always him first," Matt jokes.

Leaving Jayden, I move over to Matt and wrap my arms around his neck as his come around me and find my ass. I grin up at him. "Good morning, baby."

His grin widens. "Call me that again."

I raise a brow. "Baby?"

He nods. "I like the sound of it coming from you."

I bite my lip to hold back my growing smile. "Good morning, baby."

He leans down and kisses me. "Good morning, Bug."

Stepping out of his arms and pouring myself a cup of coffee, I check the stove behind him and see pancakes and lick my lips as he chuckles and shakes his head. I take a seat at the kitchen island beside Jayden's highchair and make faces at him while he plays with his cereal, occasionally pushing a few pieces into his mouth.

"So," I start, and Matt looks at me over his shoulder. "That gala I've been helping Maggie with is next Saturday. Maggie wants me to go and see what I helped with and said I could bring someone. Would you—will you be my date?"

He turns the element off and places a plate of pancakes in front of me. "Of course, I'll be your date. I'll be your date to every event."

I grin as he hands me a fork.

"Now dig in before they get cold."

I take a bite and moan around the chocolaty flavour. "These are so good."

"I'm glad you approve."

We eat, talking to each other and Jayden, and when we finish, I clean up the kitchen while he takes Jayden upstairs and gets him changed.

When Matt comes back downstairs, he wraps an arm around my waist and pulls me into him. "Now, do Jayden and I get to enjoy your company today?"

"I'm sure I could be convinced," I say, and he pinches my side.

"These two handsome faces aren't enough for you?" he says playfully.

"These two handsome faces are all I need," I say, much more serious.

All his joking falls away as he leans down and presses his lips to my forehead, whispering, "I'm glad."

We head to the living room and play with Jayden until he's ready for his first nap, and then Matt and I settle on the couch with me tucked into his side as we watch a movie. Matt manages to convince me to spend another night with him and Jayden, and I'm quickly realizing I don't think I ever want to leave.

CHAPTER 35

Zoey

The evening of the gala, I stare at myself in the mirror, pleased with my choice in dress. It's a black and hugs my body with thick off-the-shoulder sleeves, and a slit comes halfway up my right thigh. When I spin, the light catches the small glittery pieces within the fabric of the dress. My black heels make my legs look longer than they are and my ass look amazing.

Grabbing my clutch, I head downstairs to meet Henry and Maggie. I'll be riding with them there to help Maggie with the final set up, and Matt will meet me there. Maggie made sure his name is on the list.

When I'm halfway down the stairs, Henry smiles up at me. "You look beautiful, Zo."

"You clean up well, big brother. Where is your gorgeous wife so we can get going?"

His jaw drops slightly, and I turn to watch Maggie come down the stairs. I turn back to Henry, and he's covering his mouth and shaking his head as he stares in awe at his wife. When she stops in front of him, he mutters, "How in the hell did I get so lucky?"

She goes up on her tiptoes and kisses him. I love that Henry and Maggie found each other and are still in awe of each other, even after having been together for eleven years. I only hope Matt and I can have that, too.

"Ready to go?" Maggie asks, and I nod.

We follow Henry out to the car, and he drives us downtown to the Convention Centre where the gala is being held. When we get there, we do everything we can to help Maggie with finishing touches. As guests start to arrive, Maggie begins making the rounds and greeting people. I grab a glass of champagne and take everything in. I can't believe we were able to turn this space into something so beautiful.

Shiny silver stars intermixed with faerie lights hang from the ceiling. Soft burgundy drapery hangs from the walls, covering some of the harsher tones. Tables surround the perimeter of the dance floor at the front of the room, each draped with a black tablecloth with three tall vases in the centre filled with water and floating candles. The lights are set perfectly so you can still carry on conversation with people with the soft music that's playing, but you can also watch the candlelight bounce off the shining stars.

As I make my way around the room, I spot Matt, two flutes of champagne in his hand. When he sees me, he stops, his jaw dropping as he motions for me to spin. I giggle as I do it, and he makes his way to me as quickly as socially acceptable without running or shoving people out of the way, it only has me giggling even more.

He hands me one of the flutes, and his free arm wraps around my waist, his hand landing just above my ass, staking his claim without being overly inappropriate.

I shake my head as I look up him, my smile never leaving my face. "You know, if you really want to show everyone I'm yours, you should kiss me."

He grins down at me. "You're brilliant and right, I should kiss you," he whispers before our lips meet. It's a socially acceptable kiss, even though I know neither of us want it to be.

When he pulls back, I ask, "How was Jayden when you dropped him off?"

He shakes his head and chuckles. "I swear that boy doesn't care when I drop him off at Mom's. He's so spoiled by them that he'd be happy if I dropped him off with Grandma every weekend."

I cup his cheek. "He loves you."

His hand covers mine. "I know, and I'm happy he enjoys going to my mom's."

"He'll be excited when you pick him up tomorrow." I drop my hand from his face and take a sip of my champagne.

"You mean when we pick him up. And he's going to be more excited to see you."

I raise a brow. "We?"

He runs his teeth over his bottom lip and nods. "Yup. My plan is to woo you enough tonight that I can convince you to go home with me, and maybe if I do a good enough job you'll spend the weekend."

My shoulders shake as I silently laugh. "Someone's ambitious."

"When it comes to you, always."

"Well let's make the rounds and see how well you do tonight."

He mock salutes me and takes my hand as we talk to people we've never met. After thirty minutes of socializing, I hear a familiar voice and grin widely as I spot Liv and Josh talking to a couple. I quickly make my way to Liv, and when she spots me, we throw our arms around each other. Josh ends his conversation and shakes Matt's hand.

"I'm so happy to see you," I say as I squeeze my best friend.

"Well, if you didn't let my brother steal you away, you might see me more."

I shake my head as I step back. "Don't act like your husband hasn't done the same. Plus, with Cate, you've got your hands full."

Josh and Liv share a quick look before she agrees.

"Zoey, this place looks amazing. You and Maggie did good work," Josh says.

"Thanks. The real judge will be how much money we manage to raise tonight."

He nods. "Either way, that job is still yours if you want it."

I'm radiating with excitement. Being able to do what Maggie and I have done for the last few weeks all the time would be a dream come true. "I'd love to take the job."

Josh smiles and offers me his hand, and I shake it.

"I'll send the signed contract to HR on Monday," I say.

He nods. "We'll get you started in the new year."

"I look forward to it."

Matt takes my hand and kisses my cheek before we all make our way to find our seats. I'm glad the four of us are all together. We take our seats, and two more couples join us. A tall man, probably in his late fifties, offers his hand to each of us, introducing himself as Hank, and his wife is Loretta. Loretta seems so excited to meet new people, asking the four of us all sorts of questions.

"And how do the four of you know each other?" she asks.

"Josh is my husband, Matt is my brother, and Zoey is my best friend," Liv answers as Josh's arm goes around the back of her chair and she leans in closer to him.

"Oh, how lovely. And who invited you guys tonight?"

"Maggie Williams is my sister-in-law," I say. "I've been staying with her and my brother and helped her with some of the planning for tonight. Matt's my plus one." I smile at him, and his thumb grazes over my shoulder from the back of my chair.

"I got mine through my company," Josh says, and Loretta's eyes widen slightly.

"Are you Joshua Lincoln?" He nods, and she nudges her husband, who was in conversation with the other couple beside him. "Honey, this is Joshua Lincoln."

"Ah, the new owner of the Cyclone," Hank says, nodding. "I have to say, I'm surprised the team sold so quickly."

Josh shrugs and smiles softly at Liv. "What can I say, my wife and I both have a love for the game and the team."

Matt gives Josh a playful slap on the back and grabs his shoulder. "Glad to know your best friend didn't play a factor."

Josh just shakes his head and takes a sip of his drink, but Loretta raises a brow. "You married your brother's best friend?" she asks Liv, who blushes slightly, tucking her hair behind her ear.

"I did, and my dear brother is now dating my best friend. It's funny how that all works."

"You all seem to be handling that much better than my brother would have." She laughs.

"If I trust Josh with my life, no reason I shouldn't trust him with my sister's. He's good to her, and I have a beautiful baby niece that he dotes on."

Loretta leans forward. "Oh, please tell me you have pictures of this adorable little girl."

Josh is already unlocking his phone and showing her the dozens of recent pictures he has of Cate.

She ohhhs and awwws at the pictures and turns to Matt and me. "Your babies are going to be just as cute, I can tell already."

I blush, hard. My cheeks are so warm, and I feel the tips of my ears heating, too.

"If they look anything like Zo, of course they will," Matt says.

I bite my lip. Him just acknowledging us having kids together is such a turn on.

As the waiter's come around with dinner, Loretta joins her husband in conversation with the other couple, and I lean into Matt and whisper, "You've succeeded."

He grins down at me. "Have I?"

I bite my lip and nod before making sure I get in real close so no one can hear what I'm about to whisper. "You have, and I expect you to have me calling your name all night long while you fuck me."

"That's a guarantee, baby."

I sit properly in my seat and dig into my steak. Everyone enjoys dinner, and dessert is served before the evening transitions into the auction. A silent auction has been taking place all night along one wall of the event space, but the bigger items are being done in a live auction on stage. Maggie climbs the stairs to the stage and greets the guests, thanking everyone for coming and for their donations for tonight's event before handing it over to the MC who runs the auction. I can't wrap my head around the money some of the items go for. It's insane.

After the auction ends, a band takes over, and people head for the dance floor. Matt offers me his hand, and I place mine in his as he leads me to the dance floor. I lay my head on his chest and close my eyes as we sway to the music.

A few songs in, I feel a tap on my shoulder and a soft, "Excuse me."

Matt stiffens against me, and anxiety radiates off him. Lifting my head, I look beside me and see this beautiful blonde woman, several inches taller than me, with full curves. She offers me a soft smile and looks up at Matt. He's not looking at her fondly. In fact, he's practically glaring daggers at the woman.

"Can I cut in?" she asks, and I'm not sure what I'm supposed to do, but Matt's grip on me tightens.

"I'm in the middle of something, Hazel," he practically growls, and rage fills me. I look up at Matt, the question in my eyes, and he nods in confirmation. I fist my hand in Matt's shirt in an attempt to not turn around and slap this woman. I never really thought about what I'd do if I ever came face to face with Jayden's mother, but the only thought going through me right now is violence.

She took so much from Matt by not telling him, robbing him of the opportunity to experience the pregnancy, and then she just dropped Jayden off at his doorstep. She deserves nothing nice in this world. A calming presence comes to my side, and I see Josh and Liv. I know the second she finds out who this woman is, she won't be calm, though. Matt's eyes haven't left Hazel, and I don't even think he's noticed his sister.

Plastering on the fakest smile and staying as calm as possible, I say, "Why don't we take this conversation outside?"

Her eyes dart to me, and her smile drops for a second before it returns. "I only need to talk to Matt."

I grate my teeth. I'm not letting her talk to him by herself. I'm not letting her even attempt to take my man or my kid away from me. I don't care if Jayden isn't my biological child, he has become a part of me. I care more for him than I do myself, and I'm not losing him. You'd have to kill me and put me six feet under if you wanted a shot at it.

"Like I said, why don't we take this conversation outside."

Frustration seems to radiate off her as she looks at Matt, and he shakes his head. Taking my hand, he leads the way out of the event space. I make eye contact with Liv, and she knows immediately to follow us. As soon as Matt deems us far enough away from the doors, he stops and plants his feet shoulder-width apart and crosses his arms over his chest. I have no idea how she ended up here at the gala, but I want her as far away from us possible. I want her gone.

"What do you want, Hazel?" Venom fills his voice, and Liv's shocked inhale fills the hallway.

"To talk." She side-eyes Josh, Liv, and me. "Alone."

Matt shakes his head and scoffs. "Anything you have to say to me, you can say to them."

"And who are they?" she says, disgust filling her voice.

"My family. Jayden's family."

I take a step closer to Matt, loving that he's lumped me in as his and Jayden's family. I try to show some of the strength Matt is by not going after this woman, but it's hard.

"I'd like to see my son," she says, and I say, "No," before anyone else has a chance to.

If she could shoot fire out of her eyes, I'm sure I'd be burnt to a crisp right now, but I don't care. I pull my shoulders back and stand taller.

She scoffs. "And who the fuck do you think you are to say I can't see my son?"

"The one who's taken care of him when he's been sick. The one he reaches for in the morning when he wakes up and wants to put him to bed. The one who reads him books before putting him to bed and plays with him. And he's not your son, you gave him up."

She looks at Matt. "You're going to let her speak to me like that?" She pops a hip like she thinks Matt will choose her over me.

Matt nods. "She's only saying the truth."

She eyes me up and down before returning her gaze to Matt. "You let this woman around our baby? Maybe I shouldn't have left him with you if you make such bad choices."

She's gone too far. I take a step forward and lower my voice to one that's unrecognizable even to myself. "You better watch yourself before you end up with my palm across your face. Matt is an amazing parent. He's stepped up when you didn't even tell him he had a kid. You took away the experience of the pregnancy, the birth, his first few months, all because you're a selfish little bitch. Matt's a better parent than you could ever be. You gave up your rights, so why don't you turn around and take your ass out of here right now and never show your face around here again."

Her jaw is slack as she stares at me then Matt then back at me. "You can't speak to me like that," she shrieks.

"She can," Matt says. "Unlike you, Zoey won't abandon Jayden. I know without a doubt that no matter what happens between her and I, she will always be in his life. But my plan is she'll be there, with us, always. She will be the female role model he'll look up to, because she's a good person who supports her family and the people she loves. I'm not letting you into his life only to abandon him again. I'm not putting him through that. You gave me the papers saying you didn't want him anymore, and I'm going to honour that. You should know there are certified copies of those papers with Josh and Liv"—he tips his head towards them—"my parents, my lawyer, a cop friend, and another friend. No matter what you do, there are enough people who know that you can't fight it."

"He's my son," she tries to argue, but I shake my head.

"He's not."

"And he's yours?" she says in outrage.

I take a step closer. "He is. I will die before I let you try to take him or walk into his life, only to abandon him again."

Her entire demeanour changes as disgust fills her expression, and she looks at Matt. "You know what, I only gave this a shot because I was in town and you were a decent fuck, but it's not worth this. You can keep your psycho bitch and the kid, I'm heading back to Winnipeg next weekend anyways."

I raise a hand and take a step towards her, but arms wrap around my waist. She laughs at me. "Go," I say. "Before I give you what you deserve."

She rolls her eyes and leaves the building, and it takes everything in me not to go after her. The arms drop from around my waist, and I take a deep breath, turning and tucking the strands of hair that fell behind my ears. I drag my hand downward in front of me as I close it in an attempt to centre myself. When I open my eyes, the three of them are staring at me. Liv looks worried, Josh looks kind of impressed, and Matt, I can't pinpoint the look.

"You good?" Liv asks, and I nod.

She hugs her brother and whispers something to him before Josh shakes his hand and they head back inside, leaving Matt and me alone.

CHAPTER 36

Matt

The second Josh and Liv are through the doors, my lips are on Zoey's. I kiss her as if my life depends on it, giving her everything, every piece of me. She grips the front of my suit with one hand as the other finds the back of my neck, and I walk her backwards until her back is pressed against the wall.

I'm breathless when I pull back. I stare into her eyes, and I know I'm madly in love with her. If everything before tonight didn't already tell me that I was, I know in this moment, without a doubt, that Zoey Williams is the only woman I want to spend my life with.

"Can we get out of here?" I ask in a whisper, and she nods.

"I just need to tell Maggie and Henry that I'm leaving."

I nod and kiss her one more time before interlacing our fingers and following her as she leads me back inside and to Henry and Maggie's table. She kisses them each on the cheek, and I shake their hands before we make our way out of the venue and to my car.

I feel like I'm shaking as I navigate the streets back to my place. It's taking everything in me to not just blurt the words I love you. I need to tell her how I feel.

We get inside, and Zo makes her way to the kitchen, grabbing a glass of water before she turns to me. "Are you okay? I know I may have overstepped back there, and I'm sorry if I did, but—"

"I love you," I blurt, cutting her off, and she stares at me, mouth open. "You can't be that shocked, can you?"

She gives her head a little shake and closes her mouth. "No, I guess not, just not what I thought you were going to say."

I round the kitchen island, needing to be close to her. I need to touch her in some way. Her breathing picks up the closer I get, and I love that just my proximity brings this reaction out of her. I stop when I'm in front of her and cage her in with a hand on the counter on either side of her.

"Zoey, Bug, I'm hopelessly, madly, life-alteringly in love with you."

"I didn't overstep?" she whispers.

I shake my head, my hand coming up to cup her cheek. "No, Bug, you stood up for your family. You did what you thought you needed to do to protect us. I'll never fault you for that."

She rolls her bottom lip between her teeth. "I love you, too," she whispers. "I love you both. In a way that I don't know how I'd live if anything happened to either of you, a scares me shitless kind of love."

I grin so wide my cheeks hurt. "Good."

She chuckles. "Good?"

"Yeah, good, because then when I ask you to move in, I know you might say yes."

She stares up at me, shock evident on her face. "You're asking me to move in?"

I nod. "Do you really think I picked this house without thinking of you moving in? This kitchen is because you said you wanted one that had plenty of storage. You said you wanted a dining room large enough to host your family and a large walk-in closet you could try to fill." I lean down and kiss her. "All the bedrooms is because I want us to fill them."

A stray tear falls down her cheek. "That was weeks ago," she whispers.

"Zoey, when I said I was in this with you, I meant it. I want it all with you. I want you to move in, make this place yours, ours. One day, I'll get down on one knee and ask you to marry me. We'll get married, and then I want to fill this house with kids." My hand finds her stomach, flattening over it. "I can't wait to watch you grow our kids. Please tell me you want all of that."

She nods so vigorously I'm not sure how it doesn't hurt her

neck. "All of it. I want all of it, Matt. I want the house, the marriage, the babies, with you. Only you."

I kiss her, slowly this time. I have the whole night, hell, the rest of my life to devour her. Right now, I want to take my time, to show her how much she means to me. My lips move across her jaw and down her neck.

"You look absolutely amazing in this dress," I say as my hand finds the slit and makes its way up her leg. "When I first saw you tonight, I thought about how good it's going to look on the floor of my bedroom."

Her head falls back as she grants me better access to her neck and chest. My lips continue to move across her soft skin.

"Why don't we go see if you're right," she says as I nip at her shoulder.

"I think we should start right here," I say against her skin as my hands grip the fabric of her dress and slowly bring it up her legs. "I think I want to taste you right here on the kitchen island where you're supposed to eat meals."

Her hands find the counter, and she pushes herself up onto it and spreads her legs. "Eat me then, Matthew. Devour me like I'm your favourite fucking meal."

"Gladly," I say as I push her dress up enough to show me the black lace panties waiting underneath. My finger hooks under the fabric between her legs and pulls it to the side before my fingers slide into her. "So wet for me."

She kisses me as her hips roll into my hand. "Now put your mouth where it's supposed to be," she says as she breaks the kiss, and I grin as I lean down and run my tongue through her wetness. She falls back on her elbows as she watches me.

I do exactly as I'm told and devour her. I bring her to the edge until she's trembling beneath me and pull back, allowing her orgasm to fade before I have her chasing her release again. When I go to bring her back from the edge, her hand comes to my head, and she grips my hair painfully tight as she holds my head still. The fact that she knows exactly what she wants and is willing to take it from me is such a turn on. Everything Zoey does is such a fucking turn on. I'll never get enough of her.

I bring her over the edge, loving the way she calls my name over and over as the orgasm ripples through her. It's so strong she can't hold herself up and more as she falls back against the island. Pride washes through me that I just made her do that.

I don't even let her catch her breath before I'm dragging her across the counter until her feet are on the ground and I can throw her over my shoulder. I quickly make my way up the stairs, pulling her heels off and dropping them beside the bedroom door then placing her beside the bed. The second her feet touch the floor, she's kissing me. My hand finds the back of her dress, and I pull down the zipper, allowing the dress to pool at her feet. I undo the clip that's been holding her hair and toss it to the side.

She steps out of the dress, kicking it to the side, and I take a step back, taking in every inch of her. Her skin is flush and looks amazing against the black of her matching bra and panties. Her lips are swollen from our kiss as a mischievous grin spreads across them.

"What are you thinking, Bug?'

"I'm remembering standing here while you crawled to me."

I bite my lip, getting harder in my dress slacks. Zoey is the only woman I will ever crawl for, and if she wants me to do it again, I will.

"Are you asking me to crawl for you again?"

She nods, her pupils dilating even more, if that's possible. "I want you do it naked, though."

I loosen my tie and pull it over my head, tossing it across the room before slowly undoing the buttons of my shirt then pulling it off and dropping it. I pull my socks off and take my time undoing my belt and my dress slacks before shoving them down my legs with my boxer briefs, my erection popping free, and kicking them to the side.

Standing in front of her fully naked, I drop to my knees and then my hands and slowly make my way towards her. I let her enjoy every second of it.

"You look so fucking gorgeous, baby," I say.

"You've never looked hotter than you do right now, crawling to me like a good boy."

God, this woman is only making me harder.

"What else would make me your good boy?" I ask, and her chest rises and falls faster.

"Take my panties off," she commands, and I do it without hesitation, helping her step out of them. "Now my bra." I stand and do as I'm told. "Now, do you want to watch me ride your cock or do you want me on all fours as you fuck me from behind?"

If I haven't said it before, Zoey is a dream come true.

"I want to watch you ride me."

She smirks. "Then be my good boy and get on the bed."

I do, reaching beside the bed to grab a condom, ripping open the package and rolling it down my cock.

The second it's on, she throws her leg over me and positions herself, running the tip of my cock through her wetness. "You look so good like this, at my mercy."

"Only for you," I say as she slowly sinks down on me, taking me inch by inch until I'm fully inside her.

She rolls her hips, and I moan. "Damn right, only for me." She falls forward, and her nails dig into my chest as though she's trying to leave some physical mark as to her claim on me. I'd tattoo *Property of Zoey* on myself if that would make her happy, because every piece of me belongs to her.

She rides me slowly, enjoying the feeling of me stretching her as my thumb finds her clit. Her head drops forward. "Fuck, Matthew, you fill me so well."

I lean up and kiss her. "You were fucking made for me, baby. I want to feel you come. Ride me the way I know you want to, take everything, it's yours."

She kisses me fervently as she increases the speed. She pulls back as she leans back on my legs, and my eyes move to watch how good her pussy looks filled with me.

"Like what you see?" she asks.

"Yes," I pant.

"Slap my clit," she tells me, and my eyes find hers as she bites her lip. When I don't do it right away, she tells me again, and this time I do and she clenches around me as a low moan leaves her. "Again," she pants, and I listen. She clenches again, and I watch as the muscles in her legs tighten. Fuck she's close.

I reach up and grab her jaw, pulling her forward, and she comes with me willingly until her lips meet mine. We fight for control, tongues and teeth clashing as we both chase our release. I hold back, needing her to come, needing for her to feel that release before me.

When she clenches around me one final time as her fingers dig into my skin, I finally give in to my release, moaning as I empty myself into the condom. I don't stop kissing her until we've both finished and we're panting for breath.

She rolls off me, panting as she stares up at the ceiling. I roll and face her, placing gentle kisses on her arm and shoulder, and she turns her head to look at me, a soft smile on her face. I tuck a piece of hair behind her ear and smile at her as I whisper, "You're my dream girl."

Her smile brightens, and she rolls to face me. "You're my dream guy."

I didn't think my grin could get any bigger, but it does. "Move in," I say.

"Is that a demand?" she asks playfully.

I shake my head. "A plea. Move in with me, please."

She nods and kisses me. "I'll move in. I'm giving you fair warning, though, you may lose your closet."

I laugh. "It's all yours, baby." I kiss her, and I'm already hard again. "Can I take you on all fours now?" I ask between kisses.

She doesn't answer, merely breaks the kiss and rolls onto her stomach and slowly lifts herself. I don't waste any time grabbing another condom and positioning myself behind her. I don't go slow or soft with her. I grip her hips so tightly she'll have bruises, and I fuck her. I fuck her in a way that will leave her knowing she's mine. That even though I will crawl for her and do whatever she asks and be her good boy, she's fucking mine.

She holds her hands flat against the headboard to prevent her body from moving any further up the bed as my hips relentlessly pound into her. She moans loudly, muttered fucks often following them. I spank her, and she clenches around me.

"Yes," she moans. "Be a good boy and show me who I belong to."

I reach forward, my hand finding the front of her throat, and pull her back against my chest as my left hand finds her clit.

"You like giving orders," I say and nip at her neck. "But you also like knowing you're mine. You want me to fucking claim you, don't you?"

She nods, and I pinch her clit.

"I want words, Zo."

"Yes, claim me."

"I'll be your good boy, but you're mine, Zoey. Body, mind, and soul, you're mine."

Her arms reach back and wrap around my neck. "Yes, Matthew, I'm yours. You're mine, and I'm yours."

My hand comes down on her clit, and she moans. I kiss her as my hips continue pistoning into her. "Fuck, I love you," I mutter against her lips, and she smiles, but I kiss her again.

"I love you," she mutters as she breaks for air.

We shatter together, and I hold on to her tightly, loving having her pressed against me. I place gentle kisses on her lips and she smiles softly.

"I'm yours," she whispers, as if she knows I need to hear those words when we're not in the height of fucking.

I tuck her hair behind her ear and whisper, "And I'm yours."

She falls forward, and I carry her to the bathroom. She does her business while I turn the shower on and then she follows me in. I wrap my arms around her, just holding her as the warm water washes over us. My mind goes over the evening's event, and as I remember how possessive Zoey was, claiming Jayden and not taking any of Hazel's shit, I grin.

She looks up and me and asks, "Why are you grinning?"

"Because I love feisty and possessive Zoey."

"God, I really let the heat of the moment take over." She shakes her head and closes her eyes.

I kiss her temple. "I love that you felt that strongly about Jayden and me. Family isn't always blood, and you're Jayden's family. You're my family."

She turns in my arms and cups my face. "You're my family. I love you both more than life itself."

I turn and kiss her palm. "I hope you know I feel the same."

She nods, and I kiss her softly before we help each other clean up and climb into bed with her wrapped in my arms. When she starts snoring, I smile to myself, knowing I'm committed to a lifetime of listening to her snore.

CHAPTER 37

Matt

When we wake up in the morning, Zoey is completely wrapped around me. I've never woken up as content as I am right now. When she stirs, I kiss her nose, and she scrunches it, causing her eyes to squint. She looks adorable first thing in the morning.

"Morning, baby," I murmur as I tuck her hair behind her ear, and she smiles.

Her eyes flutter open, and she whispers, "Good morning."

She stretches, and when she's done, I roll and hover over her. "So, breakfast and then we can go pack your things?" I ask, and her eyes widen.

"Pack my things?" she squeaks.

I nod. "You said you'd move in, which means we need to get you packed."

Her laugh is one of disbelief. "You really want to do that today?"

"Yes. I want you in here as soon as possible. I don't want you sleeping anywhere that isn't this bed with me."

"And if I say I want to wait a few weeks?"

I drop beside her and try to think of a way to convince her she shouldn't wait. Her laughter pulls me from my thoughts, and when I look over at her, she's beaming.

"You're cute when you pout," she says.

"Does that mean you'll move in today?"

She laughs and shakes her head, but a contented sigh eventually leaves her. "Yeah, I'll move in today."

Excitement fills me as I roll back over her and start kissing my way down her body. She spreads her legs, giving me more room so I can settle between her thighs as my mouth continues making its way down her stomach. "Maybe we can practice the whole making babies thing first," I say against her skin.

Her hand comes to my jaw, and I stop my movements and look up at her.

"Matt," she breathes, and I tense. "I want to be married before we have more kids."

I grin at her use of the word more, accepting Jayden as both of ours. "We can do that."

She nods and bites her lip. "I'm not ready for marriage, though. I want to settle into a career. I want to build a home first."

Nervousness is written all over her face, but I get where she's coming from. Marriage and kids are not something to blindly jump into. I kiss back up her stomach until I'm hovering over her and kiss her cheek.

"You want marriage?" I ask, and she nods. "And kids?"

She nods again.

"Then we're on the same page. I'll go at whatever speed you want. All I care about is that we want the same things, and that you're happy." She nods, and I grin, my thoughts going back to what I was doing. "I would still like to practice the whole making babies until you're ready."

She rolls as much as she can between my arms that are caging her in and reaches into the nightstand, producing a condom. "Then let's practice," she says as she rips it open and rolls it down my hard cock. She cups my face, and something in her eyes has me not moving and just watching her. "Make love to me," she whispers, like it's a prayer.

I nod and kiss her slowly. My hand slowly exploring her body before I position myself at her entrance then slowly push inside her. I watch her face closely, making sure to capture every change. I always hoped I'd find someone I'd fall in love with and want to start a family with, but I never imagined I could feel as deeply for someone as I do Zoey.

She scratches at my back as I slowly move in and out of her, savouring every moment. I place gentle kisses on her skin as I whisper, "I love you," over and over, and she whispers it back. I feel her building, and I'm right there with her. We're so in sync right now, I can only hope we experience this over and over for the rest of our lives.

Her eyes shut as she squeezes them, and she silently convulses around me, pulling me over the edge with her.

I kiss her nose as she slowly opens her eyes. So much is held in those beautiful brown depths, and I'm the one who gets to spend their life exploring them.

"Shower then packing," I say, and she nods. I help her up, and she follows me into the bathroom. As I lather her in soap I say, "Just think, this is the last shower you have to leave smelling like me."

She smiles. "But what if I want to smell like you?"

"Then I guess you'll have to spend a lot of time in my arms."

She blushes, and her eyes shine. "I guess I will."

Henry's surprised to see me walk in his front door with Zoey, but he offers me his hand and I shake it, kissing Maggie on the cheek when she greets me.

"What brings you two here?" she asks, and I know it isn't that we aren't welcome, but rather that we've never been inside together.

Zoey rings her hands in front of her, her eyes bouncing between Henry and Maggie. "I'm actually here to pack my stuff."

Maggie smiles widely as she hugs Zoey tight. Henry's eyes are on me, though. When Zoey and Maggie separate, I wrap an arm around her middle and hold eye contact with Henry. "I love her. I'll do everything I can to give her the life she deserves."

He stares at me for a few seconds before he nods and looks back at Zo. "You're always welcome here, Zo. This will always be a safe space for you."

She nods and hugs her brother.

"I still expect you for Christmas Day," he says as she pulls back.

She looks at me over her shoulder and smiles before looking back at Henry. "Can we bring Jayden?"

"Of course, you can," Maggie says before Henry even has a chance to answer. "I still need to meet this adorable boy of yours."

Zoey is glowing as she smiles back at her. "He is the most adorable thing. You'll love him. Oh!" she exclaims as she reaches for her phone in her back pocket. "I have pictures."

Her and Maggie bend over the counter and stare at her phone as they go through all the photos, and I follow Henry as he jerks his chin to the living room. We sit on the couch, and he clasps his hands in front of him as leans on his thighs.

"So, what are your plans?" he asks.

"I want to marry her one day. She wants to take our time and to get settled in her new career before we do that. I'll do this on her timeline. We want the same things. I just want her. She is the one person who makes me feel like me and feel sane."

His eyes move over my shoulder, and I know he's looking at his wife. He's got the same look Josh has when he looks at Liv, when Caleb looks at Bailey, and when Grayson looks at Hannah. That look of pure adoration where you're not sure how you'd survive without the other person, and I know I have the same one when I look at Zoey.

Henry nods and claps me on the shoulder, and I take it as his sign of acceptance. "I never asked her to view Jayden as her own, that was all her, and it's only made me fall for her more."

When Zoey and Maggie are done looking at pictures, she comes and grabs me so we can start packing her room. She's decided to just take some of it now and come back and slowly grab more. She's packing a suitcase when I find a box hidden in her closet that I remember from when I helped her move months ago.

"Kept everything in the box?" I ask, and she looks at me over her shoulder to see what I'm talking about.

She shakes her head. "No, I pulled a few out. They're in the nightstand drawer."

I open the box to see what she chose to leave behind, and sitting right on top is that box I couldn't help but stare at back then.

She sees me staring again and shakes her head. "It's brand new."

"I figured because it's still in the box, but I'm curious as to why you bought it in the first place."

"Because I enjoy using it on my partners."

I nod as the thought of her using this on me fills my mind, and I'm fucking hard. She notices me adjusting myself in my pants and grins like a fool, stopping what she's doing and stepping closer to me. Her fingers slowly crawling their way up my chest.

"Do you like that thought, Matthew? Are you picturing yourself lying on your back on the bed, legs spread as I slowly fill you with that silicone cock? You'd look so good letting me fill you like a good boy."

"Fuck," I moan. I toss it in her suitcase. "That's coming with us."

Her jaw drops slightly. "Seriously?"

I grip her jaw and stare into her eyes. "I'll do whatever you want. You obviously want that, and I'm just your good boy, completely at your mercy."

"God, how are you this fucking hot?" she whispers.

"Because I'm yours," I whisper back and kiss her. I break the kiss before it can go too far. "I'm not fucking you at your brother's. Let's pack this stuff and go grab Jayden."

She nods, and we quickly grab a few more things and take everything to the car. She hugs Maggie and Henry goodbye, and we head to my parents' to get our boy.

CHAPTER 38

Zoey

Matt and I agree to spend Christmas Eve with his family and Christmas Day with mine. I've heard about the Carter family Christmases. It's Liv's favourite holiday. She'd come to school when we were growing up and tell me all about what they did. It was never about the gifts she got, but the experiences she got to have with her parents and brother and sister. This will be my first Carter Christmas.

Henry and the boys always made sure we created some Christmas memories. We'd play games, watch Christmas movies, and when Henry met Maggie, she'd bake with me before the holiday.

I decide to make one of Maggie's cookie recipes to bring with us, as well as a pie. I've always loved Matt and Liv's parents, and Liv has always said they love me, but it's different knowing them as my best friends' parents and now meeting them as my boyfriend's parents.

I stand in the kitchen, looking around, trying to make sure I've grabbed everything. I triple count Jayden's bottles and make sure the desserts are packed in a canvas bag and the gifts are by the door. Matt is patting Jayden's back as he watches me.

"Bug, why are you so worried?"

"This is the first time I'm seeing your parents as your girlfriend, and this is the first time I'm spending a family holiday with you guys. This is different than Canada Day, this holiday is all about family."

Matt slowly makes his way towards me, cupping my face when he stops in front of me. "You are family."

"An honorary Carter isn't family," I say, going back to that conversation we had months ago.

"You'll have the name as soon as you tell me you're ready to have it. You are family in every sense that matters. My parents love you. They'll be so happy to have you join the family. Please don't be nervous, Bug."

I take a deep breath and voice the thoughts I've tried to ignore. "My parents never did anything with us for the holidays. We were lucky if they even remembered our birthdays or any other holiday. Your parents are so involved with you and your sisters, and now with Cate and Jayden. I don't know what it's like to have that."

Matt nods in understanding, and his thumb lovingly strokes my cheek. "I'm sorry you've had to deal with and experience that, Zo. I hope all your future Christmases are positive memories and my parents, Jayden, and I can be a part of that." He kisses my nose, and I relax a little. "I love you, Zoey Williams, and we will create many more memories to replace all your not-so-positive ones. Just give us some time."

I nod, and he wraps his arm around me, pulling me into him. "I love you, too," I whisper into his chest.

Taking a deep breath, I step out of his arms. I shake out my arms and grab the few things I need then meet Matt in the entryway.

When we arrive at the Carter family home, Matt squeezes my knee before getting out and rounding the car, opening my door and getting Jayden out while I grab our bags. We make our way to the front door, and Matt gives me a look, checking in. When I nod, he opens the front door and I follow him in.

The house smells amazing as we step inside, filled with the scent of the real tree. We slip our shoes off, and I follow the smell of food wafting from the kitchen, where I find Mrs. Carter. She smiles widely when she sees me and stops what she's doing to wrap her arms around me and kiss my hair.

"How are you, dear? I'm so glad you're spending the day with us."

"I'm good, thank you, Mrs. Carter."

Her hand comes under my chin in a very motherly way, and I smile. "No need to be so formal. You can call me Maddison."

Her words have any tension I had left in my body leaving. Matt joins us, and Maddison smiles more at Jayden than she does Matt, I think. She kisses Matt on the cheek quickly, and then her hands are deftly undoing the buckles on the car seat and taking Jayden out.

"How is my grandbaby?" she asks, and Jayden smiles at her as he babbles.

Matt tips his head to the living room, leaving Jayden with his mom. We move into the living room and greet his dad, who is coming down the stairs with a wrapped box as the front door opens and Josh and Liv walk in. Stopping at the bottom of the stairs, Mr. Carter kisses Liv's cheek and then Cate's, who's in Liv's arms, and shakes Josh's hand before coming into the living room to greet Matt and me.

"Where's your boy?" he asks.

"Mom," Matt says with a smile, and Mr. Carter nods in a knowing way. "I was chopped liver when I went into the kitchen, she just wanted her grandbaby."

"Because he's adorable," I say, and Matt feigns pain.

"And I'm not?"

I shrug. "Your cheeks aren't as pinchable."

He pinches my ass, and I squeal. "You can pinch my cheeks whenever you want, baby."

I can't help but to throw my head back and laugh. The way he wiggles his brows, I get the innuendo.

"I'll remember that," I whisper, and he kisses my cheek.

Mr. Carter takes Cate from Liv, and she pulls me away from her brother and into the kitchen. She says hi to her mom, kissing her on the cheek before she drags me to the den.

"Okay, so now that the boys aren't around, tell me everything." She scrunches her nose and shakes her head quickly. "Okay, not everything. You know what I mean."

I laugh. "So, you don't want to know what Matt and I did last night?"

The look of disgust on her face is priceless. "No, no I do not want to know." She pulls her leg up on the couch and wraps her arms around it, holding it to her chest. "You know, I love that we've always been as close as siblings and now you'll be my sister-in-law."

"Not for a while," I say.

"I see the way my brother looks at you. I know he wants to marry you. I'm surprised he hasn't jumped on that already."

I play with the hem of my shirt. "I told him I wanted to wait. I've spent too much of our relationship not knowing what I wanted to do with my own life, feeling lost. I don't want my life to be our relationship. I love Matt, I do. But I want to make sure I'm my own person before I'm his wife."

Liv smiles. "I admire you, Zo. Not everyone is strong enough to admit that, let alone follow through on it. You're family. You'll always be family, no matter how long you decide to wait to get married."

I hug my best friend, and the boys come in with babies on their hips. I grin at Matt. "Now don't you two look good, two best friends with babies at the same time."

Matt rolls his eyes and joins us, placing Jayden on a tummy time mat on the floor. Josh puts Cate beside him and takes a seat beside Liv while Matt picks me up, taking my seat and settling me in his lap. I notice Liv and Josh are watching Cate pretty intently.

"Something wrong?" I ask.

Liv shakes her head. "No, but she's started showing signs of crawling soon and neither of us want to miss it."

"Already? God, I can't believe she's growing up so quickly."

"Tell me about it. I realized I have to start thinking about her birthday soon, and I cried for a solid hour. I'm not ready for my baby girl to grow up."

Josh runs his hand over her hair and kisses the top of her head, and I know he's thinking the same thing.

We eventually fall into conversation as we watch the kids play. Gianna pops her head in a few times, but spends her time in the kitchen with Mrs. Carter. Cate looks like she'll crawl a couple times, but not tonight, apparently. After dinner, we all gather in the living room for gift exchanges. Liv and Josh insist on going last, handing all four adults gifts the same size. We open them, and I'm crying before I get the box fully open.

"Really?" I ask, and Liv is crying, too. Putting the box aside, I wrap my arms around her. "I get to be an aunty again," I say through my tears.

Liv nods. "And you're the best aunty."

Everyone hugs, and I stare at the copy of the sonogram that was in the box with a shirt that says: *Two-Time Best Aunty.*

I lean on Matt's arm as I stare at it, and he kisses the top of my head. "One day, that will be us," he whispers, and I nod, wiping at my tears. I can't wait for us to get to experience that together. I look up and kiss him softly, and he wraps his arms around me.

Liv tells us she's just shy of three months and doesn't want to tell anyone outside of her family for a few more weeks, and that just brings more tears to my eyes. I'm family.

As Matt and I start to yawn, we decide to call it a night. We pack up and say our goodbyes before heading home. Home. Something about calling the place where Matt and Jayden are home is special. We always called my parents' place home growing up, but it didn't have that warm and inviting feeling or the feeling of safety I get when I'm at Matt's. And at Henry's I knew I was always welcome, but it was very much Henry and Maggie's place.

When we get home, I get Jayden settled in bed, loving this part of our routine. I've taken nights for the most part, and Matt takes the morning, knowing I'm not a morning person. I've gotten more accustomed to it with Jayden now, but it's still not easy.

While I'm rubbing Jayden's back and rocking him, Matt joins me, quickly adding something to the mobile that he's moved from Jayden's tummy time mat to above his crib. I'm surprised to see he's adding a little ladybug right to the centre of the mobile. He smiles at me.

"Why?" I ask.

He puts his finger under my chin and tips my head back. "Because you're the centre of our world. He needs something to remind him of how lucky he is to have you in his life."

He kisses me and heads back into the bedroom, leaving me reeling in all the best ways. I kiss Jayden's forehead and get him settled in bed. I stare down at this perfect little boy, knowing I'm just as lucky to have him.

When I venture into the bedroom, I laugh as Matt points to the mistletoe he hung above the bed. "You're a dork," I say. I love that he can go from saying such heart-warming things to having fun with me like this. It just shows me how comfortable he is with me, and with our relationship.

He grins and wraps his arms around me, pulling me into his chest. "Maybe, but you love me." He leans down and kisses my nose.

"That I do."

He pulls me down onto the bed with him, pulling a giggle from me. "You've got to kiss me, Bug. It's the rules."

I kiss him as I smile against his lips, so happy he is who I'm spending the rest of my life with.

CHAPTER 39

Eliza

It's New Year's Eve, and we're all at Matt and Zoey's this year. Apparently, Zoey begged Liv to be able to host now that she had a space big enough, and Liv happily obliged. I love that they're now family. They were always close before, but now with Matt and Zoey dating, and the fact that we all know she'll be walking down the aisle in no time, it's different.

They're so happy, and so is Hannah. I've loved watching my friends fall in love and bringing Bailey into the fold when her and Caleb started dating. I've become an honorary aunt to Charlie, Cate, and even Jayden, something I never thought I'd get to experience as a kid. Being an only child to two very over-baring and controlling parents means I haven't experienced a lot of what my friends have, and now that I'm creeping up on thirty, I want to break out of this box I've confined myself in.

Mac, the goalie for the guys' team, stops at my side. Zoey wanted to fill this house with people to celebrate the new year, which means she invited the whole team and their significant others if they have them.

"And why are we hiding over here?" he asks, his British accent causing goosebumps to erupt across my skin. Something about this man has given a reaction ever since I first met him. He's no model, but he's conventionally attractive with strong features and dark-brown hair he keeps styled and out of his face, but I think it's this air of mystery around him. No one knows much about him. Liv's told me he's a typical goalie, meaning he's not typical at all. They all have their own eccentricities.

"Didn't feel much for socializing," I say, and he hums softly.

"Then why are you here?"

"My friends. How about you?"

"I have my reasons."

I turn and face him, taking him in. He takes a piece of cubed cheese and puts it in his mouth before walking away, and I stare after him. The more I stare, the more I wonder, could Mac be the one to help me break this box I've put myself in?

Epilogue

MATT

One Year Later

Fuck, I'm anxious. I've debated about when the best time was to do this for months. Was it at an early morning coaching session because that's where Zoey and I started spending more time together? Or at one of my games? Did she want her family there, or mine? I don't think I've antagonized over a decision this much ever, but I have to get this right.

We spent Christmas Eve at my parents' place last night, and we're heading to Henry and Maggie's in about an hour. It seems like this is going to be our tradition now. I didn't sleep well last night at all. I think I got maybe an hour of actual sleep. The rest of the night, I was tossing and turning, and I can't blame Zoey's snoring. It actually calmed me a bit.

I can't stand trying to sleep anymore. I throw the blankets off, and as I throw my legs over the edge of the bed, Zoey asks, "What's wrong?"

I plaster on a smile and look at her. "Nothing, baby. Just go back to sleep."

She shakes her head, worry filling her expression. "No, something's wrong."

I love that she knows me so well, but I hate it in this instance, because I can't keep any secrets from her. I let out a breath and drop my head between my shoulders. I feel her shuffle onto her knees and move closer to me. Her hand comes to my back, slowly rubbing it before she runs her fingers through my hair and kisses my shoulder.

"You know you can tell me anything," she says, and I can't fight my smile. Zoey is the one person I want to tell everything. The good, the bad, the mundane. She's who I want to tell.

"I know, Bug."

"You're worrying me," she whispers, and that's the last fucking thing I want.

"Give me one minute?" I ask, and she nods.

I rush downstairs and grab the present I hid at the very back of the tree under the tree skirt so she wouldn't see it and take the stairs two at a time on my way back up.

She's sitting up in bed when I enter the bedroom again. When she spots the box in my hand, her jaw drops and tears start to gather in the corner of her eyes. My girl is smart, and I knew as soon as she saw the box, she'd know exactly what it was. I've held onto this for so long, waiting for her to tell me she was ready, and when she told me a few months ago, it took everything in me to not just grab the box and ask her then. I wanted to make this perfect for her. I promised we'd make happy and positive Christmas memories, and I wanted to make this one of them.

"Is that..." Her voice fades as her tears start to fall, and I nod.

She scrambles onto her knees again and rushes to the end of the bed to meet me. "Yes, yes, yes," she says as her arms wrap around my neck.

"Baby, you didn't even let me ask."

She pulls back and wipes at her tears. "You don't need to. I know my answer will be yes. I love you so much, Matthew. I can't wait to be your wife."

I cup her face, my thumb swiping under her eyes. "I had a whole speech planned and everything."

She sniffles, and it's the cutest fucking thing. Humour and heat fill her eyes as she smiles at me. "Do you want to say your speech, or do you want to fuck your fiancée?"

I kiss her softly and whisper against her lips, "You're not my fiancée until you're wearing my ring."

She holds eye contact with me as she grabs the box and rips into the wrapping paper. Her eyes widen when she finally looks down at the ring in the box.

"Do you like it?" I ask hesitantly.

"It's perfect. This is exactly what I would have picked."

It's a simple princess-cut stone set on a band lined with diamonds. The size of the main stone isn't showy, but the light hits all the stones and it shines, just like Zoey. I take the ring out of the box and slowly slide it onto her finger, the small possessive part of me coming out as I get to claim her as mine. She's going to wear something that tells the world that Zoey Williams is mine.

I lean down and kiss her, my hands coming to her hair as I grab fistfuls of it and devour her. I'm panting when I finally break the kiss, and I press my forehead to hers.

"Do you want me to be your good boy or do you want to be claimed?"

"Claim me, Matthew."

Fuck me, this woman is everything. I quickly push down my boxer briefs, and she tosses her nightgown to the side, letting me take in every perfect inch of her. She leans back on the bed and pushes herself closer to the headboard.

"Spread your legs for me, baby, I want to see how wet you are for me."

She grins as she does as she's told, and I hold back my groan as I see she's glistening.

"You're perfect," I say before my tongue tastes her. I didn't think simply being able to call her my fiancée could make her taste better, but I swear it does. I don't take my time, I want to watch her writhe and come on my tongue.

She bucks her hips, chasing her high, and I love that she'll take what she needs from me. When she calls my name as her orgasm tears through her, my ego and pride swell. Zoey Williams builds me up in a way where she is the sole person who could destroy me, and I wouldn't have it any other way.

She reaches down and pulls me up, kissing me, licking herself off my lips and tongue. I groan into her mouth and reach into the nightstand, pulling out a condom. I need to be inside her right now. She grabs the condom from me, breaking the kiss to rip it open and roll it down my length.

"Fuck me," she moans as she runs the tip through her wetness.

"Yes, ma'am," I say and watch as her pupils dilate.

I thrust inside of her, loving the way she immediately contracts around me. I start slow, letting her adjust before I pick up her right leg and press it to her chest, letting me hit a part of her I wasn't before. She looks down her body, watching as I stretch her and licks her lips.

"Do you like what you see? Do you like the way my cock is stretching your tight little pussy?"

She clenches and nods. My free hand finds her clit, my thumb circling it. Her head drops back as though the pleasure running through her is too much for her to be able to hold it up.

"You're perfect," I say, and her eyes find mine, filled with warmth and love. I kiss her. "So perfect," I whisper against her lips between kisses.

She cups my face and forces me back as she stares into my eyes as I continue to fuck her. "You're perfect, too," she says as her eyes start to roll back in her head. "I love you so much."

I need to kiss her again. Words aren't enough for me right now. My lips crash against hers, and she fights me for control as she scratches at my back. I make her fight for control, but when she's obviously won, I hand it over. She pushes at my shoulder, and I roll us, just like she wants.

She grins as she pushes herself up and starts riding me as her hands come to her tits and start rolling her nipples. The light catches on her engagement ring, and it's got me ready to blow.

"FuuuuccccKkkk," I groan. "You look so good in nothing but my ring while riding me, baby."

"I know," she purrs and rolls her hips before leaning forward. "And I can't wait to see you wearing my ring while I fuck you."

"I'm yours," I say, and she lights up.

"And I'm yours."

I'm not going to last much longer; her words alone almost send me over the edge. I find her clit, and two swipes is all it takes before she's falling over the edge, taking me with her. She collapses on my chest, and I don't think I've ever been this happy. Zoey's agreed to marry me. Just the thought has me grinning.

She rolls off me, and I follow her, hovering over her and peppering kisses across her cheeks, neck, and chest. I whisper, "thank you," and she shakes her head as she grabs mine and forces me to look at her.

"You don't need to thank me for loving you, Matthew."

"Yes, I do. My life wouldn't be what it is without you."

She rolls her teeth over her bottom lip. "Then, Thank you." I open my mouth to say something, and she stops me. "If you're thanking me, then I'm thanking you. Matt, you and Jayden make me feel complete in every way. You make me feel safe and loved, and I'll never take that for granted."

I stare at her, not sure how she's real or what to say. I settle on rolling off the bed and picking her up as I carry her to the bathroom and turn on the shower. I wash her hair and body, and when I'm done, she does the same for me. As the water washes away the soapsuds on my back, I wrap my arms around Zoey and hold her to my chest. I love how perfectly she fits against me.

She shuts off the water, and we dry off as Jayden wakes up and I can hear him through the baby monitor. He's grown up so quickly, and he's so attached to Zoey. His first word was mama, and while I had wished it was dada, I'll never regret getting to see Zoey's reaction to it and getting to hold her that first night as she cried tears of joy. She tried to tell me she could tell him to call her Zoey or Zo, and I told her over and over that she'd earned the right to be called mama. She's been there for him and defended him since he came into my life. She loves it so much, and I know at first she felt bad that he's a mama's boy, but now she lets herself enjoy it.

She grabs her robe and moves into his room, smiling as she picks him up out of his crib and kisses his cheek. "Does someone want some nummas?" she asks, and he grins as he flaps his arms and says, "nummas," over and over.

I kiss my son's cheek and head downstairs to get him something small to eat before we head to Henry and Maggie's. They're making a big breakfast before we do presents. Zoey's whole family has really embraced Jayden and even me as part of their family. I know it wasn't easy for them to accept Zoey joining a ready-made family, but she made it clear she wasn't leaving, and I've been told several times that it's just too hard to say no to Jayden's cute face.

When Zoey joins me in the kitchen with Jayden, I ask, "Do you want to call Liv now or after we tell your brother's?"

I watch as she bites her lip to hold back her smile, but she can't fight it any longer. "Now."

I nod and take Jayden while she grabs her phone and video call my sister who is already up with Cate.

Liv smiles and says, "Merry Christmas," as she answers the phone. It takes her a second to realize Zoey is holding her hand in front of the camera, showing off her ring, but when she does, I'm glad I'm not in the same room as her, because she's freaking out.

"Oh my God! He did it? You're officially getting married!"

Zoey nods, and Liv asks to hear the whole story. I kiss my fiancée's cheek and smile as she moves to settle on the couch and tell my sister all about it. I look at our Christmas tree in the corner of the room that has a *baby's first Christmas,* and a *baby's second Christmas,* ornament front and centre and I can't wait to add more of those to the tree and more kids to this house.

Life with Zoey is everything I could ever dream of.

The End

Make sure to check out Matt and Zoey's bonus epilogue here:
https://BookHip.com/WMFXBPB

Dicktionary

Chapter 24
Chapter 28
Chapter 29
Chapter 30
Chapter 34
Chapter 36
Chapter 37
Epilogue

Acknowledgements

I want to first thank my readers for going on this amazing journey with me and picking up Matt and Zoey's story. Some of you have been here since Josh and Liv, and some of you are picking up *Taming You* as your first book by me, and I'm eternally grateful for all of you. Authors really are nothing without their readers, so thank you for being here.

Writing a book is a scary journey, and I wouldn't be able to do this without all the amazing people who have been in my corner for this journey.

Sydney, thank you for being you. Thank you for all your love and support and just being a genuine friend. I am beyond grateful for you, and I don't have all the words to express how thankful I am to have you in my life. Thank you for being the ultimate hype-girl. I can't wait to meet you in person, and for more virtual movie sessions and buddy reads.

I've recently been able to dive back into reading, and I need to thank Alisha for being such an fun buddy reading friend. Thank you for letting me send you all my unhinged reactions as I read and an endless stream of TikTok's. Thank you for being a part of this journey and a fun escape when I need it.

Chelsey, thank you for being my friend and being here with everything that is going on in your life. You will forever be my twin flame, and I'm so glad that we have two visits planned this year, because having you so far away is hard.

To my at home besties, thank you for all your love and support. You are really the best friends a girl could as for and know that I'm beyond grateful for each of you.

To my Beavers and the SMUTTERING, thank you for being a supportive group that I can always turn to. I appreciate you all more than I can say.

There are so many people behind the scenes that help bring a book to its final product. Thank you to my amazing beta readers who dove into this story last minute and showed me all their love for Matt, Zoey, and Jayden. I'm so glad that I have you as part of my team. Thank you to my editor Andrea who read through some of my shake my head mistakes that I missed and helping make this book the best it can be. Thank you to Kim, who put together a gorgeous cover, and Paige, who brought Matt and Zoey to life.

I can't wait to share more of this journey with everyone!

About the Author

Living in the Vancouver area of British Columbia with her husband, Alex enjoys spending her free time reading, watching Hockey (go Canucks), watching Disney movies and crime TV shows, and spending time outdoors. She started writing in 2023 when her first story just wouldn't leave her mind. From there, the ideas of a series formed and she's never looked back.

She enjoys talking to other authors and romance lovers. Her TBR is never-ending, but that doesn't stop her from adding at least one new book every day. Alex looks forward to experiencing more in the indie author community and can't wait to share her books with the world.

Connect With Me:

https://www.instagram.com/authoralextaylor/
https://www.threads.net/@authoralextaylor
https://www.tiktok.com/@authoralextaylor
https://www.facebook.com/profile.php?id=61552508379128
www.authoralextaylor.com
alex@authoralextaylor.com

Also by Alex Taylor

DESTINED LOVE SERIES

Always Been You

Saving You

Keeping You

Taming You

WILLOW VALLEY SERIES

Finding Home - Coming July 17, 2025

Printed in Great Britain
by Amazon

60269782R00157